HOSTILE ENVIRONMENT   A NOVEL BY VIC CHARLES

HOSTILE
ENVIRONMENT

SUNSTONE PRESS

SANTA FE
New Mexico

Cover design and illustration by Beth Evans

First Edition

Printed in the United States of America

10 9 8 7 6 5 4 3 2 1

Library of Congress Cataloging in Publication Data:
Charles, Vic. 1954-
    Hostile environment / by Vic Charles.
        p. cm.
      ISBN: 0-86534-230-X (paper): $16.95
      I. Title.
PS3553.H3235H6   1995   94-48712
813' .54—dc20   CIP

Published by SUNSTONE PRESS
        Post Office Box 2321
        Santa Fe, NM 87504-2321 / USA
        (505) 988-4418 / *orders only* (800) 243-5644
        FAX (505) 988-1025

Preface

For over two hundred years the United States has sought new and innovative solutions to crime. This search has been routinely scarred by prison riots, death and destruction. No new ideas. No new programs. And clearly no solutions have been found which will keep people out of jail and prison.

The average person in today's society grasps little, if any, understanding of what actually occurs behind prison walls. Most people do not care. Yet, many strongly favor longer prison sentences and stricter penalties.

This novel was written to give a realistic picture of what actually happens in the hostile environment called jail.

—Vic Charles

1

There was no question in Ivers' mind. The prisoner had set the fire on purpose. There was a chance it had been an accident, a very slim chance, but for someone to intentionally set a fire in a locked cell defies rational explanation. Things that happen in a jail don't have to make sense. They just happen. The smoldering sheets and papers were quickly extinguished with a dry chemical extinguisher. Although the fire was out, smoke still wafted from the open cell door into the dayroom and a heavy pall of dark clouds blanketed the area. Acrid fumes bit and stung lungs with each breath taken.

The dayroom was a large concrete enclosure centrally located in the housing unit. Each prisoner had access when their cell door was open. At night all individual cell doors remained locked. Normally the air in the dayroom was clear and breathable since the jail's ventilation system constantly recycled air throughout the facility. Sensors in the ventilation system had detected the smoke and instead of recycling the air, it was now exhausting the smoke and pumping fresh air into the jail.

Lieutenant Frank Ivers shouted instructions to the corrections officers who had responded to the emergency and they moved to the other forty-seven rooms and began evacuating the prisoners. Ivers wished he could just open a window and exhaust the smoke but unfortunately jail windows do not open. In jails nothing opens to the outside world. Seventy-seven disgruntled and dangerous prisoners stood together in the dayroom waiting for the ventilation system to perform its duty.

Sweat-drenched corrections officers wearing the self-contained breathing tanks deposited them heavily on the dayroom floor. The sweat, combined with the smoke, left black streaks on their faces and necks. Alien faces, tight with fatigue and exhaustion.

Ivers caught Officer Robbins' attention and motioned to him. "Everyone out?" asked Ivers, peering through the dense smoke.

Robbins nodded and moved next to Ivers as the prisoners walked aimlessly around the dayroom. It was two AM and all the inmates had been asleep when the fire was started.

The one who had set the fire was no one in particular. Just a prisoner. He might be crazy or he might be someone who wanted attention. Setting a fire was his method of having a temper tantrum. As the smoke finally began to clear the prisoners were escorted back to their cells and the doors locked. Ivers pulled his radio from the side leather holder and called the master control center. The moment the fire had been reported, Lieutenant Ivers had ordered an immediate check of all rooms and housing units in the jail. There was always the possibility that the fire had been set as a diversion for an escape attempt in another unit. The master control officer's metallic voice came across the radio advising Ivers that all nine hundred prisoners were secure and accounted for.

Ivers replaced the radio and turned his attention to the prisoner who had set the fire. He had been pulled from his cell as soon as the fire was detected and had now regained consciousness and was sitting up staring with wide-eyed bewilderment. After years of experience Ivers knew what would come next so he moved quickly to the prisoner's side just as he bounded to his feet.

The prisoner ripped the oxygen mask from his face and charged blindly. Ivers met the charge like a professional linebacker, knees flexed, back straight, shoulders squared. Flesh against flesh impacted, the collision echoing across the dayroom. The prisoner toppled backwards and fell to the floor. Robbins had followed closely behind Ivers and as the prisoner hit the dayroom floor Robbins was on top of him. They rolled and grappled on the concrete floor as Robbins looked for an opening in the wild tangle of arms and legs. The prisoner had twice the strength of a normal person although he was only of medium height. Worse, he did not seem to feel pain. Ivers joined the two and grasped the prisoner by the hair. This provided enough leverage for Robbins to pin one arm behind his back. Within seconds several other officers joined the trio and the prisoner was securely handcuffed.

Ivers lifted himself from the floor. He now knew why the prisoner had set the fire. The prisoner was psychotic. "Crazier than a shit-house rat," Ivers mumbled to himself. Out of breath, Ivers panted instructions to the officers who held the prisoner. "Take him to the psychiatric unit and place him in the seclusion cell until the shrink comes on duty in the morning."

Until then there was nothing else that could be done. Ivers looked around the now empty dayroom. The smoke had cleared, all the prisoners had been returned to their rooms, and the unit was once more quiet. There was nothing more to be done, but to write a pile of reports.

Ivers took the elevator to his office on the first level, closed the door behind him and sat down heavily at his desk. He had been lucky tonight. The smoke could have easily killed several prisoners. But there was more. With all the prisoners in the dayroom there could have been a riot. A hundred bad things could have happened. A hundred things could have gone wrong.

Fishing a cigarette from his pocket, he wondered idly what the new jail administrator would be like. Would he know anything about jails? Would he be able to do anything about the crowded situation?

The jail was packed. Prisoners were sleeping two and three to a cell when there should only be one. Either the population had to be reduced or a new jail had to be built. But the prospect of building a new jail was not something any politician wanted to face. The millions of dollars to build a jail on an already overburdened budget would be political suicide. Instead of doing something, the problem was ignored. A great drama was being played. The actors pretended that the problem did not exist.

Everyone who worked at the jail knew it was only a matter of time before the situation became deadly critical. Something very bad was going to happen. Prisoners could not be stacked like cord wood and expected to behave. Even now the situation was explosive. It was only a matter of time before a riot and a takeover attempt of the jail by prisoners would occur. It was no longer a matter of "if" it would happen, only a matter of "when". And people would get hurt, some would die.

Ivers stubbed out his cigarette and turned to the papers on his desk. It was no good thinking about it, not when he had reports to do. Maybe the new administrator would be able to do something. Could do something before someone died.

2

Avery Beck had just fallen asleep when the harsh buzzing of the alarm clock stabbed into his subconscious. He had tossed and turned throughout the night unable to sleep and had fallen into a troubled, restless doze around five o'clock through sheer exhaustion. Avery fumbled for the off switch and after several seconds stopped the jarring noise and lay back in bed thinking. Ann, his wife of twenty years, stirred restlessly next to him. She had been with him in good times and in bad but this was one time she couldn't help. Avery Beck was on his own.

He was frightened. Avery did not want to admit it to himself, but he was frightened, there was no denying it. He knew he was not prepared for this new job. Avery Beck was forty-two years old, six feet even, with dark hair, dark eyes, and a quick legal mind. He was an attorney, not an administrator and certainly not a jail administrator. The last eight months panned by in his mind slowly and he found himself focusing on the events which had led to this day.

Sam Waterston had made a bid for mayor and Avery had been solicited by Waterston's camp to act as a legal advisor. He had provided legal advice in his usual competent manner. Waterston had won the race and was now the mayor of Coronado, Arizona.

Avery was no stranger to politics. During the campaign Avery worked hard and hoped for a "plum" job should Waterston be elected. In the days following the election Avery had hinted to Waterston's aides about his desire for a position in the city's legal department. But instead of a plum, he had been awarded a pit. He remembered the meeting two weeks ago with Sam Waterston as if it were yesterday. Avery had sat in nervous anticipation in Waterston's office waiting. He could still hear Sam's exact words, "Avery, I want you to take the top slot at the jail. There are some pretty serious problems there from what I understand. I've received several complaints from the ACLU citing brutality and the overtime expenditures at that place are unbelievable. Avery, I need someone I can trust, someone with a legal background. I know this isn't exactly what you had in mind, but it's where I need you the most."

Avery was shocked. The only picture he could see in his mind when he heard the word jail was a monolithic structure of brown concrete and steel, full of dangerous people, centrally located in downtown Coronado. It was a place that radiated fear and apprehension. No one knew what happened in a jail except for the select few who worked there. Inside there existed a fraternity that worked beyond the public view. Avery had never practiced criminal law and never even been inside a jail. He had concentrated on the clean antiseptic law of corporations, taxes and business, not crime.

Leaving Waterston's office Avery searched his mind for everything he knew about jails. Jails were not nice places. Jails contained dangerous characters. People were assaulted, raped and died in jails. If you were bad, you went to jail. A dozen times Avery had considered calling Waterston to turn down the offer, but he hadn't. Now it was two weeks later and his first day as jail administrator would begin in an hour. During those two weeks he had read everything he could find about jails and there was no shortage of literature. It seemed every week a prison or jail riot erupted somewhere in the United States. Each incident precipitated a crisis, followed by emergency funding to shore up what was termed as "a breakdown in the system." In general the public cared little about the subject. It was an ugly topic, not fit for discussion by the civilized people of the world. Those who took an interest couldn't agree. Some advocated stricter punishment while others supported rehabilitation programs and reforms. But the majority didn't care and these were the people who were shouldering the tax burden to pay for the system. Avery had also spoken to several criminal lawyers to get information about the Coronado jail. The information he received was as varied and as opinionated as the people to whom he had spoken.

Two days before Avery had lunch with Jeff Powell, the outgoing administrator and had been briefed by him. Powell had been civil and informative but of little help. He had made vague comments and references to staffing, security, jail crowding, budget, litigation and the union. But Powell's briefings made little sense to Avery.

Powell had occupied the top post for the past twelve years and had established himself as something of a legend among jail managers nationally. Waterston's administration had decided it was time for Powell to retire. Too many complaints surrounding Powell's autocratic style of management had reached Waterston's ears and he wanted his own man at the jail.

Powell was a big man, barrel chested and outwardly pleasant. Avery thought that gazing into Powell's blue eyes had been like looking into a vast, empty void. There was nothing in Powell's eyes which betrayed any human emotion. What had been even more disconcerting was his restlessness. Throughout the briefing, Powell had been tense, strained, sensing, observing. Avery felt Powell was the kind who examined every word and every situation looking for an avenue to attack and exploit. But there was something unnerving and animalistic about Powell that intimidated people and Avery had been no exception.

Powell told Avery, "You will be in charge of an all-adult, male-female detention center. Ninety percent of the people confined in this institution are here waiting to go to court and have not yet been found guilty of anything. The facility was designed to hold eight hundred prisoners. Right now you have nine hundred and thirty two prisoners. You will not receive any cooperation from the police, the courts, or the state government. You will be the target of dozens of law suits filed by every person who is smart enough to know the system. Your own staff will stab you in the back. Speaking of which, you have a total of three hundred and twenty-seven staff. Don't trust anyone. If you do not run this facility with an iron fist, it will collapse around you. Make no mistake about it, you will be the one held responsible. If you do not maintain a strong hold on your power and authority as administrator, someone will step in and take it away from you. If you give someone a break it will be construed as weakness, something you do not want."

Avery had been appalled by Powell's frankness and hard line approach. Still, Powell had been in the business for over twelve years and he had listened carefully and taken mental notes.

Avery hauled himself out of bed, showered and dressed in a conservative gray suit. After a quick cup of coffee and a fifteen minute ride downtown, he parked his car in the slot designated "Jail Administrator" and entered the Coronado County Jail for the first time.

It was the tenth day of January and the time was six-thirty in the morning. Avery entered through the unlocked front doors and turned left towards the double glass doors leading to the administration offices. A corrections officer was on duty at the counter in the front lobby and Avery nodded to the uniformed officer as he passed. The officer stared without acknowledging his greeting. Avery sensed hostility but couldn't explain it. He toyed with the notion of turning back and speaking to the man but decided against it.

He extracted the key given to him by Powell and unlocked the main doors to the administration area. It was deserted. Staff were not scheduled to report for work until eight o'clock. Powell had given Avery a master key that would open every door and office in the entire administrative area. Once through the main doors he navigated his way through a cluster of desks marking the secretarial pool and unlocked another set of glass doors. These protected the foyer outside his office. It was a buffer zone. No one entered without an appointment. Inside the foyer Avery unlocked one last door and entered his office.

He circled a large desk, moved to a gray chair, sat and unrolled the blueprints of the building on the surface in front of him. It seemed the natural place to begin. First learn the physical plant and then the operation and integrate the two. According to the blueprints, the jail had two principal entrances and one exit. At the rear was the booking section, sometimes called the receiving and discharge area. It was here prisoners entered the jail through a set of double doors called the sally port.

In a lot outside these doors, the police parked their vehicles and then escorted, dragged, and sometimes carried people they had arrested inside. The officers entered one set of electronically controlled doors with their prisoner, locked their guns in a bank of lockers provided and proceeded through a second set of similar doors. The set could not be opened at the same time, providing a fail-safe security system. No one was authorized in the booking parking lot or booking area unless they were part of a law enforcement agency or a member of the jail staff. After the police officer had entered the booking area with the prisoner, the booking process began. The prisoner was escorted to a long metal counter topped by thick plexiglass extending to the ceiling. This was where the first reality of jail seeped into the alcohol and drug saturated brains of those social outcasts.

At the counter the prisoners were instructed to empty their pockets, remove all jewelry and take off their shoes. During this process they were asked a battery of questions ranging from medical problems, social security number, date of birth and occupation. Once their personal data had been obtained and entered into the computer, the police officer supplied the charges. The prisoner was then searched. This completed the first part of the booking process. The prisoner was then escorted to a small room where a paramedic performed a cursory examination and completed a medical questionnaire detailing the prisoner's medical condition. If, and only if, the prisoners cooperated, they were afforded a telephone call. Sometimes it became necessary to encourage cooperation. Encouragement and attitude adjustment came in many forms.

To Avery Beck all of these things were unknown. Booking was nothing more than a stenciled name on a piece of blue paper. In time he would learn many of the operations of the jail, but there were some things he would never learn. Some things were guarded carefully by the line officers and never found their way up the chain of communication to top management.

Avery continued to study the blueprints and learned that the majority of the ground floor was occupied by the administrative offices, the booking area and medical and supply services. The upper six floors constituted the housing areas where prisoners were kept for months and in some cases, years. Scanning the blueprints, he whistled softly under his breath realizing he had entered a city. Lying on the desk in front of him, the plans suddenly became a guidebook to the city of the Coronado County Jail. A vast computer network linked all the areas into one central information file. Anything anyone wanted to know about a prisoner was no farther away then a few taps on the keyboard. Maintenance crews, when not physically present, were as near as a telephone call. Heat-ing, cooling and electrical systems were all serviced internally. The jail's power supply was backed up by two huge generators in case of a power outage.

A pharmacy, a dental office, a medical unit and a mental health ward provided for medical and psychological needs. The jail store sold candy and cigarettes, and was located next to the jail's laundry. It was all here, everything. An entire city within a city. All the services Coronado provided for its residents, the Coronado County Jail provided for its own unique class of citizens. The only difference between the two was that the Coronado County Jail never closed.

It was an autocratically governed mini-city. From the time a prisoner was incarcerated, every possible need and requirement had been anticipated. But what Avery Beck failed to comprehend was that this city was governed by a separate set of rules and was populated by a different type than the city outside the jail. Twelve inches of reinforced concrete and steel physically separated the two. In actuality, it was more than concrete and steel. An entire set of ethics, moral principles and unwritten laws governed the population and staff on this side, and Avery Beck was the new mayor.

He leaned back in his chair and surveyed his office. It was large, modestly decorated with several off-white upholstered couches along the wall. From his large walnut desk he continued a mental inventory of his new surroundings. On the wall was a case containing an array of homemade knives, called "shanks", which had been confiscated from prisoners during the past years. Many were ingenious deadly devices manufactured from pieces of wire, bone, metal, wood and anything else the prisoners were able to obtain. Each shank required weeks to make without the benefit of tools. Gazing at the thirty-five knives and the potential for destruction they carried, Avery shuddered involuntarily.

He pulled his attention away from the glass case and examined the phone console. It had direct lines to all the jail's division managers. To his right was a computer console which allowed instantaneous data on all of his citizens and staff. To his left was a desk set radio unit where he could monitor all radio transmissions within the various areas of his jail-city. A large window to his right afforded a view of everyone entering and exiting the front doors. An organizational chart on the wall directly in front of him graphically depicted the precise number of people and the different divisions in the jail. The security unit was the largest division with two hundred and forty uniformed officers, including lieutenants and captains. Their responsibility was to keep the people in and maintain order. The operations unit consisted of forty-three employees who operated and supervised the kitchen services, maintenance activities, social workers, the jail store, the warehouse, the recreation section and other units marked with abbreviations foreign to Avery.

At seven o'clock, a half-hour after Avery arrived, Sam Dennison, one of the two deputy chiefs of the detention center, arrived and entered the administrative area. Dennison unlocked his office door and moved directly to the computer terminal on his desk. He punched several keys and the Shift Captain's log appeared on the screen of his console. It consisted of anything and everything considered out of the ordinary which occurred during an eight hour watch. An escape attempt, a disturbance, a fire, anything requiring documentation was indicated.

Documentation was a commandment in the jail. Everything was a potential liability, and anybody could sue for anything. Therefore, everything was committed to writing. Finding several incidents of interest, Dennison punched another button and a copy of the log was printed. He removed the sheet and high-lighted several specific entries, including the detention center's current population. With copies of the logs in hand, Dennison entered Beck's office and spoke, "Chief, I have last night's shift logs if you want to take a look at them." Avery took the papers and scanned the high-lighted areas quickly.

"At nine last evening an individual was brought into booking who refused to cooperate. The individual kicked, bit, and punched several corrections officers before he could be restrained. During the restraining process, the individual suffered a laceration to the scalp requiring sutures. The individual has been transported to the local hospital for treatment."

Avery looked up to comment, but Dennison had disappeared. Avery continued to read.

"At two o'clock in the morning, an individual named Marsha Fieldman was transported to the detention center and booked for domestic violence. Prisoner Fieldman had been drinking with her husband during which time an argument had occurred, and Prisoner Fieldman had broken a beer bottle over his head. The husband has been transported to the hospital and she has been transported to the jail. While in jail, Prisoner Fieldman refused to cooperate and was placed in leg-irons and handcuffs."

Avery finished reading the logs and wondered what it was he was supposed to do with them. Obviously Dennison had given them to him for some reason, but Avery had no idea what it was.

Dennison reappeared several minutes later with two cups of coffee in white styrofoam cups and placed one on Beck's desk.

"Cream and sugar?"

Beck shook his head. Dennison took a seat on one of the couches and sipped coffee idly while studying Beck.

Avery knew Dennison was a deputy chief in charge of operations but knew little else about him. After several moments of uncomfortable silence Dennison spoke.

"I don't want to seem like a kiss-ass or anything, but you've just walked into a snake-pit. Stand with your back to the wall at all times and be careful. Some people are happy you're here, some aren't, and some don't care one way or the other."

"Which category do you fit in?" asked Beck.

"None. My job here is to support the boss, do what he tells me to do and look out for his back. When I'm not doing that I run operations. Like I said, I don't want to sound like a kiss-ass but if there's anything you need give me a shout."

Avery thanked Dennison as he left.

By eight o'clock various unit managers and the clerical staff began drifting in. Most detoured to the coffee room and poured themselves a cup of the infamous jail brew, hot, black, and unbelievably strong. Although Avery had already met a number of the jail employees, today everyone shied away, unsure and off-balance, not knowing what to expect nor what was expected. He compared this behavior to people who had been in a war zone for an extended period of time. It were reminiscent of battle weary veterans he had seen while in Vietnam--aggressive, cautious, defensive and careful. Avery knew these people were not his enemy. He had no idea what the future held, but he anticipated a long painstaking transition period before he would be able to penetrate their carefully built defenses. There would surely be power struggles and personal ambitions. There would be some pseudo-politicians, employees with connections to various local politicians. These people would be the hardest to deal with, the untouchables--or so they believed. If he disturbed their carefully built position, they would complain to their city councilman and Avery would be called to account for his actions.

Today would be the single most important day of his career and would set the standard for success or failure. Avery was no novice, nor was he naive, quite the opposite. He was intelligent and had the natural ability to eliminate the side elements of a problem and get to the heart of a situation quickly. But he was the new kid on the block and some of his actions might be perceived by some of the employees as an invasion of territory and it could upset the balance of power which many of the employees had worked years to develop. To compound his dilemma, Avery had received virtually no guidance from the mayor's office. His only instructions had been to "keep things quiet."

"Great," he muttered as he scanned the Captain's logs again, then placed them on his desk, glanced at the blueprints and then back to the organizational chart on his wall. He knew he needed to see the jail operations firsthand, which meant a tour. Avery picked up the phone and punched the direct line to Dennison's office. The phone was answered on the first ring. "How about a tour of the facility?"

Dennison's response was short and to the point, "When?"

"Now."

"I'll be right there."

The phone went dead and in less than a minute Dennison was at his door waiting. Avery took a deep breath and pushed himself away from the desk. It was time to take the plunge.

3

Jack Stilwell cruised slowly past the twenty-four-hour conve
nience store in his late model Chevrolet one more time. He
had already driven by four times. The floodlights at the front
of the store turned the empty asphalt parking lot into a sea of black.
Smaller lights at the front of the parking lot illuminated the six
gas pumps standing in a row like neon sentinels. It was like he
knew it would be.

One clerk, an old fart, was mopping the floor and doing the
things he was supposed to do. At two o'clock on this Tuesday morning, January eleventh, the streets were nearly deserted. An occasional vehicle drove down the street but no one stopped at the convenience store. The police had settled down to their usual coffee
and donuts. Weekends were bad times to commit crimes which
was why Jack always picked a weekday. Weekends all the rookies
and super cops were on duty and the old timers were off enjoying
barbecues and picnics in their thirty-year-mortgaged backyards.
Weekdays the majority of the police were "old timers." They had
developed habits and patterns of behavior including their two-in-
the-morning donut meeting. It was during these meetings that
past episodes of bravery were retold over and over again. The old
timers had been through it all before. In their younger days they
had been super cops, racing to the scene of a crime, handling several cases at one time, losing sleep to appear in court only to be
outsmarted by some attorney. They had learned the futility of it
all and their idealism had been replaced by a cold harsh reality. Do
your time, write enough citations to keep the sergeant off your
back and mind your own business. They had given up the fight,
realizing the hopelessness of the battle. The streets were ruled by
criminals and lawyers. As policemen they could not make a difference. It was a lesson the younger officers would have to learn on
their own. It would take time, but they would learn. The old tim-

ers left the blood and guts stuff to the rookies. It was a simple process of blue evolution. Jack Stilwell chuckled to himself. "Blue evolution," he muttered. "Not bad."

Jack Stilwell was not smart but he was clever and he was dangerous. Big and muscular, he had done three two-year terms at the state penitentiary for armed robbery and burglary. Jack was a career criminal. Prisons and jails did not frighten nor deter him. He considered these places of confinement nothing more than rest stops in his life. Six feet two inches tall, one hundred and eighty-five pounds of muscle with medium length blond hair, Jack Stilwell could take care of himself. He held no regard for others and lacked compassion for anyone or anything. Sociologists would have called him a classic sociopath. He lived for instant gratification and now he was thirty-three years old and needed money. The thought of getting a job and earning money was a concept his mind never entertained. There had been times when he had been forced to play the game for the parole board but it had been nothing more than a game.

Jack Stilwell guided the Chevrolet sedan around the corner and parked along the side street in the darkness. Rule number one: never drive to the front of the store and park in the light of the store you plan to rob. Rule number two: never drink or do drugs before a robbery. Rule number three: always make sure all taillights and headlights are working properly. A good criminal never helps the police establish probable cause. Rule number four: never look like a criminal. Shave, wear casual clothes and look respectable. It was a game, only a game.

These four rules were the basis for Jack Stilwell's success and they must have worked because after a string of forty-two robberies, Jack was still free.

He parked, turned off the lights, killed the engine and left the keys in the ignition. The last thing a smart robber needed was to be fumbling around in his pocket for car keys after a robbery. From under the front seat he pulled a dark blue, snub-nose thirty-eight revolver. An important tool for any armed robbery. Jack slipped the revolver casually into his back pocket, walked to the front of the store and entered.

Paul Frazer had almost finished mopping the floor when he heard the door open and saw a tall, well built, blond haired man enter. There seemed to be no cause for alarm. The man was conservatively dressed and did not display any nervousness. Paul Frazer was sixty-two years old, a veteran of World War Two, the father of three children and was married to the same woman he had married forty-two years ago. He had five grandchildren and was eligible for social security. He had elected to work three more years in order to reap the full benefits of social security.

During the past five years, Paul Frazer had been robbed seven times. The last time taking the money had not been enough for the robber. Frazer had been clubbed, kicked and beaten. After three months in the hospital and weeks of physical therapy, he had returned to work.

Frazer, slight of build, gray hair and sporting thick glasses was determined never to be robbed again. Unknown to his wife and family, Paul had purchased a small semi-automatic, twenty-two caliber pistol for fifty dollars from a pawn shop after his release from the hospital. This he kept in his pants pocket at all times while working. He had never fired the pistol and was uncertain how it operated but the slight bulge and the additional weight provided a comforting reassurance and a false belief for Paul Frazer a false belief that he was capable of equalizing any future encounters with robbers. Frazer had developed a habit over the past month of reaching into his pocket and squeezing the hunk of deadly blue steel resting there. A surge of confidence and security was generated each time he conducted this exercise. Paul leaned the mop against the wall and walked to the front counter where the blond man stood waiting patiently.

"Can I help you?" Paul asked routinely.

This man did not look like a robber--clean shaven, moderately dressed, no smell of alcohol, glue or paint. In Paul Frazer's mind the man standing in front of him was a typical late night customer.

Stilwell casually asked for a package of Kool regular cigarettes and reached toward his back pocket for his wallet. Paul Frazer nodded his head and reached up to retrieve a package of cigarettes from the display above the counter. Paul found the desired brand and placed them on the counter.

"That will be..."

Paul Frazer stopped in mid-sentence. The blond man was holding a gun and it was pointed directly at him.

"Give me the money, Pop. Don't get cute and hit any alarms and everything will be just fine."

Stilwell had rehearsed this line a dozen times. Rule number five: never use the same line twice. The police relied heavily on something they called modus operandi. If a robber used the same line time after time, the police would be able to tie the crimes to one person.

Paul Frazer just looked at the gun and froze. The pain of his recent beating during the last robbery flooded his mind. He was scared, but he was also determined. Without a word Frazer opened the cash register and began laying money on the counter. Several bills floated to the floor behind the counter. Frazer bent over to pick them up and pulled the twenty-two caliber semi-automatic from his pocket, and straightened up with the pistol in his hand and fear in his heart. Stilwell spotted the pistol. Without hesitating he pulled the trigger twice.

Two thirty-eight caliber slugs buried themselves in the chest of Paul Frazer. The first bullet ripped flesh and bone and tumbled through the heart putting an abrupt end to its sixty-two years of pounding. The second slug buried itself an inch to the left of the first. To Paul Frazer the second bullet made no difference. He was already dead. The impact propelled him back several feet. For a moment Frazer regained his balance and stared at the robber with a confused expression and then collapsed to the freshly mopped floor. It was a clean kill with very little blood. Only a small stream of red trickled from the wounds. Paul Frazer would never have the opportunity to collect his full social security benefits nor would he ever know that in order to fire a twenty-two caliber semi-automatic pistol, the user has to first chamber a round and, second, release the safety. The pistol in Paul Frazer's hand had been nothing more than a hunk of cheap metal, a piece of metal in which Paul Frazer had stored false hopes. He had realized the weapon's potential but had never taken time to learn how to release its killing potential.

The two blasts still echoed in Stilwell's ears as he stuffed the cash into his pocket. It looked like a fair amount of money. The fact that he had murdered the clerk made no difference. There would be a bigger investigation because of the murder but there were no witnesses. It all evened out in Stilwell's mind. Snatching the package of cigarettes on the counter, he turned and walked calmly out of the store to his parked car. It could be as long as several hours before the robbery was reported. It all depended on how much business the store did that night. Stilwell climbed behind the wheel of his Chevrolet, keyed the ignition and drove slowly through the residential area until he reached the freeway bordering the city of Coronado. He pulled onto the highway and drove carefully, frequently checking his speed and consciously using his signals every time he changed lanes. Stilwell turned on the radio, lit a cigarette and enjoyed the drive. Jack Stilwell was a very contented man. Any trace of guilt or remorse for the murder of Paul Frazer was nowhere to be found in his mind.

For Jack Stilwell, life was simple. It was survival of the fittest.

4

Avery Beck followed Sam Dennison out of the administrative area into the lobby. A corrections officer on duty eyed Beck carefully until Dennison introduced him as the new Jail Administrator. The officer nodded politely, making no effort to hide his lack of interest. Dennison turned to Avery and spoke.

"From this point on only authorized people are allowed--all jail staff, attorneys, police and court personnel."

Dennison moved to a large red metal door and waited. A faint click sounded and Avery followed him into a corridor.

"This is the master control corridor and the man sitting in the glass cage in front of us controls all radio communications, as well as access and exit through this door, and the other door in front of us. The officer assigned to Master Control also has an intercom system and phone system which he uses to speak with the different levels."

"Inside the Master Control Center is where all the keys not in use are kept. This facility probably has somewhere in the area of about three hundred different keys, all of which must be inventoried and accounted for every eight hours. Past this second door is the jail."

Dennison moved ahead with Avery following. The moment the first metal door had slammed shut Avery had felt a slight increase in his respiration and an irrational feeling of claustrophobia. Avery told himself it was silly and tried to concentrate on what Dennison was saying.

The two men moved through the second metal door. Dennison was pointing to an office marked "Records" and saying, "This is where all the prisoners' records are kept. It's also the place where court dates are set, release orders are filed and all paperwork regarding any prisoner we have in custody is maintained."

Dennison moved past this entry and stopped in front of another locked metal door. He pushed a small button by an intercom and a metallic voice from the speaker responded.

"What do you want?"

Dennison made a face at the intercom and spoke, "Dennison-R&D."

A metallic click echoed in the hallway and Dennison pulled open the door. He held the door for Beck and explained, "This door along with every other door on the ground floor is controlled by the master control center. This door is not opened until the officer in master control ensures the person wanting to enter is authorized."

Beck failed to understand how the officer in master control could verify the identity of anyone. The master control center was several feet down the hall and around the corner. Avery commented, "What if someone else were to say they were Dennison, how would the master control officer know the difference?"

Dennison looked at Beck for a second trying to understand his question. Everything had become second nature to Dennison after fifteen years and Beck's question was unexpected. After several seconds, he pointed to the ceiling where a closed circuit camera was mounted. "The master control officer sees everyone who comes in and out of this door."

Dennison then led Beck into the Receiving and Discharge area. Here was a long metal counter, a row of cells, and about six or seven uniformed officers typing, escorting, and searching prisoners. One prisoner was locked in a cell. He was screaming something about his energy escaping through holes in his feet. He was being ignored. Beck's first instinct told him someone needed to do something about the man screaming in the cell. He wasn't sure what, but he felt something should be done. Beck questioned Dennison about the man and Dennison responded dryly, "As long as he keeps screaming and yelling everyone knows he's all right. It's when he gets quiet, then we have to keep a close watch on him."

Beck wasn't sure he understood what Dennison meant but declined to press the issue. It was after this exchange that the smell in the booking area found its way to Beck's conscious mind. Stale urine, the smell of feet, sweat, fear and dried blood all intermingled into a nauseous blend.

Dennison continued to speak, "Everyone who comes to jail comes here first through those double doors, called the sally port." He explained the entire booking process in great detail--charges documented, the body search, the medical exam.

"After the paramedics are finished with the screening process the prisoner is allowed to make a phone call. I suppose I should mention, there are eight different cells located here in booking. Each cell has a toilet and will hold ten people comfortably. On busy nights we sometimes put fifteen to twenty people in these cells. Generally, no one will be held in booking for more than four hours. If it looks like they are not going to bond out then we dress them out, which means we take their clothes and dress them in a set of blue jail coveralls, and then we send them upstairs."

"I mentioned bonding earlier. Each charge carries a specific bond amount set by the courts. A bond is a monetary promise to appear in court. If the person is arrested for commercial burglary and the bond is five thousand dollars and the person has five thousand dollars, he can put that money up as a promise to appear in court. If he doesn't have the money, he can call a bonding company who is in the business of posting bail for people. On a five thousand dollar bond, the bonding company would probably charge about five hundred dollars, and then sign the person out. There are only two other ways for a person to get released before going to court. The first is through a pre-trial release process. Court personnel conduct interviews with people arrested and if they have ties to the community and appear to be a good release risk, they are given a court date and released on their own recognizance. Most staff refer to this process as ROR. If they fail to show up for court, a warrant is issued and they are arrested. The last way to get out of jail is to escape. We've been fortunate. We haven't had any escapes in the past four years. One thing many people forget is that the majority of people in jail have not been convicted of anything. They are here because they're poor. If they had the money to bond, they'd be out."

Dennison hesitated for a moment, wondering if Beck understood anything he had said.

"If a person is unable to bond out or be released on his own recognizance, then he gets dressed in a pair of blue jail coveralls, which means we take his clothes, and we send him upstairs to the classification unit on the first floor. He'll stay there for maybe twenty-four to forty-eight hours. Most everyone goes to court the next day. If the court does not release the person, then our classification people will look at the charges, the age of the offender, past criminal history, and anything else available, including any record of his previous behavior while incarcerated. Based on this information the prisoner will be assigned to one of the housing units. Some people will not be allowed to live in the regular units because of their charges, or maybe because of their looks."

"What do you mean because of their looks?"

Dennison shrugged his shoulders, "Some of the people we get in here are halfway through a sex change operation or they've been taking hormone shots. We get people who have the basic body parts of both sexes and nobody really knows if they belong in the male or female unit. When that happens, we place them into protective custody for their own safety."

Dennison ushered Beck out of the booking area and stopped at an elevator on the ground floor. When they entered Dennison pushed the first button marked "One". The ride was short and both men exited.

"This is the first floor. The classification unit is on the south side and general minimum custody prisoners are on the north side. Each housing unit on every other floor is identical to this one."

Beck found himself standing in a hallway with a huge sliding metal door to his right, another to his left, and another hinged metal door directly in front of him. Dennison moved to the hinged metal door and knocked. The door was opened and Beck followed Dennison inside. The room reminded Beck of an underground war room. It was dark, with a huge console of different colored lights and switches carefully laid out on a metallic control panel.

Dennison explained, "This is DL-1 Control. The officer assigned to this post monitors the prisoners and corrections officers assigned to the floor on both sides through this one-way security glass." Dennison motioned to the large windows facing the housing units on each side of the control room.

"The console with the lights allows the control room officer to lock or unlock each individual room door. Each side of this detention level has a total of forty-eight rooms. Each room has a toilet, a bunk, a sink, as well as a window. The south side is used for classification. The north side is where the minimum custody people are housed. As you can see, the people on the south side are all wearing blue coveralls and the people on the north side are wearing green. Green coveralls mean the prisoner is a trusty and can be used to work in the kitchen, the laundry, clean floors, or whatever else needs to be done in the facility. We have a total of eighty-three sentenced trusties who work daily in this facility."

The feeling of claustrophobia had increased since Beck had entered the control room. The darkness, the undefined smell of something, and the constant squawking of the radio had made him nauseous. The corrections officer had greeted Dennison when they entered, but had turned back to a stack of papers and was busy working, ignoring the two of them.

Dennison made some comment to the corrections officer in the control center and led Beck outside to the lighted corridor. There was a great deal more to see, but Dennison had detected Beck's discomfort. He looked at Beck and decided his new boss had seen enough for one day. Both returned to the ground floor. Riding the elevator in silence, Dennison wondered what Beck thought of the facility. Beck wondered what the hell he had gotten himself into.

5

Twenty-seven years ago, Mr. and Mrs. Prescott Macon had proudly announced to their family and friends the birth of their first child, Donald Prescott Macon. Today, Donald Prescott Macon was a name which was not spoken in the Macon household.

Donald was born the eldest of three children in an upper-middle class home. He had not been exceptionally bright, just average intelligence and was forced to work hard in school. There was nothing significant surrounding Donald's childhood. He went to school and he came home with no interest in sports, extra activities or even the normal adolescent curiosity about girls. Two years before graduation Donald had tried working several part time jobs. Each job ended in sudden dismissals. He had tried. He had tried very hard. Each failure had devastated him emotionally. Donald had always been shy, but now his confidence wavered and he began to withdraw deeper and deeper into himself. Life was hard. People were cruel, but his parents continued to encourage him. Donald had always been close to his parents. Now he found himself drifting away. Their encouragement only made him feel worse. There was no way he could explain the fear and the confusion he was feeling. Failure was terrifying, and to fail in the eyes of his parents only compounded the shame. Donald had always read a great deal, but now he found himself reading to escape. Reading had become his only escape from the pain of reality and it allowed him to be the hero. The masterful hero who commanded everyone's lives. He knew what was right and what was wrong. It was all clear. In his own life, Donald no longer knew what was right and what was wrong. He only knew he was frightened. Frightened of everything. Family gatherings took on a new form. Everyone participated except Donald. He did not feel well. It was all right, he would just stay home and maybe watch television or read. Besides, someone needed to keep an eye on the house with all the burglaries in the neighborhood. Donald's parents understood. Donald needed to be alone. He needed time to think, to straighten things out. He was a good boy. He would be fine. With the family gone, Donald would pace through the house. He wished he had gone. He was lonely. He wanted his parents. He wanted things to be like they had been ten years ago. Things had been so simple then.

Alone in the house, depressed--at nineteen--Donald began drinking. It was something to do. It was nothing more than curiosity. As the pain inside grew, he found a little whiskey helped to wash away some of the ache. Donald learned quickly that large quantities of alcohol could magically release the anguish he was experiencing. Donald Prescott Macon, the average young man from an average middle class environment, became an alcoholic.

It took his parents six months to discover the truth. After hours of tearful discussion, Donald was sent to Suncrest Hospital. His parents explained they were only trying to help. They loved him. For three months Donald stayed at Suncrest attending therapy sessions and mechanically going through the motions of institutionalized living. At the end of the ninety days the Prescott's medical insurance ran out and the hospital officials pronounced Donald cured.

Donald returned home.

Donald was not cured.

He was filled with more guilt than ever. His parent's house seemed alien and foreign. Watchful eyes and furtive glances followed him. Forced cheerfulness and apologies filled every conversation.

Donald needed help.

His parents' wanted to help.

Donald wanted his parents help.

The Hospital claimed they had helped.

There was nothing anyone could do...Donald left home.

There was no help to be found.

Several times during the next eight years, Donald unsuccessfully tried to return home and put his life in order. Each time his parents found it harder and harder to accept the young man dressed in rags, reeking of body odor and urine. Donald would stay for one, sometimes two days until the pangs of alcohol withdrawal forced him to leave and search for something to quiet the aching.

Metal dumpsters, cardboard boxes and empty buildings were places Donald called home. The past became a blur made fuzzy by the alcohol. Donald did not want to remember the past. There was only one goal in life--to seek, to find, and to consume enough alcohol on each day to keep the remnants of disjointed memories and disappointments at bay. The future would take care of itself. Life now was uncomplicated and simple.

In this new world, subcultures existed among the street people. Most of the people who lived on the street were nonviolent and interested in only a drink, a place to spend the night and occasionally, food.

Alongside the peaceful dwellers existed a separate group of predators. They were cruel and aggressive, prone to sudden acts of violence and rage. These acts would oftentimes erupt unexpectedly and culminate in the senseless beating of those around them. Some were mentally ill. Others merely vented their angers, failures and frustrations through physical force.

One common thread bound them together. They were all outcasts of society and they all sought the relief of alcoholic oblivion.

Donald had been beaten, rolled by other drunks and had been hospitalized in the county hospital four times within the last eight years. He had come to accept the beatings as a way of life and a penance for his failures.

Each wino established a route and staked out certain territories where booze, food and shelter could generally be found. To invade another's territory was a violation of street people ethics.

The tenth day of January had been exactly like any other day. Donald had panhandled, begging for money until five in the evening. He had made enough money to purchase a cheap pint of port wine. With the change tucked in his pockets he had gone to Pete's bar. It was here he sucked the few remaining drops of gold from the bottom of beer cans stacked outside at the back of the bar. Precious warm drops of life.

Mechanically draining each beer can, Donald purchased his daily pint of port wine which he hid in the oversized pockets of his cast-off gray coat. But to advertise one's good fortune among the other street people was foolhardy. The last leg of his rounds ended at the Salvation Army building. It was here he consumed his one meal a day. After supper, Donald headed to the place he called home, a dark green metal dumpster behind an all night convenience store. There was a serious danger attached to sleeping in a dumpster. If you did not wake up early enough on the day the garbage was collected you would die. Two street people Donald knew had died in the back of garbage trucks. Both had been dumped into the rear of the garbage truck and crushed.

The convenience store dumpster was a dry place when it rained and usually contained only small amounts of wet garbage. The best dumpsters were strictly dry garbage: papers, boxes and items containing zero percent moisture. These had been staked out by other street people years before. If you were big enough and mean enough, you could evict the current occupant. Donald was neither. He was only a sad, lonely wino who walked the streets during the day begging for money. He spent the nights in the green dumpster behind a convenience store.

He had been living in this particular dumpster for the past two years. The night clerk, a man named Paul, had left him alone and every once in a while he would give Donald hot dogs and other food gone stale. The old man never asked Donald any questions. Over all, Donald was comfortable. Around midnight, Donald climbed into his dumpster, shoved some of the papers to the side, unscrewed the cap and lost himself in a drunken stupor. This transported him into his own world. A world where he was successful. His parents stood across a river waving and smiling. Pride was in their eyes. Donald waved back smiling. Donald was successful. Everything was good. The sky was clear, but something was wrong. Suddenly, there was thunder. Two quick crashes shook him. Donald jumped.

It was a dream. He huddled, shaking in the darkness and listened. His hot sour breath mingled with the cold air formed a sticky mist. He had to urinate. He hated to climb out but it was winter and the dampness inside the dumpster would not be good. Donald staggered to his feet and peered out of from beneath the heavy metal lid. He was still dreaming. He must be. Walking towards him was a tall blonde man with a gun in his hand. The man was coming to kill him. The man had been sent by Donald's parents. They no longer loved him. Donald closed his eyes and began to cry. He waited for the sound of the metal lid opening and the gunshot. In terror and silent agony. He waited for several seconds.

Nothing happened.

Donald opened his eyes and eased up the lid a second time. He saw the man walk to a Chevrolet parked in the dark several feet away.

The car started and the man drove away. Donald stared after the vehicle dumbly. Absently, he recited the license number, "ASK 911." For several more minutes Donald stayed inside the dumpster and waited. He could feel the cheap wine making its way up his throat. Shaking from the January cold, the alcohol and the fright, he climbed out and emptied the contents of his stomach on the asphalt pavement. It was OK, Donald told himself, he still had half a pint left. He staggered back to the side of the dumpster and slid to the ground, unscrewed his bottle and took two long swigs. The wine burned his already irritated throat.

Donald opened his eyes slowly. It was still dark, but someone was screaming. First the thunder and now screaming. Beams of red light shot wickedly into his eyes and numbed his brain. He closed his eyes and rolled over hoping the screams would stop. All he wanted to do was sleep. Someone was shaking him, talking to him. Again he opened his eyes. A giant blue creature hovered over him. Donald blinked, wiped his eyes with the back of his hand, and felt the gravel that was stuck to his hand scratch his face. Someone was still shaking him. He tried opening his eyes again. It was a policeman. This had happened before. Donald's mind whirred. The policeman would take Donald to jail. The jail people would put him in a warm cell. In the morning they would give him an egg sandwich and let him go. Everything was going to be fine. There was no problem.

With the policeman's help Donald struggled to his feet. Through a drunken haze, he saw six police cars with red lights flashing in the parking lot. This was wrong. The police never used their red lights to pick him up. There was always just one car. Donald blinked and tried to clear his head. He felt a cramp in his stomach. The cramps would become worse, but not for hours. Everything was OK. The policeman placed handcuffs on him.

Donald's mind buzzed, routine procedure.

The policeman cuffed his hands behind his back and walked him to the front of the store. Police were everywhere. Police in uniform, police with cameras, police in civilian clothes, and there was screaming. Some woman with dark hair was standing next to a police car and screaming. Donald wanted to tell her not to scream. Everything would be fine. An egg sandwich in the morning. Instead he mumbled, "Ask 911."

The policeman was talking again. Everyone was talking. Donald could not understand the officer. Donald shook his head "yes." This was the best thing to do with police. Always say yes, yes, yes...yes to everything.

"Don't piss off a pig my motto," muttered Donald. "Ask, 911."

Most cops were good guys. Some were bad guys, dressed like good guys. Never make them mad, never piss off a pig.

Donald was led to a car and placed in the back seat. Someone reached across him and fastened the seat belt. He slumped over and fell asleep. If anything happened someone would wake him. He wished the woman would stop screaming.

The twenty minute ride downtown to the jail seemed like seconds to Donald. One second he was getting into the police car and the next second the police officer was taking him out.

Donald wanted to rub his eyes and wipe his nose but his hands were cuffed. The police officer took him to a glass door and waited for several seconds. The door slid open smoothly. Donald and the policeman entered. The officer leaned Donald against the wall and deposited his gun in a metal locker. A second door opened and Donald was in booking. It was early Tuesday morning and the area was relatively quiet. During the night the officers assigned to booking had processed forty prisoners. The cells in the booking area were occupied by a total of twenty-seven prisoners. Most had been arrested for drunk driving and had fallen into a sound sleep minutes after incarceration. In the morning they would go to court and plead their case before the judge. A fight between two drunks had erupted in one of the cells during the night. Both of the drunks had been too intoxicated to inflict any serious damage to each other and once they had been separated and placed in different cells, the booking area had returned to a semi-peaceful calm.

Donald moved to the booking counter and waited for the police officer to unlock his handcuffs.

The lieutenant in charge of the booking area, Ivers, had watched with detached interest as the second security door slid open and Donald Macon entered with a police officer. Ivers recognized Donald as a regular. Donald had been coming to jail for the past six years and had never given anyone any trouble. Unlike many, Donald was a calm and peaceful wino. The police officer removed his handcuffs and a corrections officer dressed in a blue uniform seated on a stool behind the booking counter began his routine questioning.

Name, address, phone number, date of birth, social security number were all entered into the computer. While Donald mumbled semi-coherent answers to questions, two other officers took up positions next to Donald.

George, AKA "Georgie," Byers had been a corrections officer for twelve years. Frank Willis had been a corrections officer for two years. Georgie pulled on a pair of rubber surgical gloves and began the routine search.

Donald wore two coats, three sweaters, three pairs of pants and two pair of socks. It was everything he owned. All his clothes were filthy. Searching street people exposed the corrections officer to crabs and other body vermin that infested the street people. The rubber gloves offered a minimum amount of protection.

Georgie helped Donald remove the two coats, the sweaters and the extra pairs of pants. Georgie found Donald's port wine and dumped the contents into a toilet before tossing the empty bottle into the trash. It was impossible to search a person through all this clothing but street bum or no street bum, it was necessary since one never knew when a person was carrying a firearm or a knife.

Willis watched with disgust as Georgie spoke quietly to Donald. As far as Willis was concerned, Donald was a maggot, a bum. The world would be a better place without Donald Macon and his kind. Frank Willis had no sympathy or compassion for this smelly, putrid human standing next to him. Donald Macon had not taken a real shower in months. His hair was matted and greasy. His two-week old stubble was punctuated by open sores on his face. Snot hung from Donald's nose and coated his cracked lips. His pants were stained with urine. When Willis noted the stains he moved a step backwards, muttering, "The son-of-a-bitch pissed in his pants."

Once Donald had been searched, Georgie escorted him to the paramedic's station where he was questioned again. Donald did not suffer from any chronic disease but the paramedic made a notation on the medical form. Donald would be withdrawing from alcohol in the next several hours. The jail pharmacy was alerted and an alcohol withdrawal kit was ordered for prisoner Macon. Georgie escorted Donald to one of the holding cells and helped him to the floor. Donald did not want to use the phone. There was no one to call. Georgie knew he would have to keep a close eye on Donald. The hallucinations of spiders and snakes experienced during alcohol withdrawal were all real to an alcoholic. More people died from alcohol withdrawals than from withdrawal from any other drug.

After Donald had moved away from the booking counter, the police officer provided the charges. This time it was not routine. This time Donald Macon would be held as a material witness to a homicide. Donald Macon would not be released in the morning.

Georgie had been working at the jail twelve years. At the beginning of his career he had been much like Frank Willis. The Donald Macon's of the world were nothing more than walking cesspools. Twelve years and thousands of prisoners later Georgie had found the compassion and sympathy which came with confidence and experience. In the beginning he had been frightened. Hell, everyone had been scared to work in a jail. If a prisoner assaulted a corrections officer, the officer retaliated. After twelve years, Georgie no longer retaliated. If a prisoner assaulted him, Georgie knew the chances of a drunk inflicting any serious damage was minimal. He also knew the drunk had no idea what he was doing. Georgie would maintain his distance and if a drunk tried to hit him, he just backed away. Nine out of ten times the drunk would stagger and fall to the floor. It had taken Georgie three years to understand the sadness, the anger, the hate and the frustration people felt when they came to jail. All of these emotions were often vented on the most convenient target, the corrections officer. Georgie understood he could take a prisoner's property, his clothes, even his cigarettes without having to fight, but once he took the prisoner's dignity and self respect he would have to fight. Fighting was something Georgie no longer cared to do. He had done his share. In the early days he had sent many people to the hospital. Now physical violence was reserved as a last resort.

There are many different types of prisoners. There are the Donald Macon's--harmless, hopeless, and non-violent. Then there are killers, the people who are plain mean. They'd kill a corrections officer without provocation and without reason.

And there are "lifers", the institutionalized prisoners. They are the prisoners who have been in and out of prison all their lives. These people are not inherently violent. When they are institutionalized they go with the flow. If a corrections officer challenges them, or disgraces them in front of the other prisoners, the lifer will attack. A smart corrections officer does not antagonize an old con. A smart corrections officer explains things and the old con moves into the main stream.

Still another class is the first time young adult. There are two types. The wild, uncontrollable prisoner who does anything and everything he can to develop a reputation. A reputation can be garnered in prison or jail by assaulting a corrections officer, by attempting to escape, or by attempting to disrupt the system. The other type of young offender is the scared kid. In most cases this is the one who finds himself involved in something serious. This person is frightened and can easily fall prey to the killer, the old con and the other young adults. In Georgie's opinion, the young scared offender does not belong in jail but the system says he does and it is Georgie's job to protect him.

Georgie had worked among all types of offenders. Within the past twelve years, he had been kicked, spat on, punched, bitten and cursed. Georgie had learned to handle the intense stress and pressure and was able to keep his cool. Not all corrections officers had his knowledge, wisdom, or the experience.

There were other corrections officers who had not learned to handle the stress. Like Willis. These people would either become wiser in time and minimize the amount of violence they practiced or they would burn out and quit. Most of them were scared. They came to work scared, overcompensated for their fears by employing too much force and left at the end of their shift still scared. Many wanted to quit but they were trapped. Trapped economically. Most were unskilled and would not be able to get another job at the same pay scale.

For these officers each day was another test, another battle. Georgie understood perfectly. He had gone through it himself twelve years ago. The corrections officer who used excessive force was rarely caught and disciplined. An officer never testified against another officer, regardless of the circumstances. Corrections officers referred to this creed as the "blue veil." It was an unwritten law among the corrections officers. But lieutenants and captains were different. They could and did testify against corrections officers. It was their job and it was accepted by the line staff. Most cases came down to a prisoner's word against an officer's, followed by an inconclusive investigation, and no action would be taken against the officer.

*　　　*　　　*

The jail is a strange institution, a microcosm of a calmer, saner, safer city. Like other forms of government, it has a formal chain of command and an informal chain of command. Georgie Byers rested comfortably near the top of the informal chain of command. He had not desired nor aspired to the rank of captain or lieutenant. Georgie was well respected by prisoners and the majority of corrections officers.

Although Georgie was respected by prisoners, most kept their distance. None wanted to be labeled as overly cooperative with Georgie or any officer. If the other prisoners detected a friendship between an officer and a prisoner, the prisoner ran the risk of being labeled a snitch. A prisoner who informed on other prisoners, regardless of the circumstances, was given a "jacket" and silenced swiftly. This also held true among the corrections officers' fraternity. Anyone who violated the blue veil and snitched on another officer would be completely ostracized. It was a delicate balance of formal, informal and prisoner rule inside the jail, a complex social system unknown to most of the outside world.

A formal but ineffectual system of sanctions also exists in jail. It is ineffectual because the majority of prisoners know their rights are protected by law and any form of punishment could only be done by the withdrawing of privileges from an inmate. Staff went through the steps and the prisoners snickered, knowing the jail officials could do little. In some cases corrections officers took it upon themselves to execute justice. Without some element of justice, the mean prisoners and the wild young ones, and even the old cons, would declare open season on the officers. Some used excessive force and punished prisoners by stepping outside the realm of formal sanctions. Late night visits to a cell occupied by a particularly abusive or disruptive prisoner by several officers was not uncommon. Often, the prisoner would be warned of the consequences of his behavior. If he fails to heed the first warning, then a second visit take's place and the prisoner is beaten. The prisoner then complains, an investigation is conducted, the corrections officers lie, and the investigation ends without conclusive proof needed to take disciplinary action against the officers. Corrections officers who operate outside the scope of their duties and outside the law, help to maintain the delicate balance of control in the jail.

Some corrections officers, like Georgie Byers, rarely engage in any form of physical violence. Other officers seek out physical altercations, reveling in the exhilaration. Still others avoid confrontation but see it as their duty to assist in maintaining control. Staff survival is a daily struggle. Georgie Byers moved from cell to cell checking the sleeping inmates and scribbling his initials. Each door had a jail form attached to it with incremental times listed. The officer checking the cells was required to initial the sheet by the appropriate pre-printed time. Everything had to be documented for possible later court appearances, including prisoner observation checks.

Georgie finished checking the cells, leaned against the wall and lit a cigarette while his eyes strayed to the clock in booking. Only two more hours to go.

Frank Willis watched from a distance. Bleeding hearts like Byers made Willis sick. Byers might have twelve years experience but as far as Willis was concerned, Byers didn't know shit. The only thing the dirt-balls in jail understood was force. And force meant pain. It was that simple. All the hearts and flowers crap Byers used might avoid violence but it was a lot faster to slap the fuck up side the head, put some handcuffs on him and toss him into a cell.

People in jail might not like Frank Willis, but they sure as hell feared him. And in Frank Willis's mind fear and respect were synonymous.

But Frank Willis was afraid. He refused to admit it to himself but each day he came to work prepared to fight. For Willis, each day was a test. Each day the fear inside him grew, and each day another prisoner was bullied or beaten. It was a hell of a way to make a living.

Meanwhile, Donald Macon lay sleeping soundly inside his cell, he was completely unaware that he would soon become a part of a delicately balanced world controlled by the likes of Georgie Byers and Frank Willis.

6

Avery Beck sat alone in his office trying to sort out a mass of feelings and emotions. He never knew how oppressive and confining a jail could be. Now he was faced with running one and understanding all there was to learn. His brief tour had been a culture shock, a walk from one world into another. The world outside had murderers, rapists and burglars but they were within the saner components of society. Here there was no pretense. The ugly brutality of man against man was clearly apparent. But this was enough for one day. He would spend the remainder of the day interviewing and getting to know his senior staff. Dennison, the Deputy Chief of Operations, he had met. Dennison had impressed Beck as capable, competent and to the point. Dennison's personnel record revealed a Bachelor's Degree in Criminology. He had been with the jail for fifteen years but had been disciplined several times in the past--once for submitting a sarcastic report while he was a shift captain and another time for initiating an illegal search. Dennison had begun his career as a corrections officer and had climbed steadily up to his current position of deputy chief.

The other deputy chief, Marshall Paulson, was in charge of security. According to his personnel file Paulson had retired from the military after twenty-fours years of service as a military policeman. He had been employed at the jail a scant five years compared to Dennison's fifteen. How Paulson had risen so fast and so far in the jail's administration was a mystery to Beck. Avery punched the direct phone line to Paulson's office and waited several rings.

"I'd like to see you in my office."

Paulson hesitated. "I'll be there in a couple of minutes," he replied curtly and hung up.

Avery waited. Two minutes later Paulson entered. He was about six feet tall with hints of a middle-age spread. His dark hair was cut close, military style, and his brown eyes were roving and hostile.

After Paulson had been seated, Avery began.

"Tell me what you do here, Marshall."

Paulson sat ramrod straight and replied. "I am in charge of security, and in a jail security comes first. If security is not there, the prisoners will escape and there would no longer be a need for the jail. I have two hundred and forty people under me--corrections officers, captains, and lieutenants. The last administrator, Powell, was not interested in new and different approaches. Powell kept all of us.."

Avery held up his hand and stopped him in mid-sentence.

"I will not discuss Mr. Powell with you. I have a great deal of respect for Mr. Powell. He ran this jail for a number of years and while I'm sure he didn't always do the things everyone would have liked him to do, I think it best if we let Mr. Powell retire."

Paulson sat quietly for several seconds.

"I agree," he replied and continued.

"I know you don't want to discuss Powell and I won't. I'll only say he was a very poor administrator, with a closed mind. "I have some good ideas. Some sound ideas I would like for you to take a look at sometime in the near future. We need a training academy, and we need some professionalism in the line ranks."

Paulson's ideas coincided with good managerial principles and Beck was impressed. He sounded energetic and willing to tackle key issues. Perhaps this was why Paulson had moved so rapidly through the ranks.

They exchanged idle chatter for another half-hour until Paulson rose to leave.

"I'd better get back to work. If I don't keep an eye on the captains, who knows what they might try to pull."

Beck thanked Paulson for his candor and watched him leave.

This talk had been the one high point this first day. Dennison was still a question mark. He had maintained his distance after the brief tour.

Avery let the thought slip from his mind and instructed his secretary to send in Roberto Romero, the internal affairs manager. He still had a lot of people to meet and a lot of information to digest before he formed any decisions about anybody or anything.

Roberto Romero supervised a staff of three people: two investigators and one secretary. And he kept busy. Romero was a retired police officer with vast experience and a clear head. Romero didn't need the job as internal affairs chief, but he enjoyed the jail investigations.

After twenty years as a police officer, working internal affairs at the jail provided him with a different insight into the criminal justice arena. In his early fifties, Romero was impeccably dressed and distinguished in appearance. He strode into the administrator's office and for twenty minutes, droned on about pending lawsuits, charges of excessive use of force and tips he had received concerning corrections staff selling drugs in the jail. Romero explained that a corrections officer could earn an additional two or three hundred dollars this way.

Until the pay for corrections officers increased, and corrections people were given recognition as a professional group, the problem of selling drugs in jail would continue.

Avery listened carefully and understood most of Romero's briefing. Law and lawsuits were something he understood. Roberto Romero was speaking his language. He concluded his briefing by informing Beck he was now working on a case involving a contract employee who had accused corrections officers Jason Robbins and Danny Pitts of some fairly outlandish activities. Beck urged Romero to keep him advised. After he left, Beck shook his head. What had he stepped into?

7

Jason Robbins and Danny Pitts were assigned to the work release unit for the third day in a row. Both officers had begun a career in corrections seven years ago. For each it had been a job and neither had intended to stay. After three years on the job they realized they were trapped financially. There was no place else they could go and make the same money. It was January 8th, the evening shift, and both officers were angry. Normally corrections officers were rotated to various posts throughout the facility. For some reason the shift captain had screwed them three days in a row. No one liked to work with Mrs. Kroger, a contract employee from Labs Affiliated. She was a cantankerous, old woman with blue hair and a wicked tongue. Mrs. Kroger habitually wore a pair of reading glasses perched on the end of a heavily powdered nose. When speaking she would sight down her nose through those glasses and target the subject of her dislike. Her job was to conduct urine tests on prisoners in the jail's work release program. These prisoners were released in the morning for work and returned in the evening.

The work release program had been started five years before as Powell's brain child to reduce the jail's population and to provide minimum custody offenders the opportunity to maintain their jobs and still be supervised by jail staff. Each prisoner was required to sign a contract agreeing to comply with a list of rules which included no drugs or drinking. The prisoners were closely monitored. Each day, when they returned from work, each prisoner would be searched, his clothes would be taken and he would dress in orange coveralls. Then there was the urine test to determine if a prisoner had taken any drugs while outside. Anyone who failed was immediately removed from the program. It was the officer's duty in this program to obtain the urine samples, label them, and pass them along to Mrs. Kroger. She then conducted the tests and reported any that were "dirty."

Mrs. Kroger did not like corrections officers. She made this clear. Fifty years old, over painted, and with a superior attitude.

She was exceedingly proper and considered herself more refined and dignified than the crass, base corrections staff with which she was forced to work. None of the corrections staff liked to work with her.

But Mrs. Kroger enjoyed the full support of the administration. She made this clear to all. Anytime Mrs. Kroger complained, which was frequently, action was taken against the corrections officer she accused. From the officer's perspective, it was unjust and an outrage.

This was the third day in a row Robbins and Pitts would have to deal with the piss bitch. Robbins informed Pitts he was not going to take any more abuse and he had a plan.

Robbins obtained an unused urine specimen bottle, filled it half full with lemonade from the chow hall and then labeled the bottle with a bogus name. This specimen was passed along with the rest to Mrs. Kroger.

Robbins then wandered into "no mans land," Mrs. Kroger's office, and attempted to make small talk. But she was not receptive. Robbins persevered.

"Hey, uh, Mrs. Kroger, how does all this work, you know, how do you test this stuff to find out if these guys have been doing drugs?"

Mrs. Kroger peered up from the bottles of which stood in rows at attention like miniature toy golden soldiers. She scowled and adjusted her glasses and began as if she were conducting a high school chemistry class.

"That machine over there is calibrated to detect cannabis, opiates, heroin and certain other derivatives. Not only will it detect them, but it will also indicate the precise amount."

"That's amazing, Mrs. Kroger," said Robbins as he ventured to the edge of the desk and surveyed the samples. Robbins was wide-eyed and full of enthusiasm. Finding the bogus urine bottle, Robbins plucked it out and swirled it around while holding it at eye level. He peered intently at the yellowish fluid.

"Can't you just look at it and tell if a guy's been taking dope? I mean does it look any different from regular piss, I mean urine?"

She responded in her usual manner, laced with sarcasm. "It just goes to show how much you know about these things."

Undaunted, Robbins unscrewed the cap of the specimen bottle and sniffed. The fragrant smell of lemon reached his nostrils. He looked across the desk at Mrs. Kroger and asked, "Can't you tell if somebody's been taking dope by smelling this stuff?"

Mrs. Kroger pointed a scrawny finger at Robbins and ordered, "Put that down this instant! I'll be writing a report concerning your insolent behavior, young man."

He shrugged his shoulders, looked indifferently at Mrs. Kroger and said, "Well what if you taste it. I wonder if it would taste any different than regular piss?"

With that, Robbins hoisted the urine specimen, tilted back his head and consumed the entire contents. Placing the container back on the table, Robbins smacked his lips.

Mrs. Kroger stared in shocked disbelief as Robbins announced, "It doesn't taste any different to me, Mrs. Kroger, and I've been drinking piss for a long time."

By now Mrs. Kroger had sunk back into her chair, attempting to form words. She blew droplets of spittle while she flailed her arms wildly. Then she suddenly thrust herself forward and collapsed over the urine bottles on her desk.

Robbins quickly called an ambulance and Mrs. Kroger was carted off to the hospital. Two days later she related the entire urine drinking episode to jail officials.

The case was passed to Roberto Romero in Internal Affairs to investigate. On January 11th, Robbins and Pitts were interviewed by Roberto Romero. Both claimed they knew nothing about anyone drinking urine and if crazy old Mrs. Kroger claimed they had drunk piss she should be locked up.

With nothing conclusive, Romero closed the case. He had heard some bizarre tales, but never had he heard anyone claim a corrections officer had drunk a bottle of urine. It was pretty far-fetched. Secretly, the internal affairs investigator agreed with Robbins and Pitts. The old woman had gone off her rocker.

Mrs. Kroger never returned to the jail. She was assigned to conduct drug testing at a quiet industrial complex.

Jason Robbins and Danny Pitts returned to work and became famous as the two C.O.s who finally rid the jail of the urine queen.

8

Tommy Brown was nineteen years old and tired. Tired of working at a fast food restaurant for minimum wage. He had barely managed to graduate from high school the year before. The only jobs he had been able to get during the past year were minimum wage and maximum labor jobs. He was a tall, gangly, white male with patches of fuzz on his face.

Tommy Brown lived with his parents. Both worked and were dedicated to their jobs, believing hard work was the key to success. They were lost in their own world of competition and success. They had raised their son and now it was time for him to strike out on his own and be successful through hard work. But Tommy Brown did not fit into his parent's encapsulated environment. He found his own where he felt important and accepted, an environment where people listened to him.

Shortly after graduation, he developed a loose association with five other young men who were prime jail candidates. Most were in their late teens or early twenties. Rick, the oldest, was the leader. He did not work, yet he always seemed to have money. In the beginning this had puzzled Tommy. Now Tommy knew why. Rick was a burglar.

In the evenings when all the guys would meet at Rick's place, he would brag about how easy this job or that job had been and how he had made a couple of hundred dollars in fifteen minutes. The eyes of the others shone with envy at the apparent ease in making money. But Rick was a generous burglar who offered a split for anyone bold and brave enough to work with him. All had declined. All had declined, that is, until tonight. Tonight, Tommy Brown made the decision to accept the offer. Tonight, Tommy would become a burglar.

It was January 10th. A cold wind had swept in from the north and the temperature was near freezing. Rick had selected a darkened house along a fashionable residential area as the first target.

Rick had supplied a five-dollar screw driver and had instructed Tommy about what he was to take once inside the house.

Tommy listened intently as Rick introduced him to the fine art of burglary. "Most people leave money and valuables in clothes they have hanging in the closet. Another place to look is inside dresser drawers where they keep their underwear. If jewelry is sitting out in the open asking to be stolen, it's probably costume crap. If you don't find any jewelry or cash hidden anywhere, then just grab a VCR, portable television or microwave. They're always easy to get rid of. Any questions?"

Tommy shook his head. He understood everything perfectly. Tommy climbed out of the car and walked to the darkened house while Rick waited. Hunched behind some bushes near a window, he wondered what he was doing here. He wanted money, but maybe this had been a mistake. He could walk back to the street and tell Rick it had all been a mistake. Rick would understand.

But Tommy knew he was lying to himself. Rick would not understand. Rick would laugh and tell everyone what a brave coward Tommy Brown had been. Tommy blew on his cold hands and rubbed them together to stimulate the circulation. After several minutes he reached into his back pocket and pulled out the screwdriver. He looked back at Rick's parked car one more time before approaching the window. Tommy knew what he was about to do was wrong. He knew he could be arrested. But Rick had done it dozens of times and never been caught.

Tommy reached the window, inserted the screwdriver and pried. On the third attempt the window opened a quarter of an inch and all of Tommy's previous doubts evaporated from this small victory. Excitement replaced doubt and determination blinded his ability to think rationally. With renewed vigor, Tommy attacked the partially opened window.

Five minutes elapsed before the window was opened wide enough to scramble through. Tommy stood in the dark interior of the house listening and waiting. He was breathing heavily from his exertions and his breathing echoed in his head.

Had Tommy turned and looked at the window casing closely, he would have seen the two silver metal contacts with a wire running down the side of the window.

He knew nothing about burglary and nothing about burglar alarms. Tommy then moved carefully through the living room and into the bedroom, all the while noting several electronic appliances he could take if he failed to locate jewelry or money. He checked each drawer carefully as he had been instructed. Finding no jewelry or money hidden in the drawers he moved to the closet and went through each coat pocket quickly. But there were no jewels or money to be found. Rick would have to be content with an appliance. Tommy returned to the living room, disconnected the VCR and walked to the open window. Sitting on the window ledge with his feet dangling outside, Tommy held the VCR tightly to his chest and dropped without a sound behind the bushes and then walked out proudly holding the VCR in front of him. The VCR was a trophy of success. He had successfully burglarized his first house. He could visualize Rick telling all the other guys how well he had done on his first job.

But these thoughts quickly vanished as two police officers held their guns drawn and pointed at Tommy.

Both officers yelled, "Freeze!"

And Tommy froze, holding the stolen VCR. One officer moved quickly towards Tommy while the other remained in place with his gun leveled at Tommy's chest. He was relieved of his burden, handcuffed and placed in the police car. There was no sign of Rick.

Tommy Brown was taken to the county jail and booked for residential burglary.

He entered the jail handcuffed and in a state of shock. Screams from intoxicated prisoners, urine on the floor, bright lights, people moving rapidly, uniformed people barking orders, asking questions, all compounded Tommys' disorientation. Once inside booking, his handcuffs were removed and he was ordered to remove everything from his pockets.

The realization of what was happening dawned on Tommy as the corrections officer conducted a search. Tommy spun around as the officer searched his groin area for contraband.

It was a natural reaction for Tommy to move when someone touched him. The officer perceived his movements as an act of aggression and caught him squarely on the side of the face with his fist. In less than a second, Tommy was on the floor with two officers expertly applying handcuffs.

He lay bewildered for several seconds and then blurted out.
"You fucking assholes, leave me alone. I'm not a criminal. Why
are you doing this to me?"

One of the officers jerked him violently to his feet and snarled,
"Look, you fucking little punk. You try any more shit like you just
pulled and I'm going to rip off your fucking head and shit in your
wind-pipe."

Tommy was pushed roughly back to the booking counter. With
his face smashed against the plexiglass counter top, he answered
each question through gritted teeth. Soon Tommy Brown officially
became a felony prisoner.

He was frightened. This was not how it was supposed to be.
The noise, the people, the smells--all overwhelmed his senses.
Tommy Brown was escorted to the paramedic's station and stood
handcuffed behind a staggering, drunken, disheveled old man who
was being questioned by the paramedic.

"Are you withdrawing from drugs or alcohol?"

"What?"

"Are you withdrawing from drugs or alcohol?" questioned the
paramedic.

"I can't hear you," shouted the old man, who was hard of hearing.

Exasperated, the paramedic screamed, "Are you withdrawing?"

The old man thought for a moment and replied, "Yep."

Again the paramedic shouted, "What are you withdrawing
from?"

The old man smiled pleasantly and stated, "Social security."

The paramedic stared at the old man for a second then shook
his head and motioned for the corrections officer to take him away.

He was placed in a holding cell where he would remain until he
either bonded out or was released by the court in the morning.
Now it was Tommy's turn to be questioned. Calmed down by now,
he answered each question politely under the watchful eye of a
corrections officer.

No, he did not have any medical problems. No, he was not
withdrawing from drugs or alcohol. No, he had never been treated
for mental illness. After the medical screening was completed a
different corrections officer took Tommy by the arm and escorted
him down the hall to a row of telephones.

The officer spoke to Tommy in a tight, controlled manner. "If I take these handcuffs off, are you going to behave?"

Tommy ignored the question and asked, "What's going to happen to me?"

Mike "Tombstone" Stone looked carefully at Tommy Brown. Mike had been nicknamed Tombstone by the other staff because of his preference for night shifts. Tombstone had worked at the jail for six years. Six years of experience told him Tommy Brown was a virgin, someone who had never been in jail before.

Tombstone ignored Tommy's question and repeated, "If I take these cuffs off are you going to behave?"

The cuffs had bitten into Tommy's wrist and this time he answered, "I'll do whatever you say."

"Turn around."

Tombstone removed the handcuffs expertly and tucked the cuffs in his belt. "According to the booking records, you've been arrested for residential burglary."

Tommy interjected, "But I didn't mean it, you know. I sort of got pushed into it."

"Look Tommy, I don't want to know what happened, OK? You tell me what happened and then the D.A. subpoenas me into court to testify, which I'd really rather not do. Whatever you have to say, tell it to your lawyer. Right now I'm going to explain to you what's going to happen. You've been charged with residential burglary. Residential burglary carries a bond of five thousand dollars. If you had five thousand dollars you can put that money up as a promise that you will show up for court when you are supposed to. Then, a court date will be set for you and you will be free. If you don't have the entire five thousand dollars you can call a bondsman. Usually they charge ten percent of the total amount of bond. In your case, it would be about five hundred dollars. You can call anyone you want from these phones here and try to have someone come down with the money and post the bail for you. There's a chance the pre-trial release people can release you on your own recognizance, but I doubt it. If your parents are willing to sign for you, the pre-trial release people might consider releasing you to them."

"What if I can't get out, what happens then?"

"If no one bonds you out and the pre-trial release people think you're a bad risk, then you'll be given a pair of blue coveralls and taken upstairs to the classification unit. You'll stay in that unit for a day or two, usually until you go to arraignment. Arraignment is where you plead guilty or not guilty. If you plead not guilty, a public defender will be assigned to your case and a court date will be set. Your court date will probably be about six or eight months from now, during which time you'll stay in jail. If you do stay in jail, you'll be assigned to a general housing unit by the classification officer. Why don't you make your call and see if anybody will come down and bail you out."

As much as he wanted to be tough, Tommy Brown was not a tough guy. He was a scared nineteen-year-old, who had screwed up and the worst imaginable thing that could happen, had happened. He was in jail.

He picked up the phone and called home. Tommy told his mother he was in jail. Halfway through the explanation he began to cry. Tommy Brown's mother was too shocked to speak and passed the telephone to Tommy's father. "Tommy, you're no longer a kid. You're a man, and as a man you have to learn to be responsible for your actions. I'm sorry son, but your mother and I don't have five thousand dollars. You're going to have to sit tight and try to work this thing out. Tomorrow I'll make a couple of phone calls and see what I can find out. I'm sorry, son."

Tommy Brown replaced the receiver and wiped the tears away with the back of his hand and wondered what he was supposed to do now. He watched as one person after another was brought to the booking window, stripped of their possessions, escorted to the paramedics and then directed to the phones. The only thing Tommy Brown wanted now was to go home and pretend none of this had ever happened.

After five minutes a corrections officer directed him into a holding cell. The heavy metal door slammed behind him. The cold ring announced a certain finality to Tommy Brown. Six other people were sprawled on the floor sleeping. A seventh staggered to his feet, stood over one of the sleeping figures and urinated on the sleeping man's head. Tommy Brown moved to the farthest corner of the cell, slid to the floor and waited.

Throughout the night, he maintained his vigil, watching people enter and leave. One of the sleeping figures had awakened and, for no apparent reason, had attacked another sleeping prisoner. Within seconds four corrections officers entered the cell and quickly removed one of the men involved in the fight. Then everything grew quiet again.

There was no way to tell time. What was several hours seemed like days to Tommy Brown. At seven in the morning, several corrections officers entered the cell and woke everyone up, announcing it was time for court. Each prisoner was chained to the other with a long chain containing handcuffs. In all thirty prisoners were escorted downstairs to a tunnel that connected the jail and the courthouse and provided tight security when transporting prisoners to and from court.

Everything in court happened quickly. Tommy's name was called. He stood. He was scared. A man in black robes asked him if he had an attorney. Tommy said he did not. The judge informed Tommy that since he did not have legal representation he, the judge, would enter a not guilty plea on his behalf and schedule a court date. It took a total of two minutes.

Then Tommy was escorted back to the jail. His clothes were taken. He was strip searched by two correction officers. His feelings of shame and embarrassment began all over again. But this time it was worse.

Tommy was given a pair of blue coveralls, two sheets, a pillow case, a towel, a tube of toothpaste, a bar of soap, a book of matches and a cup. He was then escorted to the classification unit along with five other prisoners and assigned a room. He could remain in jail for the next six or eight months. The blue coveralls would become his daily dress. In the coming months, Tommy Brown would learn all there was to learn about jail life.

9

January 11th was Avery Beck's second day as jail administrator. He arrived at six-thirty in the morning. The sky was overcast and threatening snow. He walked quickly from his parking space through the front doors of the jail, entered his office and immediately began making notes on a yellow lined tablet. Today he would continue interviewing the senior staff, learn something about the jail's budget and follow up on the investigation that Roberto Romero was conducting.

In one day, Avery had obtained a significant insight into the jail's operation. He was much more optimistic than he had been on the previous day. Eventually he would learn the jail's operation. It would just take time and patience. Today, Avery was confident. He had to admit the part of the jail he had seen was clean and appeared to be well operated.

His thoughts were interrupted by the sound of Dennison entering the administration area and brewing a pot of coffee. Dennison had been following the same ritual for the past four years. Report for duty at seven, make a pot of coffee, go to his office and check the events of the previous night in the captain's log. If he found anything out of the ordinary, or something that smelled of a legal liability, he would print the log, highlight the area and place the log in the administrator's basket. After that it was up to the administrator.

Today there was nothing noteworthy. He left his office and poured a cup of hot, black coffee. He hesitated for a second, thought what the hell, and poured a second cup for the virgin jail administrator. Secretly, Dennison felt sorry for Beck.

As far as he was concerned, Beck was a political hack who had taken the job as jail administrator and now was faced with a tremendous amount of liability and responsibility, with limited authority. Dennison was not a cynic, he was just a realist. The jail operated on a shoe string budget and always came last when the city administration doled out operating funds. Beck would have to figure out the impossible. The impossible was how to operate a grossly overcrowded jail that continued to grow, while the budget diminished. Dennison walked into Beck's office and sat the cup of coffee on his desk. Beck looked up, smiled, and thanked Dennison, who had already turned and was leaving Beck's office.

"Sam, wait a second, I'd like to talk to you."

He stopped, turned around slowly and stepped up to the desk and waited.

"Have a seat," said Beck, motioning to one of the couches along the wall. Beck wasn't sure where to begin. Dennison betrayed no emotion in his eyes and reminded Beck slightly of Powell. There was no physical resemblance, but it was the manner and the eyes.

Dennison was five foot ten, one hundred and sixty pounds, with short brown hair. Everything about him, including his gray suit and white shirt, said Dennison was a proper employee. Yet, there was something slightly mysterious about him something Beck wanted to get out in the open.

"I've reviewed your personnel file, along with the files of all the other senior staff members. According to your file, you've been with the jail for fifteen years. Is that correct?"

After a momentary pause, he responded, "That's correct."

"You started as a corrections officer?"

"Right."

"And then you were promoted to lieutenant, then captain, and now deputy chief."

"Yes."

"Your file indicates several letters of discipline over the past fifteen years. One for submitting sarcastic reports to the jail administrator as a captain, and one for an illegal search. Would you care to comment?"

Dennison sat for several seconds, staring. He knew Beck had every right to ask these questions, and if Dennison was in Beck's position he would be asking the very same ones. Dennison was unsure of just how much honesty Beck could handle this soon.

Dennison shrugged his shoulders, sipped his coffee, then asked. "How honest do you want me to be?"

"Completely."

He took a deep breath and began. "The letter in my file for sarcasm is because Powell wanted to fire an employee whom I considered to be a good officer. Powell ordered me to write a report recommending termination, and I refused. I did, however, write a letter stating what I thought of the employee and what I thought of Powell's action. Powell didn't like it and I got a letter of discipline for being sarcastic. The employee stayed and is still with us and, in my opinion, is still doing a good job. I considered it a fairly good trade. A letter of discipline for me, and the employee keeps his job. The second letter deals with a situation that occurred several years ago. A female attorney from the district attorney's office came to visit a male prisoner. I had learned from one of my sources that this female attorney would be bringing in some drugs. When she arrived I had her strip searched, and we found half an ounce of marijuana along with a dozen quaaludes. The district attorney's office intervened. It seems she was related to the DA--cousin, niece, or something. Anyway, no charges were ever filed. The DA was pissed, the female attorney was pissed, and the prisoner was pissed. The DA's office made a lot of noise and Powell gave me a letter of discipline for illegal search. He had to do something to get the DA off his back and since I was the one who initiated the whole thing, it fell back on me."

Beck was no stranger to politics and he could easily understand how something like this could happen. Beck decided to ask one last question.

"What's your assessment of the jail?"

Once again Dennison hesitated. Here was the new boss asking him some very pointed questions. He had been around long enough to evade answering a question directly, but he liked Beck, even if he was a virgin, and he knew Beck needed some answers.

"The situation right now is terrible. Morale is low, the facility is grossly overcrowded, we're operating on half the budget we need, and there are some certified idiots in this organization in fairly high level positions. I anticipate a serious incident within the next several months, and I think somebody is going to get killed."

"These idiots in high places. Care to elaborate?"

Dennison smiled and replied, "No I don't think that would be wise. It's better for you to draw your own conclusions and make your own judgments. I will caution you, however. Don't draw conclusions too quickly. What you see in the beginning may not be the true picture. The world inside these walls is a lot different from the outside."

Dennison rose from the couch, drained the last of his coffee and asked, "Is there anything else?"

Beck indicated there wasn't and Dennison left.

Beck still considered Dennison a mystery. What bothered him most was Dennison's reference to incompetent management staff. Was it professional jealousy, office politics, or maybe even personality differences?

Later, Avery spoke with the jail's fiscal analyst who echoed Dennison's budget concerns. There was no question the jail was grossly under-budgeted. The past four years had seen the jail progressively lose positions and money while the prisoner population had increased. Paul Rivera, the fiscal analyst, explained that the city had been experiencing shrinking revenues and basic services such as water, garbage, police and fire had to be maintained. The jail simply was not considered a priority.

"How can we change this?" Beck questioned.

Paul Rivera shook his head and responded, "It's all politics. If you have a strong tie to the mayor's office, then maybe we'll get an increase in our budget. If you don't, then we'll be operating from a budget deficit for the entire year."

"Doesn't the budget process focus on basic needs and priorities?"

Rivera smiled nervously and said, "Nothing in city government focuses on needs and priorities. Everything focuses on politics. Let me know if I can help."

Avery found himself dejected after Rivera's comments and returned to his paper work.

Then Roberto Romero appeared at his door and asked, "Got a minute?"

Beck waved him in.

"The incident I briefed you on yesterday concerning allegations made by a contract employee against two corrections officers appears to be unsubstantiated. The contract employee claims an officer drank a vial of urine."

"What?"

"We have a work release program here where prisoners are released for work and then return at the end of the day. When they return, urine samples are passed to a contract employee who tests for drugs. The contract employee claims a corrections officer drank a vial of urine in an attempt to test the urine to see if the prisoner had been taking drugs. Supposedly, Robbins was testing a theory that drugs could be detected in urine through taste. I just finished interviewing the accused officer and the other officer who was present. Both claim the contract employee is off her rocker."

Beck thought this was crazy. Why would someone accuse a person of drinking urine?

"So you consider this a closed case?"

"I do, unless I can get some other corroborating evidence. I don't believe any exists."

Beck agreed. The allegation was too unbelievable to consider seriously.

First it had been Dennison with his cryptic warning. Then Paul Rivera with his dismal budget scenario and now Roberto Romero with these allegations.

The ugly reality of operating a jail was becoming more and more evident.

10

Lieutenant Vernon Rose stood in the corner of booking and closely monitored the actions of his corrections officers. Rose was sixty-five, and had been a lieutenant for the past eight years. Everyone knew Rose could retire, but his wife wouldn't let him. She didn't want him at home. Rose was not an easy person to get along with. Demanding, tyrannical and unmoving, he focused on the small, unimportant things while major issues swept by unnoticed. At the moment, Rose was watching a corrections officer initial the cell observation check sheets. The officer pretended he did not know Rose was watching, but he could feel the old man's eyes boring into the back of his head.

The officer making the checks was Georgie Byers. He was indifferent to Lieutenant Rose but he had heard the talk among the other officers. Chris Keys had told everyone he had a plan. By tomorrow morning Lieutenant Rose would be putting in for retirement, guaranteed. This had kept everyone on edge from the beginning of the shift, watching Chris to see what he had up his sleeve.

Booking was calm. Weekdays tended to be slower than the weekends when everyone went crazy. On weekends, people drank until they dropped. Others drank and then shot each other.

By eight o'clock that evening, booking was quiet and Chris Keys approached Lieutenant Rose.

"Hey, Lieutenant, how about I do a roof check?"

A roof check of the facility was required on each shift to make sure no prisoners had gained access to the roof.

This was one of the few times Rose had ever had anyone volunteer and he eyed Officer Keys with suspicion.

"You want to do a roof check?"

"Yeah. You know, I'd kind of like to get some air."

Rose did not trust Keys, nor any of the other officers for that matter, but a roof check had to be done and booking was quiet.

Keys left the area and went straight to his car. Under his arm he carried a pair of rolled up jail coveralls. Reaching his car Chris unrolled the coveralls and placed them on a mannequin that was lying on the back seat. He had only been able to get a female mannequin, but Keys figured it was dark, and the dummy's sex would make little difference.

Carrying the mannequin back to the facility, he entered, stopped at the master control center, obtained the appropriate keys and headed for the roof.

He walked across the jail's roof to the edge. Six stories below was the booking parking lot where police cars parked. Now it was completely vacant. Keys quickly pulled his radio from the pouch, keyed the button and spoke.

"Unit three to Lieutenant Rose."

"This is Lieutenant Rose. Go ahead."

"Please step out into the booking parking lot."

Puzzled, Rose put on his regulation black down jacket and hurried to the lot. He peered up into the dark sky and waited. Within seconds, Keys' face appeared over the edge of the jail's roof.

He yelled down. "Lieutenant! I got a jumper up here and he wants to talk to you. He says if you or I call anyone else he's going to jump. He won't talk to anyone but you."

Rose was numb. This was absurd. How could a prisoner gain access to the roof? There were at least three locked doors, all electronically monitored, which a prisoner would have to pass through. And why would a prisoner want to talk to him?

Rose kept his eyes glued to where Keys had been moments before. A figure dressed in blue coveralls appeared at the edge. Rose reflexively placed his hand up in the air and bellowed. "Don't jump, whoever you are, don't jump. I'll get you some help. Just stay where you are."

The figure swayed and then leaped out into the air. Slowly, the figure did a complete turn in mid-air and crashed on the lot, splintering into a thousand pieces.

But Lieutenant Rose didn't see the prisoner strike the ground. When he had leaped off the roof into space, Rose had closed his eyes and sunk to his knees. Never in all his time had he ever seen a suicide. It was more than he could stand. The crashing sound of the body hitting the pavement next to him caused his stomach to heave. Within seconds, corrections officers rushed into the parking lot through the booking door and assisted Lieutenant Rose to his feet and helped him back to booking where he was placed in the chair behind his desk.

Chris Keys scrambled from the roof and with the assistance of another officer, hurriedly gathered the splintered pieces and deposited them in the trash.

After several minutes, Lieutenant Rose picked up the phone and slowly dialed the shift captain to report the incident. Within minutes the shift captain appeared. Rose stood slowly and escorted the captain outside to the parking lot. Several officers, including Keys, trailed along behind.

Rose searched the parking lot desperately. He knew he had seen a prisoner jump from the roof. He had heard the body hit the pavement. Now there was nothing. No blood, no body, no nothing.

Rose turned to the captain. "I know what I saw. It was right here, Captain. The body hit right here! It was a prisoner! He was wearing blue coveralls!" Desperately, Rose wheeled to Keys for corroboration.

Keys looked confused and said, "Lieutenant Rose, I'm not sure what you're talking about."

The shift captain turned to the corrections officers and ordered everyone back to their posts. Then the captain placed an arm across Lieutenant Rose's shoulders and spoke softly to him. He offered to drive him home. On the way, Lieutenant Vernon Rose agreed with the wisdom of the shift captain. Perhaps he had been in the business too long. It was time to retire.

Corrections Officer Chris Keys became a legend.

Meanwhile, Georgie Byers had not participated in the incident and did not approve or disapprove. Byers had grown numb to most everyone and everything. He existed one day at a time, and let fate take its course. So what if Rose had retired. Byers knew there would be another Lieutenant Rose. And if Chris Keys quit, or even, for that matter, if Georgie Byers quit, sooner or later there would be another Chris Keys and another Georgie Byers. It would be just the same. There was no beginning and there was no end. That was the way it was.

11

It was the evening of January 11th. The cold north wind had increased and scattered snow flakes had covered the greater Coronado metropolitan area. Jack Stilwell drove to the night club district and was perched on a bar stool at the Silver Slipper Saloon.

For the past three hours he had been popping valium with beer chasers. The convenience store robbery and the Paul Frazer murder was nothing more than a distant memory.

At the moment, Stilwell was busy talking to a bleached blonde sitting next to him. Tonia was very drunk. Stilwell paid the bar tab and helped Tonia outside into the cold wind. After depositing Tonia in the front seat, Stilwell walked behind the car to the driver's side, got in and cranked the car into life, gunned the engine several times, then pulled out of the Silver Slipper's parking lot. He had rented a room at a cheap motel and it was here he intended to spend the night with Tonia. Tonia was busy chattering about something when Stilwell spied the police car in his rear view mirror.

"Shit. There's a fucking pig behind us," announced Stilwell while reaching under his seat and pulling out his thirty-eight revolver.

"Listen, if the pig stops us don't say nothing. Let me do all the talking."

Stilwell drove carefully for another three blocks. The police car was still behind him. The last thing he needed now was a hassle with the cops. After several turns there was no question. The cop was following him.

He casually lifted the revolver from the seat and dropped it in Tonia's open purse. Although Stilwell considered his driving perfect, the beer and valium had an effect. Stilwell's car weaved several times. The police officer flipped on his red lights and moved into position.

The cops had nothing on him. Stilwell knew he was being stopped for a chickenshit traffic violation. His gun was in Tonia's purse and if she kept her mouth shut, the cops wouldn't even give her a second glance.

Stilwell aimed the Chevrolet at the curb and stopped. The police car slowed and stopped ten feet behind the parked Chevrolet Stilwell pulled out his driver's license and registration. Tonia was still chattering incoherently. After several minutes, a figure in blue exited the car and made his way to Stilwell's window. Stilwell smiled pleasantly and greeted the officer. The officer had his hand on his gun, a fact that did not escape Stilwell. The officer then ordered him out of the car.

Stilwell opened his car door slowly and stepped out into the freezing cold. The cold air struck him like an invisible fist and Stilwell staggered momentarily.

He was searched, cuffed and advised he was under arrest for driving while intoxicated. Tonia was told to get out of the car and stood, swaying, next to Stilwell's Chevrolet. The officer asked for identification. Tonia searched her purse until she located her driver's license. The officer took the license and returned to his vehicle. Tonia's social security and driver's license number were checked by computer to determine if she had any outstanding warrants or traffic tickets. Meanwhile, Stilwell stood in the freezing cold, handcuffed and silent.

He had been through this dozens of times before. If the cop wanted to talk about robberies or anything else, he would not talk without an attorney. He hoped Tonia was clean. Without his gun the cops only had him for a traffic violation. The only way the cop could search Tonia's purse was if she were placed under arrest.

After a five-minute wait, the officer returned and informed Tonia Williams (this was the first time Stilwell had heard her last name that she was under arrest for a shoplifting charge for which she had failed to appear in court.

Tonia's purse was taken and she was handcuffed. Jack Stilwell and Tonia Williams were then taken to jail.

At the booking counter, Stilwell waited and listened as the arresting officer informed the booking officer he was charging Stilwell with driving while intoxicated. Stilwell had been arrested dozens of times. The charge was not serious. At most, Stilwell would get three square meals a day and enjoy a short stay in jail.

But when Tonia arrived at the booking counter, her purse was searched and the gun was discovered and confiscated by the arresting officer. Everything now depended on the thoroughness of the arresting officer. Stilwell knew the officer would check the gun's serial number to see if it had been stolen. He had purchased the gun from an acquaintance and had no idea if the gun was hot or not. It didn't really matter. The gun was found in Tonia's possession and she would be charged with possession of a stolen firearm, not him.

After Stilwell was checked by the paramedic, he informed the corrections officer he had no one to call. Stilwell knew the procedure as well as anyone. He was looking forward to a good night's rest. Stilwell looked back and saw Tonia crying. What a pity, he thought to himself. A perfectly good night ruined.

But Jack Stilwell could care less if Tonia was charged with possession of a stolen firearm. As far as he was concerned, it wasn't any of his business. Life was nothing more than survival of the fittest.

Early in the morning on January 12th, Jack Stilwell was awakened by the corrections officer on duty and informed it was time to go to court. He hauled himself out of bed, splashed water on his face, ran his fingers through his long blond hair and waited for court call.

Nothing ever changed. Stilwell was in an eight-foot by nine-foot room. The room contained a raised concrete platform against the wall which served as a bed for the flat mattress and two white sheets. A stainless steel combination toilet and sink was positioned next to a concrete shelf. The shelf doubled as a writing table. Two security lights illuminated the off-white room. A narrow four-inch strip of window running from floor to ceiling allowed Stilwell to view the weather outside.

He had been in jail more times than he cared to count. Each room in the Coronado County jail was identical to this one. On the shelf sat a cup with a toothbrush, a small tube of toothpaste and a bar of soap. Stilwell had been allowed to keep his comb, cigarettes and matches. He lit a cigarette and puffed leisurely. It would be two or three hours before he would be able to smoke. It all depended on how long court lasted.

Twenty minutes later, a corrections officer arrived and escorted him, along with a dozen other prisoners, downstairs to the tunnel which led to the arraignment room. Stilwell eyed each of the prisoners carefully and mentally assessed the size and physical potential of each in an attempt to determine who might give him trouble later on. Nobody screwed with Jack Stilwell. If he had to knock a few heads to get the message across, he would.

He considered one a possible danger. The man was older probably around forty, guessed Stilwell. He was short and stocky, and had the hardened look in his eyes of a career criminal. This guy was a lifer. All lifers had contacts and an association group inside the jail or prison. If Stilwell took on the lifer, he would have to take on at least a dozen others. Stilwell would leave this lifer alone. It wasn't worth the effort.

In the group, there was a fairly young wino who stunk and another kid with big bright eyes, like a fawn. Stilwell smiled to himself as he looked hard at Tommy Brown. If Stilwell stayed in jail for any length of time, he would do what he could to get close to Tommy Brown. The kid was scared and needed someone to look out for his interests. In return, Stilwell would demand a few small favors.

The group soon moved into the arraignment room. Court moved quickly. The group returned to the classification unit and Stilwell knew it would be a matter of only a couple of hours before he was assigned to a permanent housing unit. During the arraignment, he had learned the lifer's name was Greg Leeks, a name Stilwell had heard before while he was in the joint. Leeks was a heavy, someone who had been around, and someone who had established a reputation.

Stilwell had been right. Leeks was a lifer who had been charged with possession of stolen property. Stilwell had also learned the young kid's name was Tommy Brown. The kid had been busted for residential burglary. The kid's age, lack of a criminal record and a non-violent crime told Stilwell that the kid would probably be assigned to a minimum custody unit. Stilwell had been popped for driving while intoxicated which meant he stood a good chance of being assigned to the same unit. Everything was moving along smoothly. Stilwell anticipated enjoying his brief stay in jail, especially if little Tommy Brown became his roommate.

Greg Leeks had done more time in the can than he cared to think about. As a kid, he had dropped out of school and worked construction until he had been busted for stealing. He had done a three-month stint in the juvenile home, been released and then picked up a week later for shoplifting. The judge had wanted to make an example of him and he had been sent to the boy's state correctional facility for a year. During that year Leeks had developed the friends, contacts and knowledge that would prove invaluable for years to come. When he was discharged, he was eighteen. He had no home, no money and no education. Leeks pulled a string of armed robberies for which he received three years' probation. But during this time, Leeks continued his armed robberies. He was again caught, convicted and sentenced to five years in the state penitentiary. Here Leeks found a large number of friends and associates he had known while in the juvenile home. Five years passed quickly and Leeks returned to the streets. Two more five-year sentences for possession of drugs and an armed robbery, and Leeks had left prison again only to return to the streets and a life of crime. Now he had been charged with possession of stolen property. The thought of returning to prison was not an uncomfortable thought for Greg Leeks. Prison and jails were easy. Everything was orderly and anticipated. The majority of his friends were in jails and prisons. Doing time was easy. In prison there were no utility bills, no rising food costs and no one to hassle him, except for an occasional overzealous corrections officer.

Leeks's thoughts turned to Stilwell, the muscular blond he had seen during arraignment. He hoped Stilwell would get released. Leeks did not like Stilwell's type. Stilwell was crazy and dangerous. Leeks had seen this type before. Cons like Stilwell spelled trouble. They upset the natural order of things. Leeks didn't want any trouble, any hassles. He wanted to get through his court crap and go to prison as fast as possible. In prison, things were more stable than in jail. By tomorrow, his friends would know he was coming. The communication system within the walls of prison and jail was phenomenal. It would be like a family reunion. Leeks returned to his room and waited for classification. Once assigned to a permanent housing area, he would settle in to the day-to-day grind of jail life. Leeks hoped he would be assigned to the sixth floor where the old timers and career criminals were housed. The young kids were trouble. They were always horsing around and starting fights. The young kids were out to make a name for them selves and they were a nuisance.

Victor Moss had screened and assigned ten prisoners from the classification unit to a general housing unit. The screening pro cess was a review of the prisoner's past criminal record, current status, whether arrested for a felony or a misdemeanor, age and the nature of the current charge. All available information was weighed before assigning a prisoner to a specific housing unit. Typically, the jail's classification system was designed to group the different types of offenders together into separate housing areas. Murderers were not housed with traffic offenders and older pris oners were not housed with young offenders. This worked well when there was plenty of space. When the jail was overcrowded, it left few options.

Victor Moss had been working at the jail for the past ten years. He had seen Jack Stilwell come and go during those ten years and although Stilwell was being held for a misdemeanor, he knew the minimum custody floor was not the proper assignment for him. Stilwell was mean, big, and strong. To assign Stilwell to a misde meanor floor would do nothing but cause problems. Within days he would bully and intimidate the rest of the prisoners. Stilwell would be running the minimum custody unit through intimidation and fear. There was no question, Stilwell would become the barn boss.

He could not assign Stilwell to the sixth floor, because Stilwell was not a felon so he decided to compromise and assign him to the second floor, it was a medium security area, populated by felony prisoners.

Reviewing the case file for Tommy Brown, Moss shook his head in disgust. Here was a young kid who had involved himself in something in which he had no business getting into. Brown had no prior arrests. Since Brown was a felon and it was his first offense, he was assigned to the second floor. After another five assignments

Moss reviewed Greg Leeks' file. Moss recognized Leeks as a regular. Here was an institutionalized prisoner, a prisoner who could take care of himself and was respected by other prisoners. Leeks belonged on the sixth floor with the other career criminals. Unfortunately, the sixth floor was too crowded. Moss knew Leeks avoided problems and did his time quietly. Although the second floor was not the appropriate place, Moss had little choice. Greg Leeks was assigned to the second floor along with Jack Stilwell and Tommy Brown.

Victor Moss signed the move authorizations and delivered them to the corrections officers assigned to the first floor, classification unit. The classification system in the jail had become a farce. Moss had tried to tell anyone who would listen that once eighty percent of the jail was occupied, the classification unit would falter. With some areas of the jail full, the classification unit would be unable to assign prisoners to the most appropriate housing unit. Mixing different types was dangerous. The classification system was designed to separate killers from traffic offenders, the young, inexperienced prisoner from the hardened convict. Each housing unit had been designed to house a certain type of prisoner. But this was not happening, and it was not Victor Moss's fault.

All his concerns had fallen on deaf ears. Now the jail was well over a hundred percent capacity. If something didn't happen fast, someone was going to die.

Moss felt as if he were sitting on top of a powder keg. But the protective custody unit of the jail, where former police officers, child molesters, homosexuals, and state's witnesses were kept was the one area where Moss would not budge. It was entirely too dangerous to mix these people with the rest of the population. This was the special offender's unit, a place where the weak, the unpopular and the homosexuals were kept for their own protection. The law clearly stated that, once individuals were incarcerated, they became the responsibility of the jail. If they hung themselves, it was the jail's fault. If they started a fight with another prisoner and were hurt, it was the jail's fault. Anything and everything that happened to a prisoner while in custody was the responsibility of the jail. If the jail housed the number of people it had been built and designed to house, the problems would be manageable.

But that was not the case. No one was interested in reducing the jail's population. The courts and the police considered overcrowding the jail's problem. Moss hoped the new administrator would be able to find some answers.

Meanwhile, Jack Stilwell was happy. Everything was working out. He had been assigned to a minimum custody floor along with the little kid. He was determined to turn Tommy Brown into his personal punk.

But the threat to Tommy Brown and the worries and concerns of Classification Specialist Victor Moss were unknown to Avery Beck. Unknown or not, Avery Beck was still responsible. He was the mayor of the jail city.

12

Wednesday, January 12th, Avery Beck drove to the jail un
der overcast skies. The dark, low hanging clouds gave
every indication of pending snow. Avery parked in his
now-familiar parking space and entered the jail. It was now his
third day as jail administrator. In two days he had learned much.
Avery Beck took his position and his job seriously and he was determined not to be just another political hack sitting at the top of a
department, pretending he knew what was going on. He was determined to learn everything. Eventually, he hoped to become a
viable administrator. What he needed was information. Paulson
had provided some good ideas and had asked Beck for his approval.
Beck had hesitated. He wondered why Powell, with his years of
experience, had not acted on Paulson's proposals. Beck might be
new to the jail but he was not new to life.

Beck felt he could trust Paulson. Paulson seemed open and
sincere, a motivated employee who appeared to have foresight and
ideas.

Dennison was another story. Dennison had answered all of his
questions honestly but without elaboration. Maybe that was it.
Maybe it was Dennison's curt manner, the fact that he never offered additional information. And then there had been those cryptic warnings.

Beck heard Dennison enter the administration area and knew
he would follow his daily routine of brewing a pot of coffee and
reviewing the log again, Dennison found nothing of interest in the
logs except the high population count that had shot to over a thousand prisoners in the past couple of days. Dennison made note of
the fact.

He then walked to the coffee pot, poured himself a cup and
started to return to his office. He hesitated and then poured a
second cup for Beck. This could get to be a habit but Dennison

liked Beck. He seemed like a nice guy. Dennison walked into Beck's office where he deposited it on Beck's desk and turned to leave, but was stopped by Beck's question.

"Anything in the logs?"

Dennison stopped at the door. "Nothing. Looks like it was a quiet night. The only thing worth mentioning is the population. It's over a thousand prisoners."

Beck thanked Dennison and watched him leave.

For the next three hours Avery studied the jail's budget trying to make sense out of a document that defied logic. He was not an accountant, but it did not take an accountant to recognize there was something wrong with the figures.

Marshall Paulson, deputy chief in charge of security, knocked at his door and entered. "Boss, we have a few minor problems in our property room. That's where we store the stuff we take from the prisoners at booking. Some of the property is missing and I have a plan to solve the problem. I want to take about eight corrections officers and assign them to the room permanently. That way, if anything comes up missing, we'll know who to point the finger at."

This was the fourth idea Paulson had presented in three days and Beck decided it was time to make a decision. "Sounds like a good idea. How soon before you can put this new scheduling into effect?"

"It shouldn't take more than a couple of days."

"Let me know how it works out," directed Beck.

Paulson strolled from Beck's office elated. It was an opportunity for Paulson to show the new boss what he could do given the opportunity.

When Paulson left, Roberto Romero entered. He had been waiting patiently outside the administrator's office. As usual, he was impeccably dressed in a gray suit, maroon tie and black wingtip shoes. Romero looked more like an attorney than an internal affairs investigator. Romero greeted Beck and then launched into a recital of pending legal cases lodged against the jail. He had already provided Beck with an overview of these cases, but several things had been discovered during his investigation which pointed to some wrongdoing on the part of staff.

Finished with his briefing, Romero leaned back in the sofa, crossed his legs and brushed some dust from the toe of his shoe. Romero's wingtips were known as the shoes with a thousand eyes. And Romero was called the man who wore the shoes with a thousand eyes, a suitable title for this particular chief of internal affairs.

Avery had understood everything Romero had said. After all, litigation had been his profession. He was comfortable with Romero because legal issues were home territory. Perhaps this comfort was what compelled him to ask, "What do you know about Dennison?"

Romero hesitated a moment. "Dennison is a damn good administrator. He's been screwed a few times and I think he's a little bitter, but he'll do whatever you tell him to do. There's probably no one here who knows more about this jail. He's patient and doesn't bull into things. He takes his time, thinks of all the angles, plans and then proceeds. He's efficient and a good organizer."

Beck was suddenly sorry he had asked. Questioning one employee about another was not the way he wanted to operate. He wanted to observe, evaluate and make judgments based on concrete facts. He did not want to make decisions based on someone else's opinions.

But it was too late to retract his question. He did not want Romero to think he had a special interest in Dennison. He asked casually, "What about Marshall Paulson?"

Romero shrugged his shoulders. "He's OK."

Beck thanked Romero and the chief of internal affairs left. Avery sat alone in his office, lost in thought. There was something strange going on and he intended to find out what. It wasn't so much what Roberto Romero had said, it was more what he hadn't said. During the conversation, Beck had studied Romero's face closely, waiting for an answer, and he was certain Romero had evaded his question about Paulson.

Picking up the phone he punched the direct line to Dennison's office and instructed him to report to his office. Shortly Dennison entered Beck's office with an unlit cigarette dangling between his lips. Beck motioned him to take a seat.

Had Beck looked into a mirror at that moment, he would have been surprised by his reflection. His eyes were set exactly as he remembered Jeff Powell's. Dennison plopped down on his favorite couch and waited.

Beck questioned, "It's Sam, isn't it?"

"Right."

Beck noted that each question he had put to Dennison was answered with one word. Beck employed a different approach. "You probably have some familiarity with the security unit." Beck discerned a slight smile on Dennison's face. Something he had said had touched a nerve. "I've received a proposal to initiate a new schedule for corrections officers assigned to the property unit in booking. I'd like to hear your thoughts on the subject." He then explained Paulson's plan.

Dennison cursed to himself. Beck had finally done it. After two days of groping and searching, he was beginning to ask the right questions. There was nothing for Dennison to do but answer. "The concept in itself is not a bad idea. How it's implemented will be the key."

"What do you mean?"

"There's no question accountability needs to be maintained in the property room. I've seen the reports of lost rings, watches and jewelry. If you implement a separate schedule affecting any corrections officers, a memorandum of understanding will need to be filed with the corrections officers' union in conjunction with the city's personnel office and this department."

"Why would we need a memorandum of understanding for something as small as a schedule change? It would only affect half a dozen people?"

"If you don't, you'll be violating their union contract and the corrections officers' union will most probably file a prohibited practice charge. You'll violate the union contract under the bidding rights clause, as well as the seniority clause, and possibly even under the clause which stipulates permanent assignments. I'm not sure on the last, I'd have to check."

"So you're telling me, before I can do any re-scheduling I have to go through all this red tape."

"Correct."

"I take it you're familiar with the corrections officers' contract?"

"As much as anybody," replied Dennison.

Dennison did not like the direction the conversation had taken. He took care of operations and Paulson took care of security. He didn't want Paulson meddling in his affairs and he was determined not to meddle in Paulson's. If the new boss wanted changes in security, then he should be talking to Paulson and not him.

Beck knew Dennison was holding back. There was more to Dennison than what appeared in the personnel file. Beck was thoughtful for a moment and then dismissed Dennison.

Beck then phoned Paulson and five minutes later he appeared in the doorway. He took a seat and Beck asked casually about how the schedule change was coming along.

Paulson launched into a long explanation of how the new schedule would work but Beck cut him off. "It sounds good, but exactly how do you propose to implement this new schedule?"

"I'm going to select the best people we have in the department and assign them to the property room. Those I select will be people who are completely honest. We won't have to worry about stolen or missing property once this whole thing is in place. It's going to make everyone in the department look good."

"Is there anything in the union contract governing schedule changes?" asked Beck quietly.

Paulson's eyes turned to smoke and when he replied his voice was strained. "I'm not sure, I mean I haven't checked yet, but it's about time we let everyone know who's running this place. The union is always trying to tell management what they can and can't do."

"If there is something in the corrections officers' union contract that covers a schedule change, then I want you to follow the proper procedure," directed Beck.

Paulson looked at Beck with unmasked hostility. And several moments later nervously stood up and walked out of the administrator's office without a word.

Back in his own office Paulson fumed. The new administrator was afraid to take a chance. A perfectly good plan was no longer worth the paper it was written on. Paulson knew the corrections officers' union would never agree to a scheduling change. He had hoped Beck would sign off on it and if the union did file a prohibited practice charge, Paulson could always claim it had been the administrator's decision. Everyone was against him. Every time he had an idea, people found fault with it. Paulson was getting sick and tired of people always putting him down. Some things were going to have to change at the jail, in spite of Avery Beck. He was the security chief, and he was going to run his operation the way it should be run, without any interference from Beck, Dennison, Rivera or Romero, and that was the way it was going to be. He had put up with a lot of shit from Powell. He was not going to put up with it any longer. Not from anyone, and that included Beck. If Beck didn't like him, well that was too bad. Decisions were not made based on personalities. They were made on the basis of merit and fact.

Back in his office, Beck was stunned by Paulson's rapid personality change. He had posed a seemingly innocuous question and the physical transformation in Paulson had been unbelievable. Beck certainly did not need a prohibited practice charge filed by the corrections officers' union. He wanted the officers to learn from his actions that he was on their side. Dennison had kept him from making a large blunder and his opinion of Dennison raised a notch.

Beck picked up the phone. A woman named Cecile answered. Beck asked for Roberto Romero and Cecile politely asked who was calling. Avery smiled to himself and responded, "Tell Roberto Romero its the Jail Administrator." Within seconds Romero was on the line.

"We need to talk."

Romero asked Beck what he wanted to talk about. "The jail."

The jail was two blocks from the internal affairs office and Romero offered to come over. But Beck told Romero he would rather come to his office. For Avery Back, it was time for a little honesty.

Twenty minutes later Beck was sitting in Romero's office asking some pointed questions. At first, Romero was reluctant to answer his questions, stating it was not his job nor his responsibility to supervise either one of the deputy chiefs at the jail. His job was internal affairs and investigations. Beck quickly informed Romero that his job was whatever he, Beck, decided it to be and right now he wanted information.

Romero answered all Beck's questions completely, including history and background. It was six in the evening before Beck decided he had heard enough and left.

That evening, Avery Beck sat in front of his television lost in thought, while his wife split her attention between a book and a favorite television program.

According to Roberto Romero, Sam Dennison had been promoted to deputy chief in charge of security four years ago. Marshall Paulson had been a Lieutenant at the time and had also applied for position, along with several others. Dennison had been selected and Marshall Paulson, as well as three others, had filed a discrimination suit against the jail, the city administration and Dennison.

Paulson had not stopped with filing a suit but had bent the ear of several city councilors. The councilors didn't want anyone making waves and they had leaned heavily on the former mayor to resolve Paulson's problem. The former mayor knew he would be running for re-election in two years and having Paulson, a member of the black community, as a part of his inner circle wouldn't hurt his chances.

The former mayor had penned a written order to Powell and Paulson had been administratively promoted to deputy chief two years ago. The usual process of interviewing, testing and seniority had been ignored. The result: Paulson had been a maverick under Powell, running to the mayor's office and to the city councilmen with inside information concerning the jail and criticizing Powell. Paulson had systematically sabotaged Powell at every move, hoping to discredit him and ultimately become the jail administrator. Powell had been powerless to take action under the former administration and had been stuck with Paulson and his subversive attitude.

When Paulson had been promoted, Dennison had been moved and placed in charge of operations. According to Romero, Paulson had been promoted because he was black and because of politics. There was no other reason. Dennison had arbitrarily been sacked as the security chief and moved to operations. Dennison had been screwed, and he knew it, but hadn't said anything to Beck. Dennison was and had been the most qualified person for chief of security.

All this explained Dennison's smile when Beck had asked him if he knew anything about the security unit. Dennison had been part of the security unit for eleven years. Of course he knew the security unit.

Although Dennison had been placed in charge of operations, which included the department's maintenance, training, safety, food service, commissary, laundry, warehouse and caseworker unit, Powell had also used Dennison as a utility man in all the other jail areas including security.

When the conversation moved to Marshall Paulson, Romero had hesitated and then informed Beck bluntly that Paulson was crazy. Romero pictured Paulson and Dennison as totally different. Paulson was retired military and believed in treating everyone like raw recruits. Dennison, on the other hand, dealt with people more gently. He knew what motivated a corrections officer. Paulson dreamed of pie in the sky programs and when they failed he blamed it on racism or personality assassination. It was a fact that Paulson was black. It was also a fact that Marshall Paulson was totally and completely incompetent. In Romero's opinion, Paulson was a walking time bomb-full of paranoia, distrust, anger.

His explosive temper, his accusations of racism, and his headlong dashes into projects with no forethought spelled disaster not only for Paulson but for the department as well. Powell had been unable to terminate Paulson without risking a racial discrimination suit and without the support of the mayor's office. Therefore, Powell had no choice but to try to make the best of a terrible situation.

In the final analysis, Paulson was a very good talker, a poor doer, and a dangerous high level employee with a great deal of power.

Romero warned Beck that the first time Beck disagreed with Paulson, or reprimanded Paulson, he would accuse him of dealing in personalities and of being a bigot, regardless of the circumstances. Beck did not comment on his earlier meeting with Paulson, but suspected Romero was correct.

What Romero had told him explained Dennison's unwillingness to talk about security issues and it explained Paulson's hostility. Beck had his work cut out for him.

There were a number of options he could employ but for the next several days he would continue to watch, observe, and listen. One thing for certain, he needed to speak with Dennison, and Dennison needed to open up. If what Romero said was true, then Dennison knew more about the jail than anyone else and Dennison needed to share this information.

In the meantime, Paulson was a walking time bomb. If Beck was to be successful he would have to keep a close watch. It was going to be a very dangerous game for Avery Beck. He needed answers.

13

While Beck sat at home torn by indecision about the loyalty and dependability of Dennison and Paulson, Lieutenant Frank Ivers was busy supervising twenty-eight corrections officers and over a thousand prisoners. On this particular evening, January 12th, Ivers was assigned to the detention levels. It was here the prisoners lived in housing units and where the majority of serious problems occurred.

Ivers had spent most of the evening running between the psychiatric unit on the fifth floor and the maximum security unit on the sixth floor. It seemed as if all the prisoners had a complaint of some sort and Ivers was expected to come up with an instant solution.

Ivers, also known as The Preacher, had been called for the third time to the fifth floor psychiatric unit. One of the prisoners, Eric The-Space-Case Moore, was convinced his room was haunted by the ghost of the man he was charged with murdering. Ivers had tried to reason with him, but to no avail. Every time Ivers left, Moore resumed screaming. This kept the other people on the fifth floor disturbed which in turn unsettled corrections officer Jason Robbins, who was assigned to the unit. Robbins would call Ivers every time this happened.

"What is it this time?"

Robbins raised his voice in order to be heard over the shouts coming from Moore's cell. "The same thing as last time, Lieutenant. I don't know what to do with this guy. He's getting everybody upset and if he doesn't knock it off soon, this whole damn unit is going to rock-n-roll."

Ivers agreed with Robbins' assessment. Already some of the other prisoners were pacing back and forth nervously. Ivers had to do something to quiet Moore.

Robbins asked, "You think a ceremony would help?"

Exasperated, Ivers replied, "I suppose it's worth a try. Get everything set up and I'll talk to Moore."

Robbins unlocked Moore's cell door and he rushed past him to Ivers and pleaded, "Help me! It's after me! You got to do something! It wants to kill me! I know it does! Don't let it get me! You have to do something! Please, I'll do anything! Just make it leave me alone, don't make me go back into my cell!"

Ivers spoke softly to Moore, trying to dissipate his hysteria. He spoke in a soft melodious sing-song fashion. Ivers had learned years ago that this helped to calm irrational people. Several minutes passed before Ivers detected a flicker of understanding in Moore's eyes. "I'm going to do something for you I rarely do for anyone, but it will require your cooperation." Just then, Robbins returned and announced that everything was ready.

Ivers took on a solemn look, bowed his head and mumbled a few words. He then motioned for Robbins and Moore to follow him into Moore's room. Moore hesitated at the door until Ivers commanded him to enter the room and face the powers of darkness.

Ivers then turned slowly to Robbins for his "vestments." Robbins had taken a long strip of white toilet paper and had drawn crosses, circles, triangles and wavy lines on the toilet paper with a blue magic marker. This strip of toilet paper was ceremoniously draped around Ivers' neck. The decorated ends hung down to his knees.

Moore had slowly inched his way into the room, and watched silently. Ivers stood with his head down, facing Moore's empty bunk. Without lifting his head, he ordered Moore to lie. Moore complied hesitantly and lay on the bed face up with an imploring look in his eyes.

Ivers closed his eyes and announced solemnly, "I am ready."

Robbins had taken small pieces of paper and shred them into an ashtray which sat on the small desk. Next to the ashtray lay a book of matches, a cup of water and a standard jail Bible.

When Ivers announced "I am ready," Jason Robbins handed the ashtray filled with shredded paper to him. Ivers mumbled a few words over the ashtray while Robbins, with exaggerated solemnity, lit the papers in the ashtray. Within seconds, the papers had burned to ashes. Ivers then handed the ashtray back to Robbins. Robbins put it down and handed the jail Bible to Ivers. He thumbed through it, stopping at no particular passage while sonorously reciting scripture at random. Then, he suddenly slammed the Bible shut, startling Moore. Ivers then passed the bible to Robbins who carefully placed it on the desk. Robbins then handed Ivers the sacred ashes.

For the first time during the ceremony, Lieutenant Ivers acknowledged Moore's presence. Looking deep into his eyes, Ivers asked, "You need to use the bathroom or anything before I seal the spell, Eric?"

Eric Moore shook his head.

Ivers explained, "If your feet touch the floor once I seal the spell, the spell will be broken. Any loud words, screams, shouts or yelling will also break the spell. Do you understand, Eric?"

Eric Moore nodded nervously.

Ivers then nodded his head and instructed Moore to climb under the covers on his bed. Moore complied quickly and waited in wide-eyed anticipation.

Ivers sprinkled the ashes across Moore's bed while he intoned the latest weather report, stock market analysis and anything else that came to mind. Ivers then turned to Robbins again and was handed a cup of water.

Ivers looked down at Moore and explained, "What I hold in my hand is not ordinary water. It is sacred water." Holding the cup to Moore's mouth, Ivers instructed him to drink.

After Moore had sipped some of the sacred water, Ivers sprinkled the remaining water across Moore's bed.

The ceremony was over. Ivers motioned for officer Robbins to leave the room and handed Eric Moore the Bible and said, "I have sealed your room against all manner of spirits, ghosts, goblins and entities. You will no longer be plagued by any manifestations, but you must do as I tell you. Do you understand, Eric?"

Eric nodded in assent.

"Good! Now take the Bible and repeat after me, Bam-Zah-Gum-Goo. That is your sacred word. It holds great power. Continue to repeat this word and never, and I mean never, tell anyone. The moment you tell someone about this word, it will lose its power. Now remember, as long as your feet do not touch the floor and you do not scream, the ghosts and demons will not be able to harm you."

Prisoner Moore clutched the Bible to his chest and fervently repeated his sacred word. Ivers slowly left the room, removed his royal vestments and said to Jason Robbins, "See that Mr. Moore is not disturbed for the rest of the night."

Robbins smiled and replied, "I guarantee no one will disturb Mr. Moore, Preacher."

Ivers was busy for the remainder of the night with an attempted suicide, a minor fight on the third floor and a multitude of complaints ranging from the temperature of the hot water to snoring roommates. Ivers only thought of Moore briefly during the remainder of his shift but he knew that in the morning the staff would have trouble getting Moore out of bed. But that was the day shift's worry, not his. His worry was to get through his shift and try to keep a cap on things.

During the past ten years, Lieutenant Frank Ivers had dealt with all kinds of prisoners. Most were cons, but there were those who were legitimately insane. Some of the truly insane ones only wanted something solid to hang on to and something to believe in, and that is what Ivers had given to Eric Moore something to hold on to and something to believe in. With no anchor in his life Eric Moore would thrash about, exhaust himself, sleep and thrash about some more. It would be a continuous cycle until he was medicated, but Ivers had provided a placebo that would work for eight to ten hours, not much longer. But it was the best he could do.

This sacred ceremony had been performed several times in the past and it had always worked. By tomorrow, word would be passed throughout the jail. The Preacher had conducted another service. In Ivers mind it was a hell of way to make a living. His thoughts were interrupted when the radio he wore on his belt announced he was needed on the fourth floor immediately.

14

January 13th, Thursday, marked Avery Beck's fourth day. His conversation with Roberto Romero the day before had helped to explain a number of things. Beck had sensed the animosity between Paulson and Dennison. Once Romero had provided his reluctant history lesson the reason became clear. How valid Romero's information was remained to be seen.

Avery spent the morning engrossed in examining staffing levels, assessing workloads and trying to determine who did what. What he hoped to find and what he did find, were three well-paid middle managers who had virtually no job functions. As far as Avery was able to determine, these people contributed absolutely nothing to the organization. Avery carefully circled the names in red. On a separate sheet of paper he listed the number of supervisors and employees working at the jail and then tabulated a ratio of well over twenty-seven line officers to one supervisor. This was preposterous. The average span of control for any supervisor was five to nine. There was no way a supervisor could be effective with this number of employees.

Beck sketched out a rough proposal which he planned to send to Mayor Waterston to address the supervisory deficiency. Beck knew money was tight so his proposal suggested the elimination of the three middle management positions and the incorporation of four additional lieutenant positions with the money saved. This would be a start in the right direction.

Beck had never met the three managers he was planning to eliminate, but it didn't matter.

While he busied himself with his reorganization, the private line on his phone rang. It was his first call on this line. Beck picked up the receiver and recognized the booming voice of the Mayor Sam Waterston.

"Avery, if you have a minute I'd like to talk to you in my office."

City Hall was only two blocks away and Beck said he would be over immediately. This was the first time he had spoken to Waterston since his appointment. Avery anticipated that Waterston wanted to get his initial assessment of the jail. He desperately needed some clarification of what Waterston expected and what Waterston wanted him to accomplish as Jail Administrator. This would be an opportune time to introduce his reorganization. It was nothing more than a trade-off of positions. It demonstrated good management. It was an opportunity for Avery to show Waterston that his faith in the new jail administrator had not been misplaced.

He walked the two blocks briskly and arrived five minutes later. The mayor's office was on the top floor of a large glass and brownstone structure nestled in the middle of the downtown area. A young woman stationed outside the office took Avery's name and suggested politely that he take a seat, explaining the mayor was in conference at the moment and would be a couple of minutes.

After he sat for fifteen minutes, he became restless. After thirty, he began to fume. Why hadn't Waterston told him he was in a meeting instead of making him wait? After forty-five minutes, the young lady with the broad smile informed Avery the mayor would see him now.

He walked into Waterston's office and was greeted by a pampered, overweight, overbearing politician with a mouthful of teeth and teased blond hair. Avery smiled inwardly. Waterston had combed his hair carefully in a vain attempt to hide a growing bald spot.

Waterston pumped Avery's hand and boomed, "Sit down, Avery, sit down! It's good to see you! I hope everything is going well over at the jail."

Avery started to reply but stopped when Waterston continued to speak.

"Avery, I'll get right to the point. I understand you have a pretty good kitchen over there in your jail."

Avery nodded dumbly and Waterston continued.

"It wouldn't be all that hard to serve up about a dozen extra meals tomorrow night, would it?"

"No, it shouldn't be a problem," responded Avery guardedly.

"Good, good! I knew you wouldn't let me down, Avery. Tomorrow night, I'm going to have a little meeting here with some state and federal zoning boys. You know how I am, always wanting to make a good first impression, so I figured a free dinner would make everyone feel right at home. Know what I mean?" Waterston didn't wait for a reply. "Whatever's on the menu for tomorrow night will be fine, as long as it's fried chicken."

Waterston laughed at his own cleverness and continued. "It shouldn't be too much trouble to have one of your staff wheel the food over here, say around seven o'clock tomorrow night, would it?"

Avery acknowledged it would be possible.

"Good! Then it's all settled."

Waterston's last comment was a clear indication that the meeting was over.

But Avery spoke. "Sam, before I leave, there are a couple of things I'd like to bring to your attention."

Waterston was visibly impatient but he waited for Avery to continue.

Avery pulled several sheets of paper from his brief case and placed them on the mayor's expansive desk. "What I propose to do, is to reorganize staff and positions at the jail. By eliminating the three positions I've indicated on the papers in front of you and using the money allocated for those three positions, I can create four additional supervisory positions." Avery stabbed his finger at the three names circled in red for emphasis and continued. "These three middle managers contribute absolutely nothing to the jail. As you can see, I am desperately in need of additional line supervisors. The ratio between employees and line supervisors.."

Avery was abruptly interrupted by Waterston's question. "Who occupies the three positions you intend to eliminate?"

Avery pointed to the names he had written in red.

Waterston studied the names, subconsciously patted his hair in place and stated, "Avery, I'm afraid there's not a whole hell of a lot you can do with these three boys. All three are tied in pretty tight with the city council and some state politicians. You start messing around with these boys and you're going to open up a hornet's nest. No, I think it would be best for you to leave these three fellows alone."

"I hear what you're saying, Sam, but these three people do absolutely nothing. Isn't there something I can do with them?" Waterston's voice was low and edged with impatience. "You try hacking away at any of these three people and you are asking for trouble, Avery. If you push the issue, which I know you won't, there's some city councilors who will make life pretty damn tough on you and me. No, Avery. These people will have to stay right where they are."

"Then what is it you want me to do as jail administrator?" Waterston placed a beefy arm around Avery's shoulders, "Just keep things quiet over there, Avery. You know, nice and smooth. No publicity."

Avery shuffled the papers on Waterston's desk back into his briefcase, thanked Waterston, and left. As he disappeared through Waterston's door, the mayor reminded him about the chicken dinners. Avery forced a smile in Waterston's direction and left.

Back in his office, Avery Beck sat bewildered. He had three people on his payroll who did absolutely nothing and he couldn't touch them. It didn't make sense. It seemed to Avery that Waterston could have stood behind him on this issue. As far as Waterston was concerned, the jail was just another city department, no different from the library. And then Waterston's comments about "Just keep everything quiet." What the hell was that supposed to mean? Keep everything quiet.

An overcrowded jail, an inadequate budget package, employees who came to work just to collect a check and a mayor who didn't know what the hell he wanted. No, Avery admitted to himself that was wrong. Waterston did know what he wanted. Waterston wanted ten chicken dinners for tomorrow night.

Beck was still furious when he picked up the phone and jabbed the button for the direct line to Dennison's office. Dennison answered on the first ring and listened quietly as Beck directed him to have the dinners delivered to the mayor's office. After Beck had finished, Dennison commented flatly, "I'll take care of it."

For once Beck was glad Dennison did not ask a lot of questions. After four days, things were not getting any better. If anything, they were getting worse. No, things were not getting worse. Beck was becoming educated on jail operations and politics.

Dennison contacted the jail's food service supervisor who was responsible for over three thousand meals a day. He stressed that the prisoners involved in transporting the food be supervised by a jail employee and all prisoners were to be showered, shaved and given a clean pair of coveralls.

The kitchen supervisor objected, saying it would involve overtime, screw up an already depleted budget, and besides, chicken wasn't on the menu for tomorrow night.

Dennison listened to the objections and then replied, "There is no room for discussion in this matter. Make sure the dinners are delivered on schedule."

15

Donald Macon could not be held in jail. That would violate his constitutional rights but the police, the district attorney's office and the courts all agreed that, technically, Donald Macon had criminally trespassed by entering a privately owned metal dumpster and should therefore be charged with a misdemeanor. By charging him with this it would keep him in jail until court and the police and district attorney's office would know where to find Donald Macon whenever they wanted to speak with him. Donald Macon was sentenced to ninety days.

If Donald Macon had some money and was a productive member of the community, he would probably have been booked, fingerprinted, photographed and released along with an apology. But Donald was none of these. He was a street person, a bum, a wino, a nobody. Now it was Donald's third day in jail. The beast in his stomach had been quieted by the pills he had been given, but the insatiable desire for alcohol was as strong as ever. He had been assigned to a room on the second floor. He had three roommates: a young nervous kid who talked a lot named Brad Wilson, another young man who spoke little, and an older man named Leeks who also said almost nothing.

Leeks had tattoos all over his arms and Donald recognized him as an old con, a lifer.

The room had been designed for only two people but additional bunks had been installed as the population expanded and now the room held four. Greg Leeks and Tommy Brown had been assigned one bunk and Donald Macon and Brad Wilson, the second.

Wilson had left the room several minutes earlier and was in the dayroom talking to other prisoners. Tommy Brown lay on the bottom bunk with his eyes open, staring into space. Greg Leeks was on the top bunk reading a cheap novel while Donald Macon lay on his side, watching the others.

Slowly, he rolled to a sitting position and placed his feet on the cool hardness of the concrete floor. The room was off-white with a stainless steel combination toilet-sink in one corner. A thin four inch strip of security glass ran from floor to ceiling on one wall, allowing the prisoners natural sunlight and a view on the outside world.

Donald stood up, walked to the stainless steel toilet and urinated. No one paid any attention. The sores on his face had begun to heal and he had shaved the day before. For the first time in years he looked almost human. His skin, leathery from years of exposure to heat and cold and poor diet made him look much older than he was. Donald returned to his bunk and sat down. Glancing across the room, he noticed Tommy Brown watching him. His first reaction was to look away but instead he tried to smile. It didn't come off well and looked more like a wicked grimace. It had been a long time since Donald Macon had smiled.

Tommy Brown kicked his legs over the edge of the bed and faced him.

"What are you in jail for?"

Donald had been in and around jail enough times to know that the less said about one's charges, the better.

"I'm here for trespassing and some other thing, but nothing serious." Leeks dog-eared a page of the book he was reading, placed it on the bed beside him, rolled to his side and peered down at Tommy Brown.

Leeks suffered no illusions. Tommy Brown was a cute kid and someone was going to make a serious effort at turning Tommy Brown into his punk. Leeks was not interested in men or young boys but he had seen it happen often enough. The kid was obviously scared. This would only attract predators like flies to honey. Leeks looked over at Macon and saw nothing more than a down--and--out--wino who had been busted for some chickenshit deal and who was in the process of drying out. Nobody would screw with Macon. Some of the younger prisoners might give him a hard time but it wouldn't be serious.

Donald saw Leeks watching him and offered a greeting.

Leeks nodded, nothing more.

Tommy Brown craned his head up. "I'm in here for burglary,

but it's really just a mistake. I was only fooling around, you know, nothing serious, but the cops caught me and I guess I'm going to be here for a while. What do you think will happen?"

Donald shrugged. "I don't know. I've never been arrested for burglary. You got a lawyer?"

Tommy shook his head. "No. The judge said something about a public defender, so I guess I'll be talking to a lawyer pretty soon. I ain't got no money, so they're going to give me a lawyer for free. I guess he'll come and see me sometime today."

Leeks dropped from the top bunk, walked to the writing table, retrieved a non-filtered cigarette and lit up. He blew a stream of dark blue smoke which twisted and danced in the air. Leeks looked back and then walked into the dayroom.

The room was large and surrounded on three sides by individual and group rooms. A dozen stainless steel tables were bolted to the floor and seats were welded to the tables.

A weight machine stood in one corner and Leeks decided he would make use of it in the future. A ping pong table was in the opposite corner and a game was in progress. Fifty other prisoners milled about, passing time. Some were watching television, others were using the weight machine, still others just stood and talked. Twenty-four hours a day this was their world. But twice a week they were entitled to go to the recreation area and twice a week visitors could come to see them in a special room under the watchful eye of a corrections officer for half an hour.

Once a week cigarettes, candy and other items could be purchased from the jail store, if you had money. Once a week a corrections officer took your jail coveralls and gave you a clean pair along with clean sheets. During the day the prisoners were locked in their rooms at eight hour intervals for a headcount and shift change. Whenever the corrections officers changed shifts, the shift going off duty counted the prisoners assigned to their floor and made sure the number matched with the number assigned to that unit. The oncoming shift did the same thing. During the evening and night shifts, additional headcounts were conducted.

Everything was planned, orderly and controlled. No decisions, no initiative, no motivation was necessary to do time in jail. This was the environment Greg Leeks had grown to appreciate.

He noticed some familiar faces but he didn't speak to them. Prison etiquette dictated no one approach an old con. You wait until he approaches you. Leeks walked through the dayroom and assessed his surroundings. He had been placed on a floor with a bunch of kids. He didn't see another lifer, just one and two time losers, and Leeks.

He drew a deep breath and realized he would have to cope with it until he could con someone in authority to sign off on a move slip.

The corrections officer assigned to the unit was dressed in a blue uniform and was moving among the prisoners. Leeks headed in his direction. "Hey, C.O c'mere."

Corrections Officer Stone, AKA Tombstone, turned and faced Leeks standing only a few feet away from him. Tombstone recognized him as an old con and stayed put.

"Yeah, you, C.O. Come here."

A C.O. who responded to a prisoner's demands could be controlled and manipulated and, generally, indicated he was a rookie. This C.O. would be difficult to con.

Leeks would test other C.O.s the same way. It was all part of the game.

"Hey man, what the fuck is this shit? I"m no fucking kid, I'm a fucking convict. If you don't get me off this floor fast, there's goin' to be some heavy duty shit coming down. I ain't goin' to put up with no shit from these kids."

Tombstone met Leeks' gaze and replied evenly. "You want to move? Fill out a Request to Move form and put it in the mail box for Classification. I'm not moving you. You get involved in any trouble and you'll wind up in lockup."

"You think you're a pretty bad dude, don't you?" This was another test.

But Tombstone showed no fear or reservation when he replied, "I"m the badest dude here. In two minutes I can have twenty corrections officers up here and lock everyone in their rooms."

Leeks couldn't let it go.

"Yeah, you're bad with everyone else, but what about one--on--one?"

Tombstone smiled. "I don't get paid enough to fight. If you

want to give me a couple of hundred thousand dollars, hell, I'll climb into the ring with Muhammed Ali, but until you're willing to cough up some dough, I ain't interested."

Leeks studied Tombstone hard for several seconds. "That's cool. No problem. But how about seeing if you can get me out of here?" Leeks changed his tact. Now he was friendly and solicitous.

"You fill out the request form and I'll guarantee the classification committee gets it. That's all I can do."

Tombstone was no virgin, or cherry boy. He had handled the situation right. He hadn't placed Leeks in a position where he had to fight in order to save face in front of the other prisoners and he hadn't gotten mad. Leeks had pushed the officer, but he had been careful not to directly threaten him. If Leeks threatened the C.O. openly, then the C.O. could do a report and Leeks would do a couple of days in solitary confinement. Tombstone was experienced. No doubt about it.

Leeks headed back to his room for another cigarette but he stopped half a dozen times to speak with some of the younger prisoners. Some had overheard the exchange and those who had not recognized Leeks as a lifer before, now knew who and what he was. Many of the younger prisoners were related to people Leeks had done time with--nephews, younger brothers, cousins. All showed Leeks a marked degree of respect. They stood a good chance of going to the can, a place where Leeks had been. None had a reputation and they hoped Leeks would be able to help then some day when they were trying to establish themselves in the joint.

The one thing feared most by young prisoners was getting a snitch jacket. They would spend the rest of their life in segregation and would be labeled. Leeks didn't have to worry about a jacket. He had already established himself. The younger prisoners intentionally maintained a distance from the corrections officers. If they were seen speaking to one it could be interpreted in a number of ways. None wanted to be accused of ratting. Older cons and lifers could speak to corrections officers whenever they wanted. This resulted in a narrow bridge of communication between the prisoner population and the official staff.

Meanwhile, Leeks had noticed a muscular blond standing near the weight machine. He had the look of someone who had done time. Leeks knew that sooner or later he and the big blond would have to reach an understanding. If not, then Leeks would have to 'take him out.' It was that simple. In jail it was survival of the fittest.

Leeks walked back to his room, climbed to the top bunk and picked up his book. Tommy Brown and Donald Macon were still talking. The conversation stopped momentarily as Leeks climbed to his bunk but he hadn't bothered to acknowledge the two when he entered.

Brown and Macon were neither allies nor potential threats so Greg Leeks was not interested in either of them. They existed and they occupied space, nothing more.

Leeks glanced up from his novel and saw the muscular blond Jack Stilwell, walk past his room. Leeks smiled inwardly. He had seen him and wanted to make sure he knew where Leeks was staying. This told Leeks the big blond was careful. And if the blond was careful, then he was also probably smart, which meant he wouldn't fuck with Leeks.

When Jack Stilwell had walked by, Donald Macon had also taken note. The big blond had been nothing more than a figure in a dream but now the dream returned to haunt him. Donald Macon felt the pain in his stomach grow. This time it wasn't alcohol withdrawal This time it was raw, naked fear.

16

Brad Wilson had been in jail half a dozen times during the past two years. Each time he had been assigned to the misdemeanor floor along with other petty thieves, traffic violators and nuisance offenders. This time he had been arrested for strong arm robbery, a felony offense and had been assigned to the second floor with the other young felons.

Several days ago he had stolen an elderly woman's purse. He had grabbed it and run, but the old woman had held on and Wilson had drug her several feet. She had broken several bones and had delayed him just long enough to be caught. Because of the injuries, the charge had been jacked up from petty theft to strong arm robbery.

Wilson knew that, in time, the district attorney and public defenders' offices would probably reach an agreement and reduce the charge to petty theft. But right now the system was playing games and he would have to do some pre-trial time. This did not bother Brad Wilson.

He was twenty years old with brown hair, blue eyes, medium build and a gigantic chip on his shoulder. Wilson had dropped out of school at seventeen and had been a thief ever since. He had stolen everything from tools to food and had made a good living at his trade. Wilson was more than a petty thief. He was a businessman with clients.

Wilson would customarily accompany one of his upper class, law abiding clients to an expensive store where the client would point out a variety of items. Wilson would return several hours later, steal the items, sell them for half price to his client and everyone was happy.

If one of his clients planned a dinner party, it was Wilson's job to supply the choice cuts of meat, at half price, of course. Brad Wilson had over fifty clients who employed him at various times to procure whatever they desired and his clientele was expanding.

Brad Wilson stole the items, turned them over quickly, and had no need of a middle-man. Everything was clear profit with no overhead.

The same people who lived in hundred-thousand-dollar houses, went to church on Sunday, and were pillars of their community were Brad Wilson's clients. The same people who shook their heads at the rise in crime and called for stricter punishment were Brad Wilson's clients.

In order to pick up a little spending money between jobs, he had stolen a purse and been caught. It wasn't a big deal and Brad knew he would be returning to the streets in a matter of months. In the meantime, he would work toward establishing a reputation for himself.

Now he was in a room with one wino, a virgin and a lifer. Brad knew he had to prove himself to the lifer. If someone like Leeks took notice of him, it could go a long way toward establishing his reputation. Wilson had no desire in life other than to be a thief. He was a good thief, probably one of the best, but sooner or later he would get caught, and sooner or later he would do some time. Wilson wanted to be prepared for that eventuality and now was as good a time as ever to begin preparations.

Jail was not a bad place for Brad Wilson. It was a place where he received approval from the other prisoners for his actions. It was a place of acceptance for people like Brad Wilson. There was always someone in jail who had a new technique or twist for stealing. Being in jail was like being in school. It was a place to learn, to grow and to expand.

Brad Wilson had watched as Greg Leeks made his way through the dayroom. He mentally made note of everyone Leeks had spoken to. To approach him directly would be inappropriate. It wasn't done that way. Wilson had plenty of time.

He had always wanted a tatoo. Each floor generally had someone who could do a tatoo for a couple of packs of cigarettes and a candy bar. Tattooing in jail was against the institutional rules and a very complicated process. First a needle had to be obtained. There were always diabetics in jail and an insulin syringe was the best, but the corrections officers kept a tight control on all needles and syringes. If that couldn't be obtained, then a paper clip sharpened to a needle point would work. Next came the problem of ink. A piece of carbon paper was best, but ink from a ball point pen could be used. As a last resort, there were cigarette ashes. The needle and the ink were generally referred to as a "rig."

The lights in the dayroom were blinking on and off and Wilson knew it was time to return to his room for lockup. It was shift change, and the C.O. wanted to make sure everyone was accounted for. Wilson intentionally made sure he was the last person back to his room. It was important to show everyone that he did not cooperate with "the man" any more than he absolutely had to. It was the first step toward establishing a reputation.

17

Corrections officers were no strangers to stress and Georgie Byers had learned to cope by ignoring it. In his mind, stress only existed if acknowledged and he absolutely refused to acknowledge stress and stressful situations. For each situation he encountered, he reacted and acted as he had been trained to do, nothing more and nothing less. It was his job.

Jason Robbins, Danny Pitts and Chris Keys faced stress through practical jokes and humor. Every day was a new scheme, a new way to beat the system without getting caught. It was a challenge. A thin line separated them from the prisoners they guarded. Mike Stone lost himself in books. Reading was a narcotic. He would leave work, pick up a novel and delve into the plot and characters. The reality of the jail was replaced by fiction.

Lieutenant Ivers found relief in exercise. He ran, swam, lifted weights and drained himself physically each day to combat the feelings of constant anxiety. Meanwhile Frank Willis reported to work every day edgy, agitated and nervous. And almost every day he hit someone. For Frank Willis, beating on people was the antidote for stress. But there was one other way of relieving stress. It was called sex and it was a common remedy.

However, Sheila Watkins handled her stress by spending time with her family and simply forgetting the jail. She had been a corrections officer for three years. The pay was not enough to raise a family, but the benefit package offered by the city of Coronado was a definite plus. Her husband, Clark, was self employed and the medical insurance in her compensation package had proven invaluable. Sheila was twenty-seven, attractive, five-foot-three, brown eyed and an intelligent officer. She had won the respect of the others in six months and had been welcomed into the fraternity of corrections officers shortly thereafter. Anyone in the fraternity was part of "us" and was privy to information not shared with "them." "Them" were supervisors, administration, prisoners and anyone else who did not belong to the fraternity.

Thirty-seven females were employed as corrections officer in the Coronado County jail. At first, Sheila had been frightened and intimidated by the prisoners but she had worked hard. Now she was a solid, well-organized officer, respected by prisoners and staff.

She had initially been reluctant to work with the male prisoners. Many were charged with rape and Sheila found it uncomfortable to be among people who had a proven history of attacking women. Then she learned the difference between jail and the streets. On the streets a prisoner could be a rapist and a beater of women but inside jail it was not considered macho. Inside, a woman in authority was a motherly figure, someone who needed protection. If a prisoner threatened Sheila or any other female, ten other prisoners would stand up to defend her. This was something no male prisoner would ever do for a male corrections officer. After three years, Sheila was no longer frightened, but she was careful. She had seen female officers fall in love with prisoners and risk their careers and futures by providing unauthorized items to their boyfriends. Many prisoners were smooth, professional con artists with dazzling muscular builds and a certain roguish, boyish attraction. Sheila had seen female corrections officers charged with bringing in drugs or fired for engaging in sex while on duty. It was a triumph for a prisoner to make it. Sheila had been propositioned, threatened and sweet-talked but she had never wavered. And she had never been taken in.

It was January 13th, a Thursday, and Sheila had been assigned to the control room on the fourth floor where the medium custody felons were housed. It was her responsibility to maintain a close watch on the other officers and maintain a log of the evening's activities. Sheila worked the three-to-eleven shift and these hours had taken a toll on her family life. When she got home, everyone was asleep and it generally took several hours to wind down after the end of a shift. In the mornings, she would drag herself out of bed, send her husband off to work, her children off to school and climb back in bed for a couple more hours sleep.

Sheila had learned quickly that Clark, her husband, did not want to hear about the jail. Clark made it clear he did not like

Sheila working there but he realized there were few alternatives Bills had to be paid.

This evening, Tombstone was working the north side of the detention level with fifty-seven prisoners and Georgie Byers was working the south side with sixty-two prisoners. Both sides had been designed to hold a maximum of only forty-eight prisoners each but this level, like the others, was overcrowded.

Sheila enjoyed working with both officers and considered them professional and competent. Neither had ever come on to her.

Some of the other female officers made life difficult for women like Sheila. Some enjoyed the excitement of having sex on the job. The pressure, the stress and the danger of working in jail all fueled some deep primitive sexual drive. This sent mixed signals to some of the male corrections officers and they would often proposition female officers. For a person to claim sexual harassment was a signal to everyone that you were unable to handle yourself, something no one would ever admit in a detention center.

Sheila had just annotated the nine-thirty headcount in her log and stood staring out the one-way glass to the north side. Something was wrong. There was a faint rumbling in the back of her head warning her that things on the north side were not as calm as they appeared. Suddenly, Tombstone approached the control room window and signaled to Sheila to let him out of the housing area. She activated the switch which moved the heavy steel door. Tombstone entered and waited until Sheila had closed the heavy metal door and then came to open the control room door. Entering the darkened control room, Sheila asked, "What's going on out there?" Her question was laced with concern.

Tombstone peered through the one way glass. "You noticed it too, huh?"

Sheila followed Tombstone's stare and replied, "Yeah. There's something going on, no question about it."

"Let's get Georgie in here and see if he's heard anything from the other side."

Sheila stood for several seconds staring out the control room window before responding. "Good idea." Moving to the control room desk, Sheila pressed the mike key on her radio and spoke, "Unit 40, please come to control."

Georgie recognized his call sign and ambled slowly toward the heavy metal door near the control room window. By the time he arrived, Sheila had activated the switch to let Georgie exit. He came to the control room door. Tombstone opened the door and he entered. Control room doors did not stay open any longer than absolutely necessary. Staff were trained to enter and exit quickly, and never to open a control room door when one of the housing unit doors was open. If a prisoner gained access to a control room, the entire floor could easily be over-run and the possible consequences were beyond imagining. The code that protected Sheila as a female would dissolve in a take-over or riot, and rape and death could be the consequence. Tombstone and Georgie would not be safe because of their gender. They too could be raped and murdered. Everyone in the jail was constantly reminded that, if taken hostage, their life, regardless of rank, was not important enough to risk a prisoner escape. These words were printed in large bold letters across the bottom of every page in the post orders manual, the book which ticked off, step by step, every function, operation and duty for each post. The knowledge that atrocities could occur at any time was something few people spoke of, but something always in the officer's thoughts.

Meanwhile, once inside the control room, Sheila and Tombstone expressed their misgivings to Georgie who walked across the control room and peered through the one-way glass to the north side. After a full minute of silence he turned to Sheila and barked, "Call the Lieutenant and get help of here right away. Tombstone! Let's go!"

Sheila instantly picked up the phone. While she waited for the master control officer to answer she asked, "What's wrong?"

Halfway out the control room door, Georgie shouted over his shoulder, "They're all wearing shoes!"

Sheila shouted that they needed help immediately, then moved quickly to the control panel and opened the heavy metal door and allowed Georgie and Tombstone into the north side housing unit.

Tombstone noted that Georgie had been right. Everyone was wearing shoes. No one wore shoes this late at night. Everyone usually wore shower shoes and Tombstone knew what this meant. It meant a fight. Part of fighting was kicking and a prisoner couldn't

kick anybody in the head with shower shoes. This looked like i
was going to be one hell of a big fight.

Georgie quickly walked toward a bay orderly he knew by name
but the orderly shied away from him. Things had gone too far fo
talking.

As Georgie turned, he saw Tombstone surrounded by ten pris
oners and felt a sinking feeling in the pit of his stomach. They ha
to hang on for a minute, two minutes at the most, before help woul
arrive. Georgie moved towards Tombstone and was conscious of a
dull roar as prisoners shouted obscenities. It was just noise, static
nothing more. Georgie kept moving and pushed his way through
the ring of prisoners and asked of no one in particular, "What d
you think about painting the dayroom blue?"

The question caught everyone off guard.

One prisoner whom Georgie did not recognize, but who appeare
to be the leader, shouted, "Fuck you, mother-fuckers! We're tire
of being treated like a bunch of fucking kids, man! If we have t
fuckin' rock-n-roll to get a little attention in this place, then we'l
fuckin' rock-n- roll!"

The circle increased and now thirty prisoners surrounded them
Both officers maintained deadpan expressions, knowing that any
sign of fear would escalate the situation.

The prisoners had been worked into a frenzy and smelled blood
Anything could set them off. Years of experience told the officers t
move and speak slowly and carefully.

"What are you talking about?" questioned Georgie.

"I'm talking about all the shit we have to put up with! You
people are treating us like animals and we ain't puttin up with i
any more! We want some fuckin' action, and we want it now!"

Suddenly the large metal door to the unit opened and ten cor
rections officers rushed in, led by Lieutenant Ivers. Many begar
shouting and ordering everyone to their rooms. Sheila also or
dered people to their rooms through the loud speaker and the feel
ing of being anonymous was destroyed as she used specific names
The prisoners complied without a need for physical force. What
had seemed like an eternity was in fact only one minute and seven
teen seconds.

Frank Willis was one of the responding officers and after all prisoners, had been secured in their rooms, he returned to where Tombstone and Georgie were talking to Ivers. Willis overheard Tombstone tell Ivers, "I'm not sure what started this thing Lieutenant. I suspect the new guy in room A-10 is behind it. He had everyone pretty worked up, but he wasn't saying anything specific. Everything was general stuff like, we're tired of this shit and `you're treating us like kids, and that sort of thing."

Ivers scribbled A-10 on a yellow lined tablet and then turned to Tombstone and directed, "Keep these guys locked up for the rest of the night. I'll brief the night shift and, depending on how these guys act in the morning, it will be the night shift captain's decision to let them back out for breakfast or feed them in their rooms. Also, I need a report from you, Georgie and Sheila on what went down here. Make sure you get it to me by the end of the shift."

Once Willis had heard the room number of the leader, he ambled to the elevators along with the other officers. He smiled as he rode the elevator back to booking. He hoped there would be some overtime available on the night shift. The maggot in A-10 would have a surprise visit tonight from some of the night shift officers. If there was overtime available, Willis would make sure he was involved. It was time for a little attitude adjustment for the prisoner in A-10 and Willis wanted to be involved.

Meanwhile, Georgie went back to the south side, checked his area and reported back to the control room. Sheila and Tombstone were already working on their reports. Georgie picked up a preprinted report form, sat down and began writing. He made sure he included everything and followed the rules of who, what, when, where, how and why. Georgie wasn't sure why, but it was his guess that Mason Roberts in A-10 had been responsible. Prisoners like Roberts, who were able to get other prisoners worked up, were dangerous. Finishing his report last, Georgie volunteered to deliver all three reports to the Lieutenant's office. Sheila and Tombstone handed him their reports. Georgie then left the control room and headed toward the elevator. Sheila turned to Tombstone and asked, "How you doing?"

"Pretty good, I think. Pretty tight situation."

Sheila's pulse rate was still up and the effects of adrenalin wer
just beginning to subside.

"So what do you think?" asked Tombstone.

"About what?"

"About the whole damn thing."

"It sucks," said Sheila, surprising even herself by the answer
Tombstone smiled and agreed. "You're right. It does suck. Bu
it's the best game in town. Know what I mean?"

"Yeah, I know what you mean. You all right?"

"Yeah, I'm all right, but you know what? I'm going to break on
of my own rules tonight and stop at Cedars and have a couple c
drinks." It was something Tombstone never did.

Sheila shrugged. "Sounds like a good idea after a night lik
tonight."

"You're invited."

Sheila thought for several seconds before answering. Ther
was no way she was going to get to sleep before three in the morn
ing. She could go home, watch a re-run on television, pace th
house, wish she had someone to talk to about how scared she ha
been tonight, peek in at her kids and then sit by herself. One drinl
and some conversation wouldn't kill her and she knew Tombston
was not one of the center's party animals. Tombstone never stoppe
to drink with the guys and he never spread rumors.

"You know, I might just take you up on it."

Georgie soon returned to the control room. "The lieutenan
reviewed the reports. No problems."

Tombstone nodded and then said, "Hey, Georgie, I'm going t
stop at Cedars and have a couple of drinks after work. Want t
come?"

"Naw, I'm going to head on home."

Sheila was busy at the control room desk but overhear
Tombstone's invitation. She was glad Tombstone had not mentione
that she might stop as well.

Near the end of the shift, Tombstone and Georgie conducted a
headcount. The count was reported to Sheila and she logged it in
Ten minutes later the officers assigned to take over their posts re
ported for duty. Georgie Byers, Mike Tombstone Stone and Sheil

Watkins walked out of the detention center and congratulated themselves on having made it through another shift, alive.

The Cedars was a middle class drinking establishment which catered to salesmen, businessmen and other professional people.

Tombstone pulled into the parking lot, turned off his lights, lit a cigarette and waited for Sheila. He met her halfway across the parking lot and they entered the Cedars. There were plenty of places to sit. Out of habit, Tombstone led the way to a corner table at the back. From here, he could see everyone coming and going and his back was to the wall. Years of working at the jail had conditioned him to always place himself at a vantage point. It was a subconscious habit employed for survival.

Sheila slid in across from Tombstone and they ordered drinks. Sheila felt awkward and wondered what she was doing here. It had seemed like a good idea but now she wasn't certain. She liked Tombstone, but she knew little about him. He rarely spoke of his personal life, as did she, and they had enjoyed a purely professional relationship.

The drinks arrived and Tombstone took a sip, and peered over the rim of his glass and asked, "What'd ya think of Georgie?" He was referring to the way Georgie handled the situation on the fourth floor earlier that night.

"Georgie never shows anything. He never looks scared, or happy, or anything. He just is. You know what I mean?"

"I know exactly what you mean. Georgie is like the Tin Man from the Wizard of Oz. Nothing inside. But I really enjoy working with him."

"Yeah, me too," commented Sheila.

Both lapsed into their own thoughts.

Tombstone had been married for six years and had one child. He loved his wife and son and had never strayed nor had ever shown any interest in another woman. In his mind, Sheila was not another woman. She was a corrections officer, a corrections officer with whom he had shared a frightening experience and she was someone who understood.

Sheila felt comfortable here with Tombstone. Words were not necessary to explain how she felt because instinctively she knew Tombstone was aware of her feelings. Sitting next to him, she felt strangely calm and was not ashamed of expressing the fear she had felt earlier.

"Were you scared?"

Tombstone smiled and lit a cigarette, "I was scared shitless."

"Me too."

"What's your husband think of you working in the jail?"

"Well, he doesn't like it and, you know, we don't talk about it very much. I guess he's interested, but I think it scares him a little that I'm locked up for eight hours with a bunch of crazy criminals. I think he worries about me. He's also a little embarrassed to mention it when we're in public. Generally, people sort of look down at people who work in jails."

"What do you do when you get off at night?" asked Tombstone

"I suppose that's the hardest part. Times like tonight, I'd really like to go home and tell Clark, that's my husband's name, Clark, what happened, but I know he wouldn't understand. Anyway, I usually go home, watch a re-run on television, check on my kids and just walk around the house."

"Sounds like me. You know, I asked Georgie one time what he did after work and you know what he told me?"

Sheila shook her head.

"He told me he goes home and goes to sleep, can you believe that? I mean, shit, how can a person just go home and go to sleep after a night like tonight?"

"I don't know. I guess everyone's different."

"Yep."

Tombstone ordered another round. Sheila started to object but then asked herself, Why? Another round wouldn't hurt and she was still keyed up. She was enjoying herself and the conversation. Tombstone knew exactly what it was like for Sheila and she knew exactly what it was like for him. Work, go home, be alone, get up in the morning, be alone, go to work and the cycle continued.

The drinks were delivered, Tombstone paid and the waitress left. Tombstone lit another cigarette. "I hope I don't offend you or anything, but why would a woman as pretty as you want to be a corrections officer?"

Sheila smiled. For some reason, Tombstone's reference to her appearance meant a great deal. Prisoners, other corrections officers and even strangers had hit on her with no effect, but now, for some reason, Tombstone's comment was important. "I don't know. I needed a job and this was the only one I could get at the time. In the beginning I had my doubts, but now I sort of enjoy it."

"You ever get lonely?" asked Tombstone, changing the topic unexpectedly.

"Yeah, all the time." Sheila did not regret her honesty. There were no longer any defenses or game playing. Tombstone and Sheila had crossed a bridge and they were now a part of each other. They were two people who had survived a situation. Two people who may or may not survive the next one. Right now, family, friends, social graces, everything had evaporated in order to allow both of them to reach out and find someone who felt the same.

Words were no longer necessary. A bond had been formed. A bond that would evaporate by tomorrow, but while it lasted, it would be cherished.

After the third drink, Tombstone paid the tab and walked Sheila to his car where the conversation continued. They were strangely drawn to each other. Both found the comfort they sought in each other's arms. Their spouses, their families, nothing entered their minds except the need to hold and be held by someone who truly understood. Someone who understood the isolation and loneliness and the fear that was faced each day.

Their lovemaking was slow and deliberate, allowing them to savor each moment. There was no longer an outside world, just the world here inside Tombstone's vehicle. Each knew they would never be able to recapture the feelings they had at this moment. It was an accident. They had simply fallen victim to a series of incidents beyond their control.

It was a sensuous, soft moment they both needed to maintain their sanity. Their sharing was a moment of closeness and understanding intertwined by the joining of their bodies.

Tombstone loved his wife. Sheila loved her husband. Right now, they needed something more precious and more fulfilling than love. They needed comfort, understanding and each other.

Afterward, there was no embarrassment. Tombstone watched Sheila walk to her car and drive away. It would never happen again. Of that, Tombstone was sure. But it had happened and now

Tombstone was ready to face the isolation and the world again. He knew he didn't love Sheila, but he did love what she had done for him.

As Sheila drove home she realized Tombstone had done something for her no one else could have. And for once, Sheila Watkins felt completely relaxed and at ease. The stress, the fears, the loneliness had all been washed away, at least for a time.

She arrived home, took a shower and fell asleep as soon as her head hit the pillow.

18

While Tombstone and Sheila were practicing the fine art of stress management, Frank Willis was planning his own stress reduction--The Joy of Beating. Overtime had been needed for the night shift and Willis had eagerly volunteered to pull a double. He mumbled to himself that it was nothing more than fate. A higher power had intervened because the higher power believed in justice. Tonight he would be doing the "Lord's" work.

After the night shift briefing and post assignments, Frank had clued in a select group of corrections officers about what had happened during the evening shift and who had been responsible.

The maggot was Mason Roberts and tonight four corrections officers, including Frank Willis, would pay Maggot Mason a visit. Once everyone had been secured in their rooms on detention level four, Mason Roberts had sat for several minutes in his room savoring his ability to create havoc. In jail, it was survival of the fittest and those who had the power controlled everything. Control the people and the power was yours.

Mason Roberts was thirty-three years old, stocky and a career criminal. It was Mason Roberts' goal to be the main man at the penitentiary some day. This incident on the fourth floor had been nothing more than a rehearsal. The people in this jail hadn't seen anything yet. Mason Roberts was smart, clever, intelligent and dangerous. Mason had been in court more times than most attorneys. He had made his mark early by learning the law and preparing suits, briefs and interrogatories. The nuisance suits had to be answered and his legal prowess had kept the officials at bay in every jail he had been. "Jail house" lawyers were respected and Mason Roberts was as knowledgeable as any civil rights attorney. In time, he would file suit against the city of Coronado and the jail citing inadequate living conditions, overcrowding, poor food and poor medical care. He would cite the eighth amendment and claim the jail constituted cruel and unusual punishment. He might not win, but it didn't matter. What mattered was his ability to control the movement and direction of the people who ran the jail. He would force them to do what he wanted through law suits and in time no one would stand up to Mason Roberts. The jail officials would grow to hate him but they wouldn't screw with him. They'd be too scared. He shed his blue jail coveralls and climbed under the covers and was asleep within minutes.

It was two in the morning and the five corrections officers were in the fourth floor control room listening to Frank Willis.

"Remember. Don't fuck up his head. Everybody use body shots."

Then the officer assigned to control activated the switch which allowed them access to the north side of detention level four. None worried about the Lieutenant arriving unexpectedly. The control room officer assigned to the fifth detention level had radioed the Lieutenant and asked for his assistance in straightening out an incorrect count. It would take at least an hour for the error to be found and the control officer could always blame it on the other shift. An hour was more than enough time for Frank Willis and his friends to do the Lord's work.

The five eased through a quiet dayroom and made their way to Mason's room. Willis keyed the lock and they entered quietly. Mason lay sleeping in his bed with his face to the wall. Willis grinned in anticipation. One carried a blanket. Willis turned and motioned for him to toss it over Mason's head. Two of them swiftly pounced on Mason's stirring form and held him while the rest pounded him repeatedly. Soon Mason's muffled screams subsided to moans. Willis spoke through the blanket over Mason's head. "The next time you start fucking with a C.O., remember there's plenty more where this came from. We're not going to put up with any son-of-a-bitch who wants to stir the shit. Just remember, Mason, we know where you live and we can get you any time we want. Think about it, fuck-face."

Four officers moved toward Mason's room door while one remained behind. When they were safely outside the room, the fifth pulled the blanket away from Mason's face and quickly left the room.

All Mason Roberts ever saw was a blue shirt melting into the darkness. It would be impossible to identify any of his assailants. His whole body ached and each movement greeted him with excruciating pain. This had never happened to Roberts before. These people were supposed to be afraid of him. He would have to rethink his strategy. He knew he wasn't seriously injured, but he was frightened. Those crazy mother-fuckers could have killed him. They could have strung him up to make it look like a suicide. The words he had heard came back to haunt him. "We know where you live and we can get you any time we want."

Roberts knew none of the prisoners would admit to having seen anything. He was alone. His choices were clear. Either conform and be like the rest of the stupid fucks in this place and live, or he could file law suits and wind up dead. It was going to be a tough decision.

Roberts rolled out of bed, doing his best to ignore the pain. Shakily, he made his way to the stainless steel toilet and urinated. His penis was the only part of his body which didn't hurt.

19

Friday morning, January 14th, Sam Dennison reported for duty, made the usual pot of coffee, unlocked his office and checked the captain's log. He noted a disturbance had taken place on the north side of the fourth floor close to shift change, but other than this, there was nothing. Dennison made a copy of the log and dropped it in Beck's basket outside the Administrator's office door.

He then moved to the coffee pot, poured himself a cup and lit his third cigarette of the day.

"You have another cigarette you can spare?"

Dennison turned to find Beck standing behind him. He reached for his pack and shook one out. It was the first time he had seen him smoke and Dennison was mildly surprised.

Dennison poured a second cup of coffee and handed it to Beck.

Returning to his office, Beck followed and asked, "Anything happen last night?"

"According to the logs there was some sort of undefined disturbance on the fourth floor. Assistance was called and everyone on the floor was placed in lockdown, meaning they were confined to their rooms. The night shift reported that they acted OK this morning for breakfast so it's my guess that Paulson will let them out. Or then again, he might not. It's his call."

Beck nodded, closed the door to Dennison's office, sat on one of the chairs and stated, "I think we need to talk."

Dennison's mind was moving quickly. Shit, he thought, here it comes. Beck's going to want me to tell him everything there is to tell about a jail in two minutes. Then he's going to ask me all sorts of bullshit questions and five minutes later he won't remember the questions, let alone the answers. Dennison liked Beck. He seemed like a pretty nice political hack. The problems with the jail, in Dennison's opinion, were simple: money, space and Paulson.

Paulson was an incompetent idiot. Paulson had bullied and bluffed his way to deputy chief by threatening to sue anyone who stood in his way. The power had gone to his head. As far as Dennison was concerned, the farther away from Marshall Paulson he could get, the better. Sooner or later the whole damn place was going to blow and Dennison did not want to be held responsible for Paulson's blunders.

"We've talked before, but each time I got the feeling you were skirting the issues and really not saying what was on your mind. There's no question I need your help if I'm ever going to make any changes around here, but you need to provide me with the information and the insight. So how about it?"

Dennison took a deep breath. "What do you want to know?"

"Everything."

Dennison smiled, stubbed out his cigarette, took a sip of coffee and said, "There's no way you'll ever know everything. A lot of things happen here that only the C.O.s know. I suspect some things, but without proof I keep my mouth shut. I will tell you what I know, sprinkled with some philosophical points and a lot of reality. First of all, you have to deal with all the political hacks in the department. No offense."

"None taken," commented Beck.

"They do no work and are constantly on the move to City Hall. Everything you do, and don't do, is reported to either a city councilor or the mayor's office. These people are interested in preserving their positions. They look for ways to undermine the administration for no particular reason other than it's a way of life for them. The Mayor and the City Council won't let you touch these guys."

Beck already knew this to be true all to well.

"The majority know who does and who doesn't work and the political hacks affect morale a great deal. Employees see these people doing nothing and getting paid well for doing nothing and they ask themselves, "Why should I bust my ass?

Anyway, I don't know what you can do about those folks. Other than the politics, you're restricted in your efforts by the union, the City's personnel rules and regulations, labor laws, and public oversight committees. When you do try to do something constructive, it's going to upset someone's apple cart and, believe me, they'll be gunning for you. That, Mr. Beck, is the reality of the situation."

Beck hadn't realized how complex running a jail could be. The innuendo, the unseen, the nuances, all became important. He could make changes, but at what price? Beck wondered idly what power he actually had as jail administrator.

Dennison continued. "In conjunction with all of these watch-dogs, protective groups and local politicians, you have the corrections officers themselves. They are a tightly knit group who trust no one outside their own circle. To convince one corrections officer to testify against another for any reason is like asking him to kill his own mother. It ain't done. This means a lot of things are going to happen which neither you nor I hear about. Some things you don't want to hear about."

"Like what?"

"I'd really rather not go into that right now, but one example would be excessive force. If you discover some one using excessive force, you are obligated to act. If you fail to act, you can legally be held negligent. Your responsibility as administrator is to ensure everyone knows what excessive force is, that the department does not condone it and that training is provided to all staff to curtail the use of excessive force. But you'll never stop it. Not here. When you take action, this pisses everybody off. Morale takes a nose dive for several months. On the other hand, if you fail to uncover a case where excessive force was used, then of course you are not obligated to take disciplinary action and morale stays high. In other words, sometimes you don't want to know. "

Dennison paused for a moment and continued. "You see, prisoners act a certain way. They want society to "do for them." This attitude is contagious and there are a number of C.O.'s who want the department "to do for them" as well. C.O.s do not trust outsiders and they perceive their situation as "us" against "them." If something goes wrong, the C.O.s blame it on the administration or the supervisors but never on themselves. We, as administrators, blame the line people, but rarely do we ever admit we screwed up. You know why?"

Beck shook his head.

"Because it's not the administration in this organization who are making the decisions. It's the pseudo-politicians and the other political groups who don't know jack-shit about running a jail. The problem we face is that we can't tell the line people just how stupid the people who are calling the shots really are. If you do, then you'll piss off the politicians and you won't last long. So the C.O.s blame the administration for everything and the communication gap grows wider and wider. Now we add stress, an unrealistic budget, a confined environment, a level of constant anxiety, laws made by rational people which are supposed to deter irrational people and we lock all these things together behind solid steel and concrete and what do you have? You have one fucked up situation, that's what you have. And then we cap it all off by having an incompetent racist in charge of security who blames his incompetence on everyone except himself and uses the black factor as a means to explain away all the failures."

Dennison sat back and waited for Beck to react. He rarely spoke this openly with anyone, but things had been boiling inside him for some time and Beck had asked for it. He had given it to him straight.

"What do you suggest?" asked Beck.

Dennison shrugged his shoulders, lit another cigarette, and replied, "Hell, I don't know. I'm not sure anyone can do anything."

"What about Paulson? Could he do something?"

Dennison smiled and asked, "Have you pissed him off yet?"

Beck returned the smile and admitted, "Yesterday. After I spoke with you about the new schedule for the property officers, I told Paulson to make sure everything was done right and he said.."

Dennison interrupted, "He said he was tired of everyone else running the facility and the union needed to find out who the boss was and he was tired of all the different personalities, and so on and so on."

Beck studied Dennison evenly and asked, "Is that his standard speech?"

"Pretty much. Sometimes he talks about racism and a hostile work environment. I think he read about it somewhere in a law book. Anyway, to answer your original question, Paulson isn't going to do anything to help. As a matter of fact, he's probably already contacted his attorney and is filing suit against you for pissing him off."

"You're kidding."

"No, that's how he operates. The best defense is a good offense. If he files suit against you, it doesn't matter if he wins or loses. What matters is that if you try to do anything to or with him, he'll charge you with retaliation. You might not back off, but those dickless wonders in City Hall sure will. It's just Paulson's way of welcoming you to the jail."

"Has he ever sued you?"

"Hell yes, at least three times."

"What for?"

"Same old stuff, hostile work environment, discrimination, and he even included harassment in one of them."

"Did he win?"

"Naw. He just files. Then, after a year or so, the time runs out and everything just falls by the wayside. And then he gets all charged up again for some reason or another and files again. I don't think it's personal on his part. He just doesn't like anybody. He even accused a black corrections officer of being prejudiced against him. I couldn't figure that one out and neither could anyone else."

Beck motioned for another cigarette and asked, "Is there anything else I should know?"

"Just what I told you in the beginning. Stand with your back to the wall and be careful who you trust. Draw your own conclusions, make your own decisions, and tell everyone else to go screw themselves. The people here have been in jail so long that most of them have forgotten how to deal with regular people. Everybody's looking for the con. Oh, there is one last thing. Your sexual habits are really none of my business but we have about four or five female corrections officers here who are scrubboards. If they get the chance to scrubboard you, they will."

"What do you mean, scrubboards?"

"Oral sex."

"And you call it scrubboard. Why?"

Dennison smiled thinly and said, "About two years ago, one female officer conducted a roof check with a male counterpart. As you know, we have intercoms all over the jail. While up there she decided to give her buddy a little head. The master control officer

116

had his intercom open and heard the entire thing go down. He said it sounded like someone was using a scrubboard. I heard about it through the grapevine and the term stuck."

"So what you are saying is, I can expect a sexual advance?"

"I'd lay money on it."

"Why?"

"It's something they can use. If a person has something on the jail administrator, then they don't have to worry about getting their vacation approved or the department taking disciplinary action against them for screwing up. Remember what I said. Everything here is a con."

"Has it ever happened to you?"

Dennison smiled, "Yeah, sure, lots of times."

"What did you do?"

"I told them all, look, Babe, you don't make enough money to touch me."

"And that was it?"

"That was it. I mean they aren't going to try and rape you or anything. They just want to have a little fun and set up some protection at the same time."

"I don't suppose you would tell me who these officers are?"

Dennison laughed and said, "I don't think so. Besides, it would ruin all the fun for you. And if no one makes an advance, well then, I haven't ruined anyone's reputation."

Beck rose, thanked Dennison, moved to the coffee pot, filled his cup and headed for his office.

Dennison watched Beck depart and chuckled. He had asked for it and he had gotten it.

Beck tried to digest what Dennison had told him. Dennison had been right about Beck's limited power to make changes. After Beck's recent conversation with Waterston, Beck suspected his power as jail administrator was severely limited.

He picked up the phone and dialed the city attorney's office. He was curious to see if Paulson had actually filed suit as indicated by Dennison. Beck asked to speak with a friend who worked in the city attorney's office. In several seconds he learned that Paulson had indeed filed a new suit against the city of Coronado and named him as a defendant.

Now Beck had to decide how to handle Paulson. Should he meet Paulson head on and let him know who was boss? Or should he encourage Paulson to be a team player and try to win his respect?

His thoughts were interrupted by the telephone. Absently, he picked it up and heard Waterston's voice at the other end demanding, "Just what the hell is going on over there, Avery?"

"I'm not sure I know what you mean," he replied.

"Well, let me tell you what I mean. This morning I was informed that one of your deputy chiefs, Marshall Paulson, has filed suit against the city and named you and me as defendants. That's what I mean."

"It's really not as bad as it seems."

Waterston interrupted with a roar, "What do you mean it's not as bad as it seems? I said keep everything quiet over there and I meant keep everything quiet. This city and this administration will not tolerate being labeled racist."

Avery started to reply but stopped. Waterston had hung up. He replaced the receiver slowly and realized he only had to get through the rest of the day before the weekend began.

Avery Beck was trapped.

*   *   *

On this same Friday, January 14th, Marshall Paulson sat in his office boiling mad. In his mind, he had been forced to contend with racism and prejudice his entire life. As a black career military man he had seen other people's names on promotion lists, but not his. Everything he had accomplished he had worked and fought hard to obtain. No one had given him a damn thing.

Had he been born white it would have been easier. No one wanted to give him a chance simply because he was a minority. Of this Paulson was convinced.

So he had filed another suit against the department, Beck and the city of Coronado. Someday he would own the city's treasury. He would make the city pay for all the harassment, discrimination and prejudice he had experienced since birth. It was only fair. Someone had to pay, and the city of Coronado had been elected.

Paulson was tired of seeing all the rich white people driving their expensive cars and living in big houses. Now it was his turn. People said he was hard to get along with. People said that he was not a team player. Bullshit! What they meant was he would not kiss their ass and play the white man's game. He was not going to play it any longer. He had the power and he knew how to use it. If someone didn't like it, then tough shit. They could quit.

Paulson had hoped Beck would be different from Powell. Powell had tried to keep him down but it hadn't worked. Paulson had gone around Powell and dealt directly with the former mayor.

If Beck wasn't willing to work with Paulson, then he would deal directly with Waterston. Paulson had the NAACP, the city's Equal Employment Opportunity Commission and two city councilmen behind him. He also had his attorney, and Paulson knew he could make life rough on the bigots who wanted to keep him down.

Paulson smiled grimly as he pictured Beck's reaction to the suit. Beck would treat him better now. He would realize that Marshall Paulson was not somebody who could be stepped on without consequence.

This morning he had typed a memorandum detailing the creation of the new property unit this memo had been distributed to the captains and lieutenants. Paulson was not going to back down. He was tired of backing down. If Beck wanted to force the issue, Paulson knew in his heart that Beck's actions would be nothing more than retaliation for the suit he had filed.

Suddenly, Paulson's thoughts were interrupted by two plain clothes policemen at his door.

They needed his assistance. The jail was holding a female prisoner named Tonia Williams. A gun had been found in her purse during booking. The serial number indicated the gun was stolen. She had stated the gun belonged to Jack Stilwell, another prisoner. Tests had been conducted and ballistics had matched the gun to the gun used in the Paul Frazer murder. The police were prepared to charge Stilwell with murder and possession of a stolen firearm.

The police explained that they had an eye witness placing Stilwell at the scene of the crime. The witness was identified as a wino named Donald Macon. The problem was, Macon and Stilwell were housed together on the same unit. If Stilwell discovered that Macon was an eye witness and was going to testify against him, Stilwell could kill Macon. The police needed Paulson to order an immediate housing change for either Stilwell or Macon and to ensure the two did not come in contact before the trial. It was also an opportunity to put Stilwell away for a long time, they stated.

Paulson listened closely but his mind wandered back to his own problems.

If he pushed the racial discrimination issue the city would never go to trial. It would cause too much bad publicity and the city was always terrified of losing. They did not want the whole world to know how corrupt and bigoted they were. The city would offer Paulson a settlement. Paulson needed to speak with his attorney. They had to come up with a settlement.

Meanwhile, the policemen were still talking. They had said something about a prisoner named Stilwell and another named Macon and they wanted Paulson to order a housing change or something.

Paulson mumbled he would take care of it, scribbled the two names on a pad and watched as the two men left. The white people of the world were finished pushing Marshall Paulson around. No honky was going to come into Paulson's office and tell him how to run things.

Paulson picked up the phone and called his attorney. He then launched into his standard speech of prejudice, harassment and discrimination.

This very morning Paulson had found a poster under his door which had read: "From now on black people in this department will no longer be referred to as negroes, coloreds or niggers. They will be referred to as Seagulls. The reason they will be referred to as Seagulls is because they cruise all night, squawk all day, shit on everybody and are protected by the Federal government. Your cooperation in this matter is appreciated."

Paulson had been livid. He knew it had come from one of the corrections officers. Paulson told his attorney about the poster and was calmly assured that it added credibility to their suit. Paulson was instructed to keep the poster in a safe place.

During the conversation, Marshall Paulson, Deputy Chief of Security, the man responsible for the safety and security of over nine hundred prisoners as well as the safety and security of over two hundred and forty corrections officers, lieutenants and captains, absent-mindedly crumpled up the piece of paper with Stilwell and Macon's named and tossed it into the trash can. Paulson had bigger and more important things on his mind.

Meanwhile, the two policemen had gone straight to booking and charged Stilwell with an open charge of murder. It had taken only ten minutes to complete the booking process because Stilwell was already in custody. The two police officers left the jail believing that Donald Macon would be separated from Jack Stilwell and would be protected by the jail staff until Stilwell's trial.

20

It was January 14th, Friday evening, and corrections officer Danny Pitts had been assigned to the psychiatric unit of the jail. Most of his evening was spent lighting cigarettes for the walking zombies who were blitzed on thorazine or some other psychotropic drug. They were not responsible enough to have matches. Most of the prisoners in this unit spent their time smoking and doing the shuffle. Pitts had heard certain drugs affected muscle movements causing them to shuffle rather than walk.

He leaned against a dining room table and waited for Joe Hicks to finish his shower. Hicks was somewhere out in the ozone. He was one of the few prisoners in the unit who required constant supervision. Most of the time, Hicks stayed in his room talking to imaginary people. Hicks was normally docile and for the most part left everyone alone. Hicks did not belong in jail but there was no place else for him, so this evening he was Pitts' responsibility.

Pitts heard the water stop in the shower and waited for Hicks to come out. The shower curtain snapped back there stood a full six feet tall man with long, unkept curly black hair, a scraggly beard and a huge pot belly. Hicks had a glazed look in his eyes and Pitts automatically knew there was going to be a problem.

Without warning, Hicks darted from the shower at a full run and began singing, I'm a Yankee Doodle Dandy at the top of his lungs. Running buck naked through the dayroom, singing at the top of his lungs, Hicks wove his way through the shufflers with Pitts right behind. After five minutes of this, Pitts called for assistance.

Hicks had taken refuge in a corner of the dayroom and was now squatting and staring at Pitts with blazing eyes. Pitts waited for assistance and several minutes later, Lieutenant Ivers arrived with C.O. Jason Robbins. "Is he taking a shit?" questioned Robbins.

"No, he's just hiding behind his imaginary wall."

Ivers removed a pair of handcuffs from his case and directed Robbins to approach Hicks from one side, Pitts the other, and Ivers would take a frontal approach. Slowly all three moved closer and Lieutenant Ivers picked up the tune and began to hum. For a fraction of a second, Hicks eyes cleared and he stared at Ivers and smiled. Ivers smiled back and hummed louder. He quickly placed the handcuffs on his wrists while Robbins brought out leg restraints to keep him from running. All three escorted Hicks back to his room.

Ivers ordered Pitts to leave the restraints on Hicks until he returned. The jail's mental health employees had left for the day and jail policy dictated in case of an emergency to contact the county mental health hospital.

The doctor on duty informed Ivers he would not prescribe any medication for Hicks until he had an opportunity to evaluate him. Ivers then directed Pitts to take Hicks over to the mental health hospital and instructed Robbins to take over on the psychiatric unit during Pitts' absence. Pitts tied a sheet around Hicks and headed for the booking area.

Booking was in chaos. More than thirty people milled about waiting to be processed. Friday nights were the worst. Waiting for the booking lieutenant to issue a vehicle key, Pitts overheard one drunken prisoner pleading with Georgie Byers.

"What am I charged with?"

"DWI," replied Georgie.

"DWI? DWI? I didn't know that was illegal."

"What do you mean, you didn't know DWI was illegal? asked Georgie.

"Look man, I just met these guys and we did some drinking but I didn't know there was a law against it?"

"What the hell are you talking about?" asked Georgie.

"Those Indians I was drinking with. I didn't know it was illegal."

"Look bud, you can drink with whoever you want to drink with. It has nothing to do with your charges."

"But you said DWI. That means drinking with indians, doesn't it?"

Georgie rolled his eyes. "No. It means Driving While Intoxicated."

Pitts chuckled and took the vehicle key handed to him by the booking lieutenant. He found his assigned vehicle in the parking lot and loaded Hicks into the rear.

Outside it was cold and clear and traffic was light. It took Pitts only twenty minutes to cover the five miles to the mental health hospital. He unloaded Hicks and entered the facility. He then signed in and took his prisoner down the hall to a dayroom area where the doctor conducted interviews and where mental patients roamed at night. Each time Danny Pitts came to the mental health hospital, he felt like he was entering the Twilight Zone. He and Hicks took a seat on one of the wooden benches lining the hallway walls. The area was deserted except for one woman in her late twenties. She was slender, about one hundred and ten pounds with long disheveled light brown hair. She was wearing a housecoat and was pacing back and forth. She clutched her stomach and repeated, "Oh, my baby, Oh, my baby," over and over.

Pitts knew it would be an hour before they could see the doctor. The interview would only last about fifteen minutes. The worst part of hospital transports was the waiting. After a half-hour of staring at the woman pacing and wailing about her baby, Hicks jumped up and began pacing with her. In thoughtful silence, Pitts watched the two walking back and forth. Ten minutes later Hicks started muttering, "My wife's going to have a baby! My wife's going to have a baby!"

Then the woman cried even louder, "Oh, my baby! Oh, my baby!"

Back and forth they walked, both lost in their own separate worlds. After another half-hour, the doctor appeared, watched Hicks for five minutes, wrote a prescription and left.

Pitts approached Hicks to escort him back but Hicks resisted.

"Wait! Wait! Can't you see my wife is going to have a baby?" implored Hicks.

"We need a doctor here! My wife is going to have a baby!"

Pitts then pulled, shoved and dragged Hicks from the hospital barely managing to load him into the van.

Pitts returned Hicks to jail, had the prescription filled at the jail's medical unit and an hour later Hicks was out. Danny Pitts stood for a moment at Hicks door watching the sleeping figure. I was sad to see people like Hicks who were so far gone they would never again be able to touch reality.

He then left the psychiatric unit, punched out and congratulated himself for having made it through the shift in one piece.

Driving home Danny Pitts never realized he was humming "I'm a Yankee Doodle Dandy" under his breath.

21

O n Saturday morning, January 15th, Avery Beck rose earl to find that a light snow had fallen during the night. H stood in his kitchen with a cup of coffee in one hand and cigarette in the other staring out the window at the distant moun tains. When Avery took time to look at the mountains, he usuall experienced a strange peacefulness. Now, it wasn't working. The had always seemed so simple, so organized, so clean, uncluttered

He glanced down at the cigarette in his hand and frowned. Wh had he taken up smoking again? He had given it up years ago bu now he found solace in smoking. Death Wish, he thought to hin self.

Now it was the weekend. Avery had looked forward to gettin away from the jail for a couple of days and clearing his mind. Bu the anxiety and undefined restlessness was still with him. Aver had gotten away from the jail, but the jail had not left his thought -overcrowding, budget, Paulson, Dennison, security.

Avery had been infected. He had been infected by a virus whic attacks people who work in a jail. It is subtle and attacks quietl without symptoms. Then it spreads slowly and systematically re sulting in stress, paranoia, frustration and anxiety. Then there i a full and complete preoccupation with the jail. It becomes a part c life. In time, Avery would find himself smoking excessively an drinking more than usual and his standard of measurement fo people would be the jail.

How would they operate in a jail environment?

Could they survive a week or even a day in jail?

And then paranoia would creep into his conscious. Every pub lic place would cause Avery to wonder if any of the people he wa seeing had ever been in jail. Would anyone recognize him as th jail administrator?

What if someone had a bad experience in jail? Would they take it out on him? Would they confront him verbally or would they attack him physically? Who could he really trust, was there anyone?

Avery yawned and studied the mountains in the distance. He toyed with the idea of dropping by the jail, just to see how things were going. Then he decided against it. Instead, he filled his coffee cup again and lit another cigarette. His wife had noticed his smoking but she hadn't commented.

Avery suddenly realized he had spoken to Ann very little during the past week. Stubbing out his half-smoked cigarette, he headed to the bedroom where his wife lay huddled under the covers. Her hair hung over her face hiding her peaceful features. Carefully Avery slid in next to her and attempted to make up for his lack of attention. For the first time in a week, the jail was effectively erased from his mind.

On Monday morning, January 17th, Avery arrived at his office five minutes earlier than usual. While dressing for work, he had been plagued with conflicting emotions. On one hand he was anxious to get to the jail and start the week. On the other hand, he dreaded the thought. But, ready or not, here he was. Ten minutes later Dennison arrived. He rarely broke his morning routine. He fixed coffee, read the logs, printed anything of interest, dropped the copies in the administrator's basket and returned to his office.

Beck walked to the coffee room to pour a cup of coffee and found Dennison waiting.

"Good morning," he said and handed the logs to Beck.

Beck took the logs made some small talk and then returned to his office. Dennison had not highlighted any of the log entries but had drawn a curious red question mark by one entry which had been made on Saturday, during the day shift. The entry stated:

"Prisoner Mason Roberts on the fourth floor complained of being attacked late Friday night by a group of corrections officers. Roberts was checked by the medical unit and multiple bruises were discovered. No serious injuries were apparent. Additionally, prisoner Roberts was unable to identify any of his alleged attackers other than stating that they

had been corrections officers. Roberts had no explanatio[n]
for the attack, and a detailed report will be forthcoming an[d]
sent to Deputy Chief Paulson along with a statement fro[m]
prisoner Roberts."

Beck called Dennison and questioned him about the questio[n]
mark and the entry.

"I'm not sure if there's anything there or not, but it is prett[y]
suspicious, especially considering the disturbance they had on th[e]
fourth floor about four hours earlier. It could be that some [of]
Paulson's boys decided to do some of the Lord's work."

"What do you mean, do some of the Lord's work?" questione[d]
Beck.

"Jail house justice. You push a C.O., he pushes back, only [a]
little harder. It sounds, and I place a great deal of emphasis o[n]
"sounds," like some corrections officers got together and decided t[o]
warn prisoner Mason Roberts to quit screwing around and to be[-]
have himself."

"Does this kind of thing happen often?"

"Not frequently, but it does happen."

"What do you usually do about it?"

Dennison didn't want to become involved in any of Paulson['s]
affairs. Dealing with C.O.s was Paulson's responsibility, not hi[s]
but Beck expected an answer. "When Paulson reports for wor[k]
tell him you want to review the report covering the incident. Hav[e]
your secretary make a copy of the report and send it to Interna[l]
Affairs. Have Roberto Romero investigate the prisoner's allega[-]
tion."

"Then what happens?"

"The investigation will probably end in a pissing contest. [A]
bruised prisoner's complaint stating he was beaten by staff. Inter[-]
nal Affairs will interview the corrections officers who were on dut[y]
the night of the incident. The corrections officers will claim th[e]
prisoner is lying. When the investigation is completed, it will com[e]
down to one prisoner's word against a dozen corrections officer[s]
The case will be filed in the event the prisoner decides to sue later[.]

"And that's it?"

"That's it."

Avery said, "Thanks," and hung up the phone.

One hour and fifteen minutes later, Marshall Paulson reported or duty and was instructed to report to the administrator's office with a copy of the lieutenant's report, along with prisoner Roberts' statement.

Paulson entered Beck's office with reports in hand and placed hem on his desk.

Beck scanned the report quickly. It detailed prisoner Roberts' omplaint, but added no additional facts. Placing the report back n his desk, Beck looked at Paulson and asked, "What's your im-ression of this incident?"

Paulson picked up the report and rapidly read the statement efore replying. "I don`t think there's anything to it. Sounds like Roberts is accusing some of our staff of beating him up in order to ue. For the record, if some C.O.s did go into this prisoners room, 'll get to the bottom of it. I will not tolerate this kind of behavior. All the C.O.s, lieutenants and captains know how I feel about this ype of thing, and if someone is responsible I'll find out who. You an take that to the bank."

Beck admitted to himself, Paulson was convincing.

"So what's your plan of action?"

"What?"

"What's your plan of action? How do you intend to proceed with the investigation?"

"Oh. Well, first I'll find out who was working on the fourth loor during the night shift and have Internal Affairs interview hem. I'll find out if anyone opened this Mason Roberts' door dur-ng the night. The control officer would know, so that's where I'll tart. I'll start with him."

"Sounds like a good place to begin," sighed Avery.

"I'll call Internal Affairs right away and get Roberto Romero working on this."

"Let me know if anything turns up," Avery instructed.

Paulson snatched up the reports and assured Beck, "If any-hing went down, I'll get to the bottom of it."

Avery watched Paulson leave his office. This morning, Paulson had been as cooperative and as pleasant as anyone he had ever met. Last week he had been combative, angry and hostile. Per-aps he needed to spend more time with Paulson. If he could gain

his confidence, he was sure Paulson would become a team playe
and work well with the rest of the staff.

Avery was soon visited by Paul Rivera, the department's fisca
analyst.

"We have a problem."

"What kind of problem?" Avery was almost afraid to ask.

"Boilers. We're going to need to buy some new boilers."

"Expensive?"

"Very. What's even worse, we're not budgeted for them. We'r
going to overspend our budget by about fifty thousand dollars."

"And if we don't buy the boilers?"

"No hot water and a thousand angry prisoners."

"Maybe the cold showers will cool them down a little," sai
Avery reaching for humor.

Rivera peered atAvery over his glasses, realized Beck had mad
a joke, and chuckled.

"Go ahead and draw up the papers," directed Avery, turnin
serious.

"Well, I'm afraid it's not that easy. See, the City has a policy fo
purchasing. First we have to write up an RFP, that's a Request fo
Proposal. In this RFP we have to list exactly what type of boiler w
need with all the specifications. Then we send the RFP to the city'
purchasing department. The city's purchasing department wil
review the request and send the RFP out to at least three vendor
who handle this type of equipment. After that, the city will wai
about a month for a response. The low bidder will get the job, an
after three more months the paper work will be processed and th
work will begin."

"Isn't anything easy here?"

"That's just the way it's done," commented Rivera defensively
Sensing Beck's displeasure, Rivera added, "Dennison told me w
needed new boilers so I'm just starting the paperwork."

"OK, OK, Paul. I understand. Get the paperwork started an
have Dennison see me."

Paul Rivera rose, passed a shaky smile and left.

Beck wondered how in the hell anything ever got done with th
red tape.

Dennison arrived twenty minutes later and Beck asked him about the boilers. Dennison responded, "The boilers we have are over twelve years old. The maintenance supervisor tells me there is an immediate need to have them replaced. Actually, they should have been replaced three years ago, but each time we included the expense in our budget, the mayor chopped it out. Now we're stuck. We have no money, we have no choice and we have no time."

"Rivera said it would take three to four months before we received approval for the purchase. Can we hold on that long?"

"I don't think we can. What Paul said is true. It usually does take three to four months and that's minimal time. A purchase this size could take up to eighteen months. No. We can't wait that long. And we don't have to."

"I suspect you know a way around the system," commented Beck dryly.

"There's always a way around everything."

"Explain."

"The purchasing procedures were written to protect the taxpayers and, hypothetically, prevent individuals within the city from hiring their relatives or some other special interest group. When all these protective regulations and rules were enacted, it bogged down the system. But there are several ways around this mess, but the most effective means is to write the RFP as a sole source."

"I'm not sure I follow," commented Avery.

"What we'll do is write the RFP to mirror the specifications of the boilers we need right down to the size of the pressure gages. The RFP will be so specific that the only company who will be able to comply with our needs will be the company we want. Since no one else will be able to provide what we need, the RFP will be labeled "sole source" and we can get around the bidding and waiting. From there it will be routine and Purchasing will sign off. I've already contacted General Dyno and they have what we need. It won't take us any longer than two to three weeks."

"Is it illegal?"

Dennison looked at Beck, started to say something, remembered Beck was a virgin, not only in the jail but in the City as well. He replied. "I suppose it doesn't conform with the spirit of the procedures but it's not illegal. It is a way to get what we need fast.

Of course, I'm sure Paul told you we'll overrun our budget with the purchase."

Beck thought for several seconds and replied, "Go ahead with the purchase. Inform Paul to send the paperwork to me when it's ready and let's get those boilers installed."

22

Leaving Beck's office after their discussion about Roberts' allegation, Paulson phoned Victor Moss, the classification specialist and instructed him to investigate the complaint and move Roberts off the fourth floor. Moss tried to explain that it would be better to conduct an investigation before making a decision to move Roberts. But Paulson replied angrily, "I've given you an order. Move Roberts and move him now! Roberts is saying some corrections officers beat him up. You and I both know some prisoners beat him up and Roberts is only looking for a way to sue the department."

Victor Moss knew Paulson didn't have actual proof. He also knew that once Paulson made up his mind, there was no use trying to reason with him.

Moss agreed to move Roberts. Where, he had no idea. There was no room anywhere else in the jail and Roberts' criminal charges and past history said he belonged exactly where he was.

Paulson hesitated a moment, trying to remember something else he wanted to tell Moss, but the thought slipped away. Paulson instructed him to keep him informed and hung up the phone.

Victor reviewed each level. There was one room vacant in the protective custody unit, but Roberts didn't belong there with the homosexuals and child molesters. The second floor was the least crowded but Moss hesitated to assign Roberts there. The second floor was not designed to house felons, but then Roberts was not a violent felon. Finally, exasperated, Moss signed a move form authorizing a move to the second floor.

There were other prisoners who needed to be assigned. On his desk was a pile of booking slips. Victor flipped through and pulled Jack Stilwell's from the pile. Stilwell had been charged with murder so this qualified him for the sixth floor, but there were no openings. Victor had no negative reports about Stilwell on the second floor and there did not appear to be a great need to move hir immediately. He made a note to himself to move Stilwell to th sixth floor as soon as a bed became available.

Satisfied that prisoner Roberts had been moved, Paulson calle Roberto Romero at InternalAffairs and explained the Roberts alle gation. Romero listened quietly and made several notes on a yel low lined pad.

Romero asked, "Have you received reports from the night shif supervisor and the officer assigned to control during the nigh shift?"

Paulson replied that had not received the reports yet. Romer knew it would be at least a week before Paulson received, read an passed the reports along to him. By then, the witnesses would b set in their stories and Internal Affairs would be working a col case. Romero had explained to Paulson a hundred times how t conduct an investigation but it never seemed to sink in. There wa no use repeating himself. Romero thanked Paulson for the cal and hung up.

Paulson then turned to a stack of papers and began shufflin, through the reports, logs and memorandums. A copy of a griev ance filed by the Corrections Officers Union was midway throug! the pile. The grievance cited a blatant violation of their contrac by the department's efforts to create a separate property unit. Th grievance detailed the section and page numbers of the union con tract which had been violated and demanded that immediate ac tion be taken on the part of management to bring the departmen into compliance with the contract.

The grievance further stated that failure to comply with th union contract would result in the union's filing a request for ; hearing before the City's labor board. The bottom of the page indi cated that a copy of the grievance had been sent to the jail admin istrator, Avery Beck, and to the City's personnel department Paulson scowled and tossed it aside. He had more importan things to do than address a complaint filed by a group of low line employees.

An hour later, Beck discovered his copy of the complaint. H initially believed the grievance had been filed in error. He dis tinctly recalled telling Paulson to ensure the union contract wa!

followed to the letter before instituting the proposed change in the property unit.

Beck picked up his phone and asked Paulson to come over. Budget overruns, union grievances, political cronies, the inability to manage the department the way it should be managed, and unclear instructions from the Mayor's officer were taking their toll on Beck's patience.

Paulson entered Beck's office beaming.

"I've initiated a full scale investigation on Roberts' allegations and I've notified Roberto Romero at Internal Affairs. It will only be a couple of days before we get to the bottom of this thing."

Beck waved to Paulson to have a seat. "I've received this grievance from the Corrections Officers Union complaining that the department has violated their contract. What's the story?"

Paulson's eyes narrowed as he spoke. "It's the same old thing. The union is trying to tell us how to run the department. They're scared of the new procedures because it will hold their feet to the fire."

"Is there any validity to the complaint?" asked Beck.

"Once this system is in place, I'll be able to track every piece of property that comes into the jail. I'll know who inventoried the property, and where it is at every step. If someone steals the property, I'll know about it immediately."

Beck wasn't sure if Paulson had failed to understand the question or if he was intentionally avoiding an answer. He repeated, "Does the union have a valid complaint?"

"No, they don't. I say let them take it before the labor board and see what happens. When the board rules in favor of the department, then we'll see how they respond. It's just a few people in the union who like to stir things up. I know who they are and I'll take care of them. It's nothing more than a personality problem. The people who are stirring everyone else up are prejudiced. They have been harassing me for a long time. If they keep it up, I'm going to file suit against the union and name some specific people as defendants."

Paulson hadn't mentioned the suit he had filed against Beck and the department, and Beck wasn't going to bring it up. Beck was now between a rock and a hard place. He felt it was important to give Paulson the opportunity to straighten out the problem. On the other hand, he had specifically instructed Paulson to follow the union policy when implementing his plan.

Beck repeated his earlier instructions. "Make sure you follow the union contract to the letter and resolve this matter as quickly as possible."

Paulson couldn't believe what he had heard. Beck was not going to back him on this issue. Beck was going to turn tail and run and leave him holding the bag. He knew he couldn't trust Beck but he never thought it would go this far.

"You're not going to back me on this, are you?"

Taken by surprise Beck asked, "What?"

This time it was a statement. "You're not going to back me on this. Instead, you're going to support the corrections officers. I should have known." Paulson wheeled and stormed out of Beck's office.

Paulson believed Beck was supporting the officers in retaliation for the suit he had filed against him and the department. He never once believed Beck would have the audacity to so blatantly discriminate against him. Paulson marched to his office, popped open his cardex file and dialed his attorney. Paulson smiled smugly to himself. Beck didn't realize it, but his retaliation only added more ammunition for Paulson's suit.

Beck had watched as Paulson left his office in a huff and was baffled. What the hell was going on here? Had Paulson lost it completely? In five minutes, he had gone from a reasonable, sane, intelligent human being into an undecipherable idiot. There was no question in Beck's mind. Some changes would have to be made. He could not tolerate Paulson's gross insubordination and temper tantrums.

Beck picked up the phone and dialed the mayor's office. It was time to lay it on the line with Waterston. Beck hesitated. Perhaps he needed more input. He depressed the switch hook and dialed Roberto Romero instead. He said he would be right over.

Beck moved from behind his desk and closed his office door. Until Romero arrived, Avery did not want or need any more problems.

Fifteen minutes later, Roberto Romero rapped lightly at Beck's door. Beck opened the door and after the two men had been seated, Romero asked, "What's up Boss?"

Beck told about Paulson's outburst and when Beck reached the part about Paulson's insubordination, Romero's lips grew tight and he stared hard at the thousand eyes in his wingtips.

Romero commented nonchalantly, "It's not unusual or surprising."

"You mean the guy acts this way all the time?"

"He blows hot and cold. Some days, he's pretty reasonable. Other times, a total maniac."

"I have to get rid of him," mumbled Beck.

I don't think the Mayor's office will let you."

"Why not?" demanded Beck.

"Well, he has some political influence, but mostly because he's black. The mayor's office will never let you fire a high ranking black employee, unless, of course, he shoots somebody or does something really bad."

"So there's no way to get rid of this guy?"

"There are lots of ways to get rid of him. One is to start documenting and fire him for just cause. Of course, that process will take about a year and a lot of documentation. The other way is to politely tell Mr. Paulson you no longer require his services as Deputy Chief and thank you very much. Both Deputy Chiefs can be demoted to the rank of Captain. As captains, they would work the line and be in charge of a specific eight-hour shift. It's the administrator's prerogative to do that. The process is clearly spelled out in the City's personnel rules and regulations. Of course, if you do that, Paulson will sue, charging you and the Mayor's office with racial discrimination. Chances are, the Mayor won't be real happy with your course of action."

Beck leaned back in his chair. He could get Paulson out of his hair but he would have to pay the consequences. Before he did anything, he would discuss the problem with Waterston and let Waterston know how damaging Paulson was to the operation of the jail.

Beck changed the subject and questioned Romero about prisoner Mason Roberts' allegations.

"Once I get the reports from Paulson I'll start an investigation. There's not much I can do until then."

Beck nodded, thanked Romero and watched him leave. Tomorrow, January 18th, Beck would set up an appointment with Waterston. Something had to be done quickly.

23

While Avery Beck sat in his office looking for solutions to problems which defied solutions, Donald Macon sat in his room terrified. Throughout the weekend, Macon had purposely avoided Stilwell. He noted that the muscular blond prisoner had taken an interest in Tommy Brown, his roommate. Donald had been in and out of jail enough to know what Stilwell was after but he had not alerted Tommy Brown.

The previous Friday, the police had interrogated Donald and he had told the police everything he knew. A statement had been prepared for his signature and assurances had been given that he would be moved to another housing unit. So far, nothing had happened and Donald Macon was worried. He knew Jack Stilwell was capable of killing him and would not hesitate if he discovered that Donald intended to testify against him. Donald wasn't sure if the police had charged Stilwell with murder and he wasn't about to ask. He stayed in his room most of the time, wondering how he had become so entangled in such a mess.

Macon was a peaceful person. He didn't hurt anyone. He took the leftover and cast off food and clothing from others and survived. He didn't want any trouble. He was a harmless wino, nothing more. His life was simple. Eat a little, sleep a little and drink a lot. He never asked anyone for anything, and he never expected anything. It was that simple. This had been the longest Donald had remained sober for the past seven years. Without the alcohol fogging his brain, he was able to think more clearly and see things he had not seen before.

Donald's mind was now clear and sharp and he knew Tommy Brown was in trouble. Another prisoner, named Brad "something or other" was sporting a new tatoo on his right arm and he had also taken up with Stilwell over the weekend. Stilwell, Brad and Tommy Brown had been together constantly.

Leeks, the lifer, had said little but Donald could tell by Leek's expression that Leeks knew what was going on between Stilwell and Tommy Brown. Tommy's public defender had only compounded the problem by telling Tommy to shave his peach fuzz, explaining that it would give him a clean-cut kid look in court. Tommy had complied and the result had been a young, feminine-looking male with smooth skin and wide, innocent eyes. If Stilwell hadn't been courting Tommy Brown, any one of a dozen other prisoners would have.

Donald had also noticed a large number of prisoners dropping by the room to speak with Leeks for several minutes and then leaving. Leeks had become instantly popular among the prisoners and daily visits had become a routine.

Another prisoner had been assigned to the second floor named Robert, or Roberts. Donald wasn't sure if it was his first or last name, and it didn't really matter. The only thing that mattered was getting away from Stilwell, getting out of jail and getting a drink, in that order.

Tommy Brown entered his room carrying a Zagnut candy bar which Stilwell had given him. Tommy's eyes were bright and clear. He had no idea what was happening around him. "Hey, Donald, look what Jack gave me," said Tommy, excitedly.

Donald looked up and saw the candy bar in Tommy's hand and debated with himself. Should he tell Tommy what was going on or should he leave it alone? It wasn't any of his business, yet he hated to see Tommy Brown turned into a punk, especially Stilwell's punk.

"You know, Tommy, maybe it's not such a good idea to be taking things from Stilwell. Know what I mean?"

Tommy shook his head. "No. What are you getting at, Don?"

Donald tried again. "All I'm saying is, things are a lot different here than outside on the streets. Sometimes when people give you things, they want something in return, know what I mean?"

Tommy shrugged his shoulders. "I ain't got any money and Jack knows that, so there's nothing I can give him in return. C'mon Donald, Jack's all right," protested Tommy.

"I suppose so," mumbled Donald, knowing his half-hearted attempt to educate Tommy had failed. Tommy ripped open the paper on the candy bar in his hand and left the room. As he walked into the dayroom, several prisoners whistled. Tommy had no idea what the whistles meant, but Donald Prescott Macon knew exactly what was up.

Donald glanced up at Leeks on the top bunk across the room. Leeks also knew what was going on and he was staring out the door into the dayroom, thinking. Without looking at Donald, Leeks spoke. "You did what you could. Unless you want to die, I'd back out of it. The kid's on his own."

Donald was unsure how to respond. The last thing he wanted was to piss off Leeks. Donald mumbled, "OK" and for the first time Leeks looked around at him.

"How long you been a wino?" Leeks asked.

The question hit a nerve. It was fine for him to refer to himself as a wino, but not another prisoner. "About seven years," mumbled Donald, not bothering to look at Leeks.

Leeks caught the edge in Donald's voice and smiled inwardly. He had gotten to the filthy little wino. Good. Leeks stretched, put down his cheap novel and rolled off the top bunk, landing on his feet athletically. Without paying Donald the respect of a glance, Leeks snagged a Camel non-filter from his pack of cigarettes and moved into the dayroom.

He asked one of the younger inmates about Roberts. Who was he? Where did he come from? What were his charges?

The inmate said the new prisoner's name was Mason Roberts. He had been moved from the fourth floor to the second floor. According to Roberts, he had been attacked and beaten by several corrections officers and had filed a complaint over the matter. The jail had responded by moving him. One last bit of information was that Roberts was a "jail house lawyer."

Leeks nodded and eased across the dayroom cautiously. He never moved anywhere without employing caution. Years of being in the can had trained Leeks to always be ready for trouble. This was how he had survived all the years he had spent inside the walls.

Leeks ambled to the weight machine and methodically began to work out. After forty-five minutes, he had built up a good sweat and the muscles in his body were rippling. Leeks had noticed a young prisoner named Brad Wilson standing nearby, watching.

Wilson had a new tatoo on his arm, and he was obviously proud of it. It was a typical jail tatoo of a peacock, not much different from the one Leeks had on his arm.

He looked directly at Wilson and motioned for him to come closer and then stared hard at the new tatoo, remembering his first one and commented, "Who did the job on you?"

Wilson had waited for this moment and was barely able to croak, "The guy in B-3 has a rig."

Leeks nodded his approval and turned his attention back to the weight machine.

Wilson moved reluctantly away and was ecstatic. Leeks had finally acknowledged his presence and even better, he had complimented his tattoo.

Stilwell watched Leeks work out on the weight machine from a distance and knew he had to be careful. Leeks was dangerous, no question about it. There was enough young stuff on the second floor for both of them and Stilwell was convinced there was no need for trouble. Stilwell could have approached Leeks directly, but that was not how things were done.

First, Stilwell would send someone like Brad Wilson to get to know Leeks. Then Leeks would send someone to get to know Stilwell. Then a meeting would be arranged. A very casual meeting. Since Leeks was older, he would decide when to call the meeting. That was fine with Stilwell. In the meantime, Stilwell would continue to work on Tommy Brown. The clean shave had enhanced Tommy's features. He was a prize, a prize that any con worth his salt would fight for. Stilwell hoped Leeks wasn't interested in Tommy Brown, at least not yet. Tommy would make a nice present for Leeks down the road. If Stilwell was released before Leeks, he would give Tommy to Leeks as a good faith gesture. It would be a good way to cap off their professional association. Tommy Brown still needed a lot of work but Stilwell knew that in the end Tommy would become a punk. Eventually, if he acted right, Tommy would become a bitch. Tommy Brown was so pretty that in time he would be able to have his pick of men and Tommy Brown would have Jack Stilwell to thank.

Mason Roberts walked to his new room on the second floor and surveyed his surroundings. A bunch of stupid fucking cons. It would take some work but Roberts was confident he would be able to control the prisoners on the second level as well as he had on the fourth floor. Prisoners were not known for their intelligence. But Mason Roberts was very intelligent. He had filed an official complaint with the department over his beating and he knew nothing would come of the complaint. The department would investigate and then file it away. In the meantime, Mason Roberts would file suit in Federal Court and charge the department with a violation of his civil rights. A clever plan.

Roberts moved carefully through the dayroom on the second floor and he recognized Stilwell and Leeks as lifers and they controlled the housing unit. That was fine. Roberts would play both sides and whoever came out the winner, that's the side he would be on. The number one rule in jail or prison was never pick a loser.

But Roberts was uneasy about the prospect of a second visit by the officers. If it happened again and he was beaten, he would feign a more serious injury. This would get him to the local hospital and allow him a week or two alone in a hospital bed while tests were run. During that time, he could enjoy the comforts of color television. Maybe he would even get a half- way decent looking nurse assigned to his room.

Mason Roberts deposited his personal items in his assigned room and paced along the perimeter of the dayroom. Everything appeared calm and quiet, something Mason Roberts intended to change.

24

Monday, January 17th, on the evening shift, corrections officer Chris Keys was assigned to the second floor as the control room officer. Chris was happy. He had heard that Deputy Chief Paulson had been contacted about his application for snake handler at the zoo. His interview was scheduled for nine AM. Paulson had been livid and demanded to know who had submitted his name. He had been told that the application was in his own name. Paulson canceled the application and stormed out of his office raving something about catching the person responsible.

There were few high points in life, but checking the job openings in the city every six months and submitting Paulson's name for the most outrageous jobs was one of them. Each time Paulson was contacted for an interview, he came unglued and launched a full-scale investigation, vowing to find the person responsible for the harassment. Each time he ran into a dead end. Keys wished he could share the practical joke with others but knew the scheme was too sensitive and too dangerous to let anyone in on.

Between calling in Paulson's name for bogus job interviews, Keys would routinely dial Paulson's beeper and leave a number. Sometimes the number Paulson called was Dial-a-Gay, other times it was Dial a Prayer. Each time, Paulson went crazy with anger.

Keys knew what Paulson's problem was. He had no sense of humor. Paulson needed to lighten up a bit but Keys knew he was not going to be the one to tell him.

Keys peered out the control room window and watched as officer Jason Robbins made his way through the prisoners milling in the dayroom. It was seven-thirty in the evening and the floor was quiet.

Robbins stopped occasionally to talk or answer questions. Most of the prisoners wanted to know when they were going to court.

This was a question Robbins couldn't answer.

Mason Roberts moved in his direction. Roberts wanted an application to use the law library to prepare his civil suit against the jail. He knew the jail had to provide him with this opportunity and if the jail denied his request, it would be a violation of equal protection under the law and his right to due process. Ultimately, Roberts could sue the jail for that as well.

Nearing Robbins, Mason Roberts slowed and called, "Hey, C.O. I need to use the law library."

Robbins looked over his shoulder and directed him to the control room where Keys was working. Keys slid a form through a small opening and Roberts picked it up.

Once Roberts had filled out the request, he handed it to Robbins and asked, "When do you think I'll get to use the library?"

Robbins replied that he didn't know and asked nonchalantly, "What are you in jail for?"

Roberts smiled and replied, "You know that commercial on TV with the phone company, where they tell you to reach out and touch someone?"

"Yeah."

"Well I did and I got busted for it."

"Obscene phone calls?"

"Yeah." Roberts sighed heavily and moved away.

As Roberts move away he thought there was something strange about Roberts but he couldn't put his finger on it.

The rest of the night was quiet. At eleven, the night shift came on. Corrections officers Chris Keys and Jason Robbins turned over their keys and radios to the night shift officers and left. They had made it through another night.

The night shift officers made their headcounts, checked all doors to make sure they were locked, returned to the control room and made themselves comfortable. Everything was quiet. On the night shift, prisoners were locked in their rooms until breakfast and breakfast was hours away. Nothing ever happened on the night shift with the exception of an occasional fire or a suicide. The potential for violence was dramatically reduced during the night shift and some officers closed their eyes and fell into the twilight area between sleep and consciousness.

The three officers working the second floor were all experienced. Nothing had happened during their shift for the past six months and there was no reason to believe something would happen tonight.

Complacency, the number one enemy of a corrections officer, had wormed its way into their hearts, minds and attitudes. Weeks, sometimes months, of boredom and routine would often give way to the unexpected, taking everyone by surprise and resulting in serious injury and sometimes death.

They understood this very well. Their false confidence, however, led them to believe that nothing would happen, at least not tonight. They were dozing, occasionally opening their eyes to check the time. For a few officers, this was a standard practice during the night shift.

Carla Terwelp was a relatively new corrections officer--thirty-three, moderately attractive, slightly overweight and a mediocre officer. She had been hired six months ago and was still on probation. Her lack of seniority had automatically relegated her to the night shift. Carla had always been overweight and plain in appearance. Men had never paid much attention to her and her life had lacked the normal sexual attractions and banter which marked a portion of most people's lives.

Carla was not especially bright, but she was sincere, and she was lonely. Working at the jail provided her with her first real taste of power. For the first time, Carla Terwelp was somebody. She had the power and the authority to command people. And, she found herself to be the center of attention among the prisoners. They complimented her daily on her beauty. This served to inflate a nearly non-existent ego. For the first time, Carla felt attractive.

There is no stereotype among prisoners. Some prisoners in the Coronado County Jail were strikingly handsome and professional con artists. They sensed Carla Terwelps' vulnerability and the power she held. It was these prisoners whom paid her the daily compliments.

On Tuesday morning, January 18th, Carla Terwelp was assigned to work the north side of detention level six where the older and institutionalized prisoners were held. Carla had requested this assignment, telling the night shift captain that she had worked

146

the sixth floor the night before. She had initiated a cleanup project and wanted to finish the project.

The real reason was prisoner Evan Richards. He was thirty-eight years old with flowing dark hair, smokey eyes and a muscular build. Any woman, anywhere, would have found Richards handsome. He was a professional con artist, gigolo and chronic bad check writer. This was Richards' fourth time in jail and he knew all the angles.

He had assessed Carla's weaknesses three months ago and with the assistance of several other prisoners, he had planted the seed.

Three months earlier, Carla had been assigned to the sixth floor for the first time. She was new and determined to take her duties and responsibilities seriously. Her first day had been a nightmare. The prisoners had refused to follow her instructions and she had been forced to call the lieutenant on duty a dozen times to maintain order. The lieutenant warned her that she needed to exert more control. She could not constantly be calling him to do the things she was hired to do. Carla had gone home dejected, realizing she could be fired.

A week later, Carla had been assigned to the sixth floor again and took her shift with a feeling of apprehension. Again, the prisoners refused to comply with her instructions. Three prisoners surrounded her and taunted her by grabbing their crotches and verbalizing their sexual fantasies. Carla had been traumatized and near tears until Evan Richards had intervened and had told the prisoners to fuck off.

With a gleam in his eyes, Evan turned to Carla and said, "Those guys are a bunch of jerks. Listen, I know you've been hired to do a job and that's all you're trying to do. I carry a little weight here and if anybody starts hassling you, let me know and I'll take care of it."

Carla had thanked Evan Richards and, true to his word, he ensured that the remainder of the evening passed without a problem. After work, she could not help thinking about Evan Richards. True, he was a prisoner, but he was a handsome prisoner and a gentleman. He couldn't be all bad. He had gone out of his way to help her. She didn't know what she would have done if he hadn't intervened.

While Carla Terwelp contemplated Evan Richards, Evan Richards congratulated himself on a well-engineered con. His three friends had played their parts well, harassing and taunting her, and Evan had stepped in at exactly the right moment and played the role of knight in shining armor. Carla would feel indebted to him. In time, she would begin to trust Evan Richards and then Carla Terwelp would belong to Evan Richards.

Evan Richards smiled to himself, rolled over and went to sleep satisfied. Everything was working out.

January 18th was now exactly three months since Carla had first met Evan Richards. They had disagreed the night before and Carla could not help but feel the disagreement had been her fault. Evan had wanted to hold and kiss her but she had put him off. He had been dejected and on the verge of tears. Carla hadn't slept well during the day. She had tossed and turned, thinking of nothing but Evan. She had then concocted this plausible story for the shift captain and he had assigned her to the sixth floor for the second night in a row. It was Carla's opportunity to set things right with Evan.

She reported for duty, took the north side floor officer's keys and radio and started her headcount. As she neared Evan's door, she felt her stomach tighten and her pulse quicken. She peered through the window. Evan sitting on his bed, reading. Carla tapped lightly on the door and Evan's dark, dreamy eyes met hers. Carla's knees weakened but she managed a smile. Evan beamed back and Carla moved on, finishing her headcount. Carla gave her count to the control officer and returned to the dayroom. The control officer logged the count in his log, leaned back in his chair and, within seconds, was lost in his own thoughts.

An hour later, Carla entered the darkened dayroom, quietly unlocked Evan's door and slipped into his room.

She now stood staring at the person who had occupied her thoughts and dreams for the past several weeks. Carla had never felt this way about a man before. Evan had told her repeatedly how much he loved her. Evan had also told her he was innocent. The charges were trumped up and once he went to court, he would be released. Then he would be free to do and go wherever he wanted and the only thing he wanted was to be with Carla.

She moved slowly across the eight feet of space separating them. Evan rose to meet her and took her in his arms. Nothing mattered now. She knew she was in love. Evan was a good man. Evan was innocent and Evan loved her. He reached up and turned off the small light. The love-making would have to be hurried but it didn't matter. Nothing mattered to Carla Terwelp except Evan's touch.

He kissed her passionately while his hand moved to her breast. With his other hand, Evan expertly unsnapped Carla's belt, unzipped her blue uniform trousers and drew them down to her knees. Pulling Carla onto his bed, Evan quickly, expertly, and methodically brought Carla Terwelp to a climax and afterwards, quickly ejaculated. Then he got up quickly. Evan could not risk Carla's being caught, not now. Not after all the work he had put into this project.

She rose slowly, wiped herself with toilet paper, pulled up her uniform trousers, snapped her belt and whispered, "I love you, Evan."

"I love you, Carla," Evan whispered in the darkness.

25

January 18th, Tuesday, Avery Beck crawled out of bed and staggered into the shower. He had smoked too much the day before and now he was suffering from a nagging headache. The hot water helped but the dull throb was still there. Avery downed two aspirins with his coffee, dressed and drove to work.

Last night, for the first time, he had spoken to his wife about the jail. She had been attentive but he knew she didn't really understand the complexities he was facing. Operating a jail was different from defending a client charged with insider trading or tax evasion. His wife had asked him the one question he had asked himself a dozen times.

"Why don't you quit?"

Avery didn't know. He had played with the idea several times but something held him. Perhaps it was his own sense of responsibility.

Avery parked and entered the administration area where he was surprised to see Dennison so soon.

"Kind of early isn't it?" questioned Beck.

Dennison nodded and replied, "I want to take off a little early this evening."

Beck grabbed a cup of coffee, lit a cigarette, and exhaled deeply. "Anything in the logs?"

"No. It looks like it was quiet last night."

"How's the boiler situation coming?"

"Paul has the paperwork done and it should be on your desk this morning. I've contacted the manufacturer we're going to use and they're ready to start as soon as the paperwork is processed."

"The population still high?" inquired Beck, changing the subject.

"Yeah, real high, and it doesn't look like anybody's too interested in helping us with the problem."

Beck took a sip of coffee and reflected for a moment. Powell's words slipped into his head again. "You're on your own and don't expect any cooperation from anyone." Beck stubbed out his cigarette, re-filled his coffee cup and walked to his office.

Dennison lit another cigarette and lingered in the coffee room for several minutes, thinking. He had done everything he could. He hoped Beck would be allowed to make the right decisions before someone died.

Beck busied himself for half the morning by signing the payroll and reviewing appeals that had been sent to him from prisoners in segregation. It was within the jail administrator's power to overturn any sanction imposed by the jail's disciplinary committee. If a prisoner was given a misconduct report for an offense, the prisoner would have an opportunity to plead his or her case before a committee. Routinely, the committee either reprimanded or sentenced a prisoner to a number of days in segregation. The prisoner then had a right to appeal directly to the jail's administrator. Being new, Avery was not comfortable overturning a decision by the disciplinary committee and he had rubber stamped each appeal he had received.

Avery then picked up the phone and contacted Waterston's office. His secretary set up an appointment for that afternoon at one o'clock. After he hung up, Beck sketched out the items he needed to address. First, he would tell Waterston about the emergency purchase of boilers. Secondly, he would discuss possible options available to him regarding Paulson. Beck knew he had to do something with Paulson and he needed Waterston's support.

One o'clock arrived and Avery Beck waited patiently outside Waterston's door for twenty minutes.

"What can I do for you, Avery?" Waterston asked.

Avery detected an icy tone and wondered what was bothering Waterston. Was it him or just something else?

Avery began, "I thought I'd let you know we're making an emergency purchase of some boilers. The old ones are over twelve years old and if they break down completely, we'll be out of hot water. This means a cost overrun of approximately fifty thousand dollars."

Waterston's lips tightened. "Where do you plan to get th money?"

"I anticipated requesting an emergency appropriation from th City Council to handle the expense."

"Think again," replied Waterston grimly. "No, Avery. You ar going to have to make up the fifty thousand dollars out of you budget. Reduce overtime, reduce food costs, cut positions, but no the ones we discussed. Do whatever it takes, but the city canno afford an emergency appropriation. Everybody is cutting back an tightening their belts. The public is not interested in seeing thi administration throw away good money on a bunch of convicts The public is interested in having water come out of their faucet when they turn them on. The public is interested in having thei garbage picked up on time, and they're interested in having nic green parks where their children can play. They are not intereste in jails."

Avery could feel the anger rising but he held his emotions i check. "Look Sam, the public is going to pay through the nos when these prisoners file federal suits for overcrowded housin conditions and inadequate housing. If the jail doesn't comply wit recommended federal guidelines we're opening ourselves up for liti gation."

"Then you had better comply with federal guidelines," state Waterston evenly.

Exasperated, Avery continued. "Sam, I can't comply with fed eral guidelines unless I have the money to do it with."

"Look Avery, I hired you to run the jail. It's up to you to figur out how to do it. If I have to deal with all of your problems myself then I hate to say it, but I don't need you. You understand what I'n saying don't you?"

"I understand perfectly," replied Avery. The fat son-of-a-bitch wasn't going to help.

"There's one more thing before I go. I have a Deputy Chie named Paulson. The man is out of control and, as you know, he ha filed suits against the City and the jail. I have to do somethin with him. The man is totally out of control."

Waterston's eyes narrowed. "This Paulson fellow is black isn't he?"

"Yes."

"And if I catch your drift, you want to transfer, demote, or fire this person because you have no confidence in him. Is this correct?"

"It's not that I don't have confidence in him. The man is incompetent. He doesn't follow orders, he blows hot and cold and he's constantly filing a suit or threatening to file a suit."

"Let's get this whole thing out in the open, Avery, and try to look at it from my perspective for a minute. We have a black male who is a deputy chief at the jail. This black male has filed a discrimination suit, citing a hostile work environment. You propose to transfer, demote, or fire this same person. You're a lawyer. How do you think a jury would look at this action?"

Avery knew Waterston was right. Any jury would see a demotion or termination as nothing more than blatant retaliation for his civil suit.

"You're right, Sam. But isn't there something we can do with this guy?"

Waterston chuckled and said, "We could always promote him."

"The bottom line is, I'm stuck with him," commented Avery wearily.

"I'm afraid so, Avery. But while we're on the subject, tell me, is there a lot of prejudice going on over there?"

"No, there's not. Most of the racial issues are created or fabricated by Paulson. I have a total of twenty-eight black employees. Of those twenty-eight, ten are in management or at management or supervisory levels. All of them are doing very well with the exception of Paulson."

"Make sure you have all of these positions well documented, Avery. Chances are, you'll need that sort of data when Paulson's case goes to court. By the way, speaking of court, the Legal Department informed me that they received an intent-to-litigate notice by a prisoner named Mason Roberts. This prisoner claims a group of corrections officers came into his cell and beat him up. I want you to check out this allegation and if what the prisoner is saying is true, then fire the people responsible."

"Our internal affairs unit is working on that case right now," he replied.

Waterston thought for a moment and said, "Maybe I was a little hasty when I said fire the people responsible. If you discover some wrongdoing let me know who they are before you take any action. We don't want to step on anyone's toes, if you know what I mean."

Avery knew exactly what Waterston meant. Waterston didn't mind firing employees who were not politically connected, but if someone's name came up who had some strong political ties, some other measure of discipline would have to be concocted.

Avery thanked Waterston and left.

Walking back to the jail, he realized nothing had been accomplished. The meeting had been a total waste of time. Avery was stuck with Paulson and left holding the bag for a fifty-thousand-dollar expenditure.

Beck was beginning to understand why Dennison kept his distance from Paulson. Dennison did not want to be held responsible for any of Paulson's screw-ups, nor did Dennison want to be labeled as creating a hostile work environment for Paulson by criticizing Paulson's poor management practices. The jail operated on an old legal concept of separate but equal. This concept had failed to work for the board of education in Arkansas and Beck could not see how the concept would work effectively here. There was no question Beck had to do something, with or without Waterston's support. Do Something! Beck had to do something. But what?

That evening, corrections officer Mike Stone was assigned to work the psychiatric unit. He conducted a headcount and reported the number to the control officer and checked the special instructions clipboard left by the mental health workers. This staff counseled and conducted therapy during the day. Often, they would leave special instructions for the officer assigned to the psychiatric unit regarding a particular prisoner. But, this evening there were no special instructions and the unit appeared unusually quiet.

Tombstone then instructed the control room officer to unlock all doors. The prisoners soon wandered aimlessly out of their rooms and into the dayroom. Tombstone had worked this unit at least a hundred times and rarely did anything change. He eased through the room, stopping briefly to answer an incoherent question and then began checking each room carefully.

They were all empty with the exception of one, which was occupied by a prisoner named Moore. Tombstone checked his list and learned Moore's first name was Eric. Entering the room slowly, Tombstone whistled softly and positioned himself away from the door and across from Moore. Experience had taught him to make some kind of noise when approaching a psych prisoner. The last thing he wanted to do was to surprise or panic a prisoner. Experience also told Tombstone never to stand in the doorway when speaking to a mentally ill prisoner. If the prisoner suddenly became panicky and felt the walls were closing in on him, there was only one exit. If you were standing in that exit, the prisoner would run right over you.

"Hey Eric, how ya doing this evening?"

Moore sat with his head down, mumbling to himself.

Tombstone tried again, "Hey Eric, what's going on?"

Slowly, Eric Moore raised his head and peered at Tombstone through hazy, bloodshot eyes. Eric's brain moved slowly and he was having difficulty focusing. The eyes cleared slightly and Eric spoke. "I'm OK, you know, OK, pledge allegiance to the flag, Billie Clinton is a fag, drink a coke everyday."

"I see," commented Tombstone gravely.

What Tombstone did see was that there were very few items in Eric's room. This was an indication that Eric had given most of his personal possessions away. A bad sign. People contemplating suicide have a tendency to give away most of their personal effects. And Eric's bloodshot eyes meant he had been crying. Another bad sign.

"Why don't you come outside to the dayroom for a while," Tombstone coaxed.

"No, I just want to stay here and think. Did I ever tell you about my girl?"

"No, you never did, Eric. What about her?"

"I knew a girl once. Her name was Maria. She gave me gonorrhea. I met her in Korea.." Eric's voice faded as his head sank to his chest. For several seconds, Tombstone stared at Eric in silence. Eric was lost in his own world, a world filled with pain and agony. He belonged in a psychiatric hospital, not in jail. Tombstone waited several more seconds and said, "I've got to be going, Eric. If you need anything, let me know. OK?"

Eric sat and gave no indication he had heard.

Tombstone took one last look and left. He didn't like the feeling he was getting from Eric. He could call the lieutenant on duty and tell him he was getting bad vibes and the lieutenant might tell him where to put his vibes. Instead, he would keep a close watch. When the night shift officer reported for duty, he would instruct him to keep an eye on Eric.

At nine-thirty, the control room officer turned the lights off and on in the dayroom, signaling the prisoners to return to their rooms for a headcount. Normally it took Tombstone twenty minutes to conduct the count unless he was hampered by prisoners hiding in corners. In this case, Tombstone would have to open the door and look inside the cell. A lump under a blanket was not enough to indicate a prisoner's presence. Movement and flesh had to be seen. Some officers were not as thorough as Tombstone, but Tombstone was a conscientious employee who took his duties seriously.

Eric Moore's room was three-quarters of the way toward the end of Tombstone's headcount. He approached the room with apprehension to find his worse fears had turned to fact. Moore had tied a sheet around his neck and the other end to the light fixture. He must have then stepped off the small writing table. With his heart pumping wildly, Tombstone reached for his radio, keyed the mike and shouted a medical emergency. Jerking the ring of keys from his belt, he burst into Moore's room.

Eric's face was purple and his bluish tongue protruded grotesquely from a bloated face. Tombstone grabbed Moore's legs and heaved, attempting to take the pressure off Moore's neck. There was nothing more he could do until assistance arrived. Forty-eight seconds later, Tombstone heard the sliding door to the unit open and knew help was at hand.

Lieutenant Frank Ivers leaped on the writing table and began untying the sheet. Jason Robbins followed Ivers and helped Tombstone hold Moore. "I've just about got it," panted Ivers. "OK. Get ready. Here he comes."

Tombstone and Robbins lowered Moore to the concrete floor. "I'll take mouth-to-mouth, you do chest," barked Robbins who was already leaning over Moore's body. Robbins felt for a pulse, detected none and gave Moore two quick breaths.

Tombstone had begun chest compressions and was counting. Neither spoke.

Moore could have AIDS. He might have hepatitis. None of this mattered now. It would be something Tombstone and Robbins would consider later. For now, their entire focus was to save a life.

Lieutenant Ivers was barking orders into his radio and ordering an ambulance. The paramedics from the booking unit arrived with their medical cart and desperately tried to find any vital signs.

Danny Pitts noted Tombstone's fatigue and moved close to him taking a kneeling position on the floor beside him.

"Get ready to switch," shouted Pitts.

Tombstone nodded his head. The movement caused large drops of sweat to drop from Tombstone's forehead onto the bare chest of Eric Moore.

"Now! Switch!" commanded Pitts who moved into position smoothly and continued the chest compression.

The paramedics placed an ambu-bag over Moore's face and Robbins was no longer required to give mouth to mouth. Robbins and Tombstone watched as the paramedics inserted an I.V. into Moore's arm and an electronic heart monitoring device was hooked to his chest. Nothing but a flat line registered on the screen. The paramedics worked rapidly, broke out the electric shock paddles, smeared Moore's chest with gel, placed the paddles on Moore's chest and shouted, "Clear!"

Moore's body convulsed on the concrete floor. A quick check of the monitor revealed nothing and a second electrical charge was released. This time, an irregular beat was detected and Moore was lifted onto a gurney and wheeled quickly to the elevator. There was nothing more to be done here. The ambulance was waiting. Moore was loaded, a corrections officer was assigned and he was whisked to the county hospital.

Ivers had followed the gurney downstairs and he then returned to the psych ward, instructed Tombstone to secure Moore's room and ordered Robbins to get the camera from the lieutenant's office. While waiting, Ivers radioed the master control center and instructed the officer to notify the Coronado Police Department of an attempted suicide and request a field investigator be dispatched to the jail.

Robbins returned within minutes. Ivers took a dozen snap shots of Moore's room, inventoried everything and instructed Tomb stone to write a detailed report. Tombstone acknowledged the in structions and closed the door to Moore's room. The door would not be opened again until the investigation had been completed.

Eric Moore may not have been worth much alive. He had prob ably been an embarrassment to his estranged family, but in death Eric Moore was worth a lot of money. Every relative Eric Moore had would sue the jail and the city of Coronado, claiming he had not been properly diagnosed or supervised and claiming these defi ciencies had resulted in Moore's death. Tombstone sincerely hoped Moore would make it. It sure would make things one hell of a lot easier.

Meanwhile, Georgie Byers was staring at Moore's room from a distance. Tombstone guessed Byers had responded along with Robbins and Pitts but had stayed outside when he noted there was plenty of assistance. Georgie had probably hung around just in case some of the other prisoners began a disturbance. Knowing Georgie Byers was on the floor made Tombstone feel better. Byers was the "Tin Man." He added a certain stability to an unstable world.

Tombstone nodded to Byers. Georgie returned the nod and left. Georgie Byers was one strange guy. But he was one hell of a good corrections officer.

26

I vers walked quickly to the lieutenants' office, picked up the phone and dialed Paulson's home. Policy required that the Security Chief be notified of every major incident. Ivers didn't waste any words. He calmly provided details surrounding the suicide attempt and finished by reporting Moore's status as unstable and critical.

Paulson informed Ivers he would be down to take charge of the investigation and hung up.

Ivers grimaced as he hung up the phone. The last thing he needed now was to baby-sit Paulson.

Ivers had no personal feelings toward Paulson one way or the other. He tried to get along with everyone. Ivers admitted to himself that Paulson was difficult, but he was the boss.

Ivers then dialed Beck's residence. The jail administrator always had to be notified in the event of a major incident.

It was now January 19, 12:03 AM Wednesday morning. Ivers identified himself and then relayed the news. Avery thanked him and hung up.

He wasn't sure what he was supposed to do. It sounded as if Ivers had covered all the bases. The police had been called, reports were being prepared and Moore had been transported to the hospital.

Avery lay in bed trying to sort things out. Why had Moore tried to kill himself? How had he managed to hang himself? Was Ivers telling him the truth or was there some cover-up?

Avery Beck had changed. He no longer accepted anything at face value. He was beginning to question everything.

Back at the jail, Ivers began his report. He wrote carefully, knowing his words would ultimately find their way to court. Ivers did not want any information that could be misinterpreted later by a clever attorney.

He finished and then reviewed Tombstone's account of the inci
dent. Tombstone had written a detailed report emphasizing th
fact he had checked on Moore's physical well-being every fiftee
minutes throughout the shift. Ivers knew Tombstone was a goo
officer.

Ivers made copies for the police and then began a second re
port. This one detailed the professionalism, dedication and quic
reaction of all corrections officers involved. Ivers singled out Pitt
Tombstone and Robbins as three officers as having performed ad
mirably and recommended a departmental commendation for thei
efforts.

Putting all the reports together, Ivers dropped them in the bas
ket, stretched and wondered if Paulson would ever arrive. Iver
remembered the first suicide he had handled. That one had bee
total confusion. But this time, everyone had done exactly wha
was spelled out in the policy manual and Ivers hoped he had cov
ered all the bases. Suddenly, the phone rang, interrupting hi
thoughts.

Ivers picked it up, identified himself and listened. At the othe
end was the corrections officer who had accompanied Moore to th
hospital. Eric Moore had been officially pronounced dead five min
utes ago at 2:17 AM.

Ivers instructed the officer to return to the facility and writ
his report. He then replaced the receiver and pulled out anothe
report form and entitled it "Supplemental." At 2:17 AM prisone
Eric Moore had officially been pronounced dead by the attendin
physician on Wednesday, January 18th at the County Hospital.

Ivers then attached this report to the others and picked up th
telephone and called Marshall Paulson for the second time. Paulso
answered on the second ring and stated he was on his way to tak
charge.

Ivers wondered what Paulson was going to take charge of as h
called Beck again. He listened quietly and ordered, "Make sure al
the reports are on my desk in the morning."

It was now three o'clock in the morning and Lieutenant Franl
Ivers was tired. He was not eligible for overtime. He just worke
until the job was finished without receiving any additional pay
Finally, after an eleven hour shift, Ivers was able to walk out of th

building. If and when Paulson arrived, he could investigate what-ever he wanted to investigate. Right now, Frank Ivers was going home and he was going to get some sleep. He had made it through another shift, alive.

Meanwhile, officer Dawn Lammers was frantically searching for a way out of a locked storeroom on the fifth floor. She had been assigned to work the women's unit on the night shift. Halfway through the tour, she discovered there were no sanitary napkins in stock for the female prisoners and had gone to the master control center to get keys for the storeroom on the fifth floor. Approaching the elevators, Dawn remembered that she had left her radio on the women's unit. Since the prisoners were locked in their rooms, she was confident the radio would be safe. Dawn took the elevator to the fifth floor, found the correct key, opened the storeroom door and entered. Behind her, the heavy metal door swung shut. The store room was stacked with soap, matches, paper towels and sani-tary napkins.

Dawn took a box, found the right key and inserted it into the lock. The lock on the outside had worked fine but for some reason the inside lock was malfunctioning.

Dawn Lammers had been a corrections officer for seven years and had been in some tight spots so this was no cause for panic. She reached for her radio and clutched empty space. She then remembered. She was locked in the storeroom with no way of com-municating.

Dawn Lammers was twenty-nine years old, tall, slender, at-ractive with long red hair. She was competent and had held her job because of her wits and her innate ability to survive.

For an hour, she continued to try different keys with no suc-cess. The control room officer probably thought she was screwing around somewhere and wouldn't call the lieutenant to report her absence. A C.O. did not rat on another C.O.

Dawn slid to a sitting position on the cold concrete floor, pulled a cigarette from her shirt pocket and lit up. She blew puffs of smoke upward and it was then her eyes fell on the fire sprinklers. They protruded two inches through the ceiling.

Dawn shrugged her shoulders, realizing she had little choice. Carefully, she stacked boxes on top of each other until she was able to reach the sprinkler heads. She pulled out her cigarette lighter and held the flame under the sprinkler for several seconds.

Even though she knew it was coming, it still took her by surprise. An alarm sounded and water saturated her in seconds. Dripping wet, Dawn slid to the bottom of the piled boxes and waited. The master control officer would be able to pinpoint which sprinkler head had been activated and would dispatch officers to investigate. In the meantime, Dawn Lammers would endure a cold shower. After what seemed like an eternity, but actually was only fifteen minutes, Lammers tromped out of the room past two officers without a word. The Lieutenant on duty asked her to write a report, and she requested time off to go home and change clothes first.

As Dawn Lammers left, several fire trucks with lights blazing and sirens whaling, pulled to the front of the jail. She winced, glad she wouldn't have to tell the fire department that it was all a false alarm.

Lammers later returned in a clean uniform, freshly applied make-up and hair meticulously in place. She then completed her report and handed it to the Lieutenant on duty. On the outside, Dawn Lammers was calm. On the inside she was scared. She had left her radio on post and ruined several hundred dollars worth of supplies. There was no question in her mind that she could be facing suspension and even termination. Her mind worked quickly. When the night shift ended, Dawn Lammers headed for the administration offices instead of going home. Deputy Chief Paulson had not yet reported for duty, but the new jail administrator was in his office.

Dawn quietly approached the administrator's door and tapped lightly.

Avery looked up from some papers.

"Could I speak with you for a moment, sir?"

Avery motioned for her to come in and placed the papers in his hand on the desk.

"Well, uh, you see I had some problems last night."

"What kind of problems?"

"Well, Sir, I got locked in a storage room and the only way I could get out was to set off the fire alarm. A lot of supplies were ained by the sprinklers but I can't afford to lose my job. I was hoping you would listen to my side of things before you decided to fire me."

Avery didn't need this with all his other problems. He wanted to tell her to leave, but instead he asked, "How did you get locked in a storage room?"

"It wasn't my fault. The lock on the door was messed up and when I tried to unlock the door from the inside, the key wouldn't work."

"I see," commented Avery gravely.

Dawn Lammers had left out the part about her radio.

In Avery's mind, it didn't seem like such a big deal. This C.O. had made a mistake. It was really the lock's fault. Now she was here pleading her case on the verge of tears. He flashed a sympathetic smile and asked casually, just to make conversation, about the supplies she had gone to get.

Lammers had been sniffling and she interrupted him to ask if he could shut his office door. "I don't want anyone to see me like this," she explained.

She slid smoothly across the carpeted floor and closed his door. When Dawn Lammers turned back, her demeanor had changed. "I'm sorry. You asked me a question."

Suddenly, Avery felt uncomfortable in his office alone with Dawn Lammers. He had been behind closed doors dozens of times with other women and this was no different. It was strictly business, he told himself. "Oh, yes. I asked what kind of supplies you needed."

Dawn smiled seductively and replied, "Feminine napkins. We were all out on the women's unit."

Avery didn't know what to say.

Dawn continued, "I don't think men really understand us women. Just because we're having our period doesn't mean we can't satisfy a man. Know what I mean?"

Avery started to reply but he suddenly he heard a voice inside his head scream, SCRUBBOARD!

Dawn moved to the edge of his desk and was still talking. A nervous smile was playing at the corners of Avery's mouth and he kept telling himself this wasn't what it seemed. It was nothing more than his imagination. Dennison's warning had ideas racing through his mind.

"I'm not talking about any kind of attachments, or anythin like that, just good clean fun," Dawn continued. She had moved the back of Avery's desk and was standing next to his left shoulde "I can do anything you like," she purred.

Avery cleared his throat. "I'm afraid there's been a mistake he stammered.

Dawn had an exaggerated pout on her face as she leaned ove Her perfume filled his nostrils and made him light-headed. Sh purred lightly in his ear. "My specialty is giving head. Anytim you want some head, let me know. Like I said, no attachments c anything like that, just some good clean fun, stress release."

Avery rose unsteadily and said, "I'm very happily marrie(Miss.."

"Lammers," Dawn interjected.

"As I was saying, I'm very happily married. And regardin that other thing about being locked in the store room, well, I'll loo into it."

Avery realized how corny "I'm very happily married" sounde(He wished he could remember what Dennison said he had used i situations like this.

Dawn walked provocatively to the closed door, placed her han on the knob, opened the door half-way and turned. "If you chang your mind, just let me know. After all, I am a public servant, an I'm here to serve."

Avery started to say "Thank you" but checked himself and ig nored the parting comment.

As Dawn Lammers left, Sam Dennison passed her and entere(with two cups of coffee and the captain's logs from the previou night.

Beck took the coffee and, nodding toward the disappearin Dawn Lammers, inquired, "Scrubboard?"

Dennison responded with a chuckle, "Scrubboard."

Avery took the logs and returned to his desk. He had never me a woman as aggressive and as open as Dawn Lammers.

Dennison took a seat, lit a cigarette and waited for the admin istrator to say what was on his mind.

"Are all the women here that aggressive?" he asked.

"Nope, just a few. If you read the logs you'll know why she wa here."

Avery found the entry describing Lammers activation of the fire alarm and her failure to have her radio with her.

"So do you think she should be fired?"

"Naw. Probably a two day suspension would be appropriate." With a gleam in his eye he added, "Provided of course, nothing went down between you and her."

Beck asked, "What do you think Paulson will recommend?"

Dennison thought for a moment and said, "I think he'll recommend termination, which I consider too harsh. Chances are, even two days suspension won't stick."

"Why not?"

"Because Paulson will probably screw it up. According to the union contract, Paulson has ten days to take action. During those ten days he has to review all reports, schedule a fact finding hearing, allow Lammers a chance to respond to the allegation and then make his recommendation to you. Nine out of ten times, Paulson screws around too long and tries to take action after the ten day limit. When that happens, the C.O. appeals and wins."

Beck considered Dennison's recommendation fair. He also realized Lammers had failed to mention she had left her radio. She hadn't lied. She had just failed to mention this fact.

"What about this suicide?" asked Beck, changing topics.

Dennison took a sip of coffee and replied, "Look, you're the boss, and I'm the operations manager. I've made it a practice not to get involved in Paulson's operations. The Lammers incident and the suicide are both issues which fall in Paulson's court."

Beck understood but he wanted Dennison's comments.

"I understand Paulson is suing you and you would rather stay out of the security operations completely. But I would like to hear your thoughts."

After a thoughtful pause he commented, "It looks like it was handled well. Of course we'll still wind up in court but I think the department and the city are in a good position. The Preacher and Tombstone were both on duty last night and you couldn't ask for two better employees. The reports look good. If the city doesn't decide to settle out of court, I'd say we have a better than even chance of winning this one."

"Does the city settle out of court often?"

Dennison smiled and replied, "All the time. After the lega beagles figure out how much money it will cost to defend the su in court, they generally opt for a settlement. Anyone, anywhere can file a suit against the city for virtually any reason and if they'r not too greedy, the city will eventually settle."

"And it doesn't make any difference whether the city is negl gent or not," added Beck.

"Not a bit."

"About the suicide, you don't think any of our staff are at fault?

Dennison shook his head and said, "If someone really wants t kill himself badly enough, there's not a damn thing anyone can de From what the reports indicate, I'd say our people did one hell of good job on this whole thing. This is a jail and, sadly enough, su cides are going to happen. Going to jail is a traumatic experience It makes people do desperate things. It's the nature of the beast.

Dennison rose and left. Avery then considered calling Watersto: to brief him on Moore's suicide. It was too early and Avery knev Waterston would not be in his office. He was not looking forwar to the briefing, but it was something that had to be done.

Later, as he was briefed, Waterston asked Avery if he had see: the morning papers. Before hanging up, Waterston roared, "Buy damn newspaper, Avery!"

27

The paper slanted the story of Moore's suicide, insinuating incompetence on the part of jail personnel. It listed all past suicides and problems at the jail for the past five years. And worst of all, the closing paragraph questioned Beck's ability and qualifications to administer a jail.

Avery read the article twice, looking for a reason for the damning attitude. Avery had the reports of the suicide on his desk and everything indicated the staff had handled the situation well. Why would the newspaper insinuate the suicide had occurred because of poor training and even poorer management?

Avery took the inaccuracies of the newspapers' suicide account and the attack on the jail's management as a personal affront. He penned what he considered to be a short, concise, and to-the-point rebuttal account of the suicide and then phoned the city's legal department. But after a ten-minute conversation, he realized his statement wasn't worth the paper it was written on. The legal department informed Avery that since this case was certain to be litigated, the city and the department were under strict orders not to comment. This placed Avery in a defenseless position. The media could criticize the department and its personnel as much as they wanted with complete immunity. The corrections officers would consider his silence as a lack of support. The general public would see Beck's lack of comments as an admission of guilt.

He tossed his statement in the trash and started an outline of the problems he was facing.

1. A pending suit by prisoner Mason Roberts.
2. A pending discrimination suit by Marshall Paulson.
3. Incompetence on the part of Marshall Paulson; unable to remove Paulson from current position.

4. Unable to reorganize the department's staff and eliminate the dead weight.
5. A possible suit by the family of Eric Moore?
6. A fifty-thousand-dollar budget overrun.
7. No support or guidance from Mayor's office.
8. An over-crowded jail, with serious potential for violence and death.
9. Negative journalism.

In less than two weeks, Avery already had nine major problems to contend with. All his plans for the jail had been cast aside. He had spent each day occupied with nothing more than survival and handling emergencies. There were no fancy management practices or theories he could employ to combat the problems he was facing. With or without Waterston's support, he had to make some decisions.

Avery began writing a plan of action to deal with the issues. There was nothing he could do about the pending lawsuits, but he could do something about some of the other issues.

Number one: call Paulson into his office and provide him with some specific criteria.

Number two: submit his plans for reorganization of the department to the city council. He would outline what he wanted to do and why. He would indicate the possible consequences if his plan was not adopted.

Number three: he would issue a press release regardless of what the city's legal department said. Avery was not going to stand by and allow the news media to slant the facts of prisoner Moore's suicide.

There was nothing he could do about the fifty-thousand-dollar over-expenditure, so he decided he was no longer going to worry about the department's budget.

Avery leaned back in his chair and studied his plan. He knew Waterston would come unglued when he discovered that he had sent his proposal for reorganization to the city council. He also knew Waterston would be livid when he opened the newspaper tomorrow and read the statement.

Avery lit a cigarette and pictured Waterston's reaction. "Fuck'em," he muttered to himself, smiling.

As the smoke curled upward, he would have been startled had he seen himself. The transformation was remarkable. Avery no longer remembered when he hadn't smoked and used profanity in expressing himself.

The spread of the jail virus had been accelerated by extreme stress and pressure. Avery Beck would never again be the same man. There was now a savage edge which compelled Avery to take chances he never would have taken before. He would no longer sit and ruminate over the obstacles. Avery Beck would strike out and would no longer avoid battle. If it took conflict to get things done, then he would play to win. Avery's mind whirled. The animalism he had detected in the former jail administrator had become his own.

28

O n Wednesday, January 19th, Georgie Byers called in sick for the evening shift. Georgie Byers never called in sick. As a matter of fact, Georgie had a perfect attendance record. Something was wrong.

Georgie had been unable to sleep the previous night. The bluish, bloated face of Eric Moore continued to dance in his mind. Moore was the deliverer. Fear, resignation, anger, hate, love, sadness, all the emotions Georgie had successfully suppressed for so many years. Now the emotions were here, surrounding him, suffocating him. Georgie could hardly breathe. Everything was closing in on him. Georgie staggered across the living room and opened a window. Georgie gulped the cold air, filling his lungs and trying to rid himself of this overwhelming depression.

Nothing was real. Eric Moore, the jail, everything was a fantasy. It was not real.

Georgie left the window open and stumbled back to a large overstuffed brown easy chair. He tried to sort out his feelings. It must be an illusion.

Only the belief that something existed caused it to exist. If you don't believe, it doesn't exist. Georgie refused to believe.

But Eric Moore's face forced its way into his mind. Eric Moore did not exist. He was dead, only an illusion, muttered Georgie. Georgie pushed Eric from his mind, exerting control. The wave of depression lifted.

In that instant, Georgie realized that he understood the very essence of life. He would always be alive no matter what happened. It was the belief which mattered, not what seemed to be fact. The fact was created by the belief.

Georgie walked to his hall closet and removed a thirty-eight caliber pistol. It was a shiny, nickel plated revolver. He slowly caressed the gun.

"It's only an illusion," muttered Georgie absently.

But while Georgie Byers sat alone in the dark, the jail life continued. It breathed a life of its own. Behind the tons and tons of concrete and steel lived a separate society. Each person struggled to carve out a niche and each struggled to survive.

Corrections Officer Frank Willis loved the jail. He could feel the jail's power through his veins. It was exciting, a challenge--a challenge which never ended.

On the January 19th, evening shift, Frank Willis was assigned to the second floor. The first order of business after headcount had been to search Mason Roberts' room thoroughly, but Willis had come up empty-handed.

He then returned to the control center informed corrections officer Chris Keys of his disappointment. "The fucking prick didn't have any contraband. That fuckin' pisses me off."

Both officers were aware that Roberts had filed an intent to sue the department for his recent beating, and both had hoped to find something unauthorized in Roberts' room.

"So where do we go from here?" asked Keys, intentionally goading Willis. Willis smiled to himself. "If Roberts didn't learn the first time, then maybe he'll learn the next."

Willis was convinced Roberts would eventually learn to keep his mouth shut. It was too soon to do the Lord's work again while internal affairs was investigating Roberts' complaint. Willis and the others must wait until things died down before they visited Roberts' room again.

"You mean, maybe another nighttime visit?"

Willis smiled and replied, "Yeah, only this time we'll make sure Roberts gets the message."

Willis left the room and swaggered through the dayroom ignoring the prisoners. He was the man in charge and the prisoners needed to know this fact. Willis eyed Stilwell carefully.

What Willis saw was a big, muscular blond with a perpetual sneer. As far as Willis was concerned, the world would be a much better place if someone planted a thirty-eight caliber slug between the eyes of Jack Stilwell.

Willis rapped on the control room window and motioned for Keys to open the detention level door.

"So how's it going out there?" questioned Keys.

"Aw, not too bad," Willis replied, answering the question an continuing. "See that big blond fuck out there by the weight ma chine?"

Keys peered through the window and noted Stilwell loungin near the weight machine. An attractive looking young kid stoo next to him. "Yeah, I see him."

"That fucker's trouble. I can smell it a mile away."

"So what are ya going to do?"

Willis smiled a crooked smile and said, "I'm goin to fuck wit] him a little, so keep an eye on me, OK?"

"You got it," assured Keys.

Stilwell noticed Willis approaching and smelled trouble. H did his best to ignore the approaching officer. Stilwell had alread heard Willis was a fucking punk who liked to throw his weigh around. Jack Stilwell didn't need any time in segregation, at leas not now. He was still working on Tommy Brown and didn't wan anything screwing up this deal. When he was done, Tommy Browr was going to be a nice, sweet, little jail house wife.

Abruptly, Willis planted himself firmly in front of Stilwell anc barked, "You lifting weights or just fucking off?"

Anger swelled up but instead of replying, he shrugged his shoul ders and eased off toward his room.

Willis sneered. Stilwell wasn't shit. He may look big and bad but when it came down to it, he was just a fucking pussy like all the rest of the cons.

Willis glanced in the direction of the control room and threw a nod to Keys. Keys had enjoyed Stilwell's backing down and it sure couldn't hurt Willis' reputation any to have Keys relate this inci-dent to the other officers.

Suddenly, Willis was in a good mood and the remainder of the shift went by without incident. But then, nothing ever happened on the second floor. The prisoners did what they were told. It was that simple.

Eleven o'clock arrived quickly and the night shift came on. There was nothing to report to the oncoming officers.

The exchange between Stilwell and Willis hadn't escaped Greg Leeks. Leeks had watched carefully from across the dayroom. Although he couldn't hear the words, it was obvious from Stilwell's reaction and the posture of the corrections officer that Stilwell had been challenged.

Leeks was surprised Stilwell hadn't decked the C.O. Then he realized why Stilwell had let the incident slide. Stilwell did not want to be separated from Tommy Brown. Leeks pursed his lips and considered the situation. For some reason, the thought of Stilwell turning Brown into a punk bothered Leeks. He couldn't explain it and knew it was none of his business. If the kid didn't stand up for himself, then no one could help him. If a prisoner stole your candy bar you had better try to kill the motherfucker.

It was how things were in prison. Leeks had seen young kids like Tommy Brown lost and won several times during an evening of cards. Tommy Browns were commodities--goods to be traded for drugs, cigarettes and even special favors.

For the past ten years, Leeks had been appropriately housed with the old timers. This was the first time he had been housed with the kids. And this was the first time he had actually witnessed a kid being turned into a punk.

Punks were something Leeks had not given a great deal of thought to. It was nothing more than a way of life. But the thought bothered him.

Leeks wondered if he was getting soft. Suddenly, the lights began to flicker off and on. It was time for lockdown. Leeks dropped the glowing butt of his cigarette on the floor and strolled casually back to his room. The night shift was coming on. It would have been so much easier if the jail people had assigned him to the sixth floor where he belonged. On the sixth floor, people didn't get punked or turned. They just did their time.

29

Carla Terwelp was excited. She had been assigned to work the control room on the sixth floor during the night shift.

But Carla approached the officer assigned to the housing unit and offered to trade assignments. The officer jumped at the chance and the switch was made. The lieutenant might say something, but they could always claim they had misunderstood their assignments and it was an innocent mistake. It was a plausible excuse, and they both knew the lieutenant on duty would buy it.

Carla conducted her headcount, returned to the control center and reported the number of prisoners. Evan had been awake when she had passed his door and he had seen her. Once she moved past, the light in his room had winked out and Carla knew Evan was waiting for her. She had to be careful. If she were too hasty, the control officer would suspect something. Corrections officers did not rat off but they did talk. If word got around that she was involved with a prisoner, the other officers would make her life miserable.

Carla then conducted a security check. It was standard routine. After the inspection, Carla returned to the control center and reported all secure.

The control room officer penciled in his log, "All secure at 0030 hours."

Carla slowly moved away from the control center and walked through the dim light of the dayroom. From his room window, Evan watched her wander aimlessly, stopping briefly to check something or other, only to move on a little farther.

He waited patiently, knowing tonight's meeting would be crucial. Evan was certain Carla had thought about their brief lovemaking the night before. Tonight, Carla would either back away, realizing she was getting in too deep, or she would be all the more eager.

Twenty minutes crawled by and then his door opened briefly and Carla slid swiftly inside.

She rushed into his arms and whispered, "I missed you so much, Evan. I wish your court case was over so we could be together all the time."

"Me too," whispered Evan passionately.

"Oh, Evan, why does it have to be like this? Why can't people see how good you really are?"

Evan brushed a strand of hair away from Carla's eyes as he replied, "Nobody believes me Carla. You're the only one who has any faith in me. Without you, I don't know what I'd do."

"I'll always believe in you Evan, always."

He reached for Carla's belt and unsnapped it quickly. Unfastening her uniform trousers, he drew them down to her knees. Evan lay back on his bed and pulled Carla on top of him. She was overwhelmed with passion. Evan muffled her moans as much as he could and once she had been satisfied, he quickly ejaculated and resisted the impulse to shove her aside. That wouldn't do, Evan thought to himself. He had to play the game.

Carla still lay on top of him forgetting where she was for several brief moments. Abruptly, she rose, wiped herself, and refastened her uniform trousers. She moved to the door and peered through the glass. No one had entered the housing unit and her radio remained silent. She hadn't been missed.

Turning back to Evan, she whispered, "I'm going to write to you. I'll use a fake name and I won't put a return address on the letters so nobody will know."

"I hope I'm around to get the letters," he said quietly.

"What do you mean?"

"Well, you see," Evan hesitated for effect. "There's some guys in here and they told me if I don't get some drugs in here soon, they'll fuck me up real good. These guys aren't kidding. They're killers and they mean what they say. I told them no way, that drugs aren't my thing."

"What did they say?" asked Carla.

"They said tough shit. Either get the stuff or they would fuck me up. That's all they said."

"Who are these guys?" questioned Carla, suddenly angry.

"No way Carla, I'm not going to get you involved in my stuff. No fucking way! These are some bad dudes."

"What are you going to do, Evan?"

"I don't know Carla. I've been trying to think of something. My real problem is that I'm not a criminal. I wouldn't have any idea where or how to get drugs."

Drops of moisture formed at the edges of Carla's eyes. Someone was going to try to kill the man she loved and she was helpless. There was nothing she could do. She had finally met a man. A good, honest, decent man who loved her as much as she loved him and some criminals were going to kill him and there was nothing she could do.

"Wait a second," said Evan. "Do you have any old prescriptions? Valium, seconal?"

Carla remembered she had a couple of old bottles of prescription drugs in her bathroom. Both were expired and outdated. One was Tylenol #3 and the other was valium. Both bottles were half full.

"I have two bottles, but what has that got to do with anything?"

Evan was intense as he spoke. Placing both hands on Carla's shoulders, Evan peered into her eyes and said softly, "My court date should be coming up any day now. If I had those prescriptions, maybe I could stall for some time. I could give them a couple of pills each day you know, just to stall for time and hopefully I'd be through court and out of jail by the time I ran out. What do you think?"

"Evan, I'd do anything for you. You know that. But I don't know about bringing something in. It's against the law. It's a felony. If I got caught, I'd go to jail."

"I know, I know," whispered Evan softly, while he pulled Carla close to him.

Evan continued, "I can't ask you to do this. I'll have to figure something out on my own. But Carla, I want you to know something. If anything should happen to me and if for some reason I never get to see you again, I want you to know how much I love you."

Carla held Evan close. It wasn't fair. The world wasn't fair and the jail wasn't fair. Nothing was fair.

Suddenly, Carla's radio squawked. The control officer was speaking, "Six control to unit twenty-eight, what's your location?" Carla squeezed Evan's hand and slipped out of his room.

Outside Evan's room Carla removed her radio and responded, "I'm in A Pod, checking for contraband."

The control officer peered through the control room window, caught sight of Carla near the shower and responded, "ten-four."

The rest of the night Carla Terwelp was in a quandary. She wanted to run to Evan's room to be with him but she knew it was impossible. She could not bear the thought that she might never see Evan again.

Five o'clock that morning breakfast arrived and Carla supervised the serving to the prisoners. Evan sat alone, eating slowly, while several of the others glared at him.

Evan looked sad and vulnerable but there was nothing Carla could do. She was totally powerless. Evan soon returned to his room while three pairs of hostile, angry eyes followed his every move.

Carla noticed and moved closer to the prisoners who had watched Evan and overheard one of the prisoners comment.

"If that motherfucker doesn't come up with some shit soon, we're going to have to fuck him up real bad."

The other two laughed loudly and agreed.

Carla Terwelp left work that morning desperate and depressed. Driving home, she continued to ask herself over and over, "What should I do?"

She knew in her heart she had the power to save the man she loved.

She parked in the lot of her apartment, unlocked her front door and walked straight to the bathroom. The two prescription bottles were where she remembered. Carla took them to the kitchen table, placed them on the table, sat down, and stared. She knew what she had to do. There was no longer any doubt her mind. The plan was clear. She would do everything she could to help Evan and if that meant taking a risk, then she would take that risk. A man like Evan came along only once in a woman's life. Carla poured the contents of the prescription bottles into a plain white envelope. Bending the top flap, she sealed the envelope tightly. Tonight, when she reported for work, this envelope would be in her purse. She would think of some reason to go to the sixth floor, even if she wasn't assigned. The only thing that mattered now was saving Evan's life.

After the dayshift had conducted the headcount, the prisoners on the sixth floor were allowed out of their rooms and into the dayroom. Evan strolled about confidently. The Evan Richards of several hours ago was nowhere to be found. This Evan Richards was confident and in control.

Evan quickly met with the three prisoners who had glared at him during breakfast.

"Well, did she notice?" asked Evan, visibly excited.

"Fuck, yeah," responded one of the prisoners.

"Believe me, man, she noticed," added the second prisoner. "I thought the bitch was going to break down and cry right here. You should have seen her face when she heard us talking about fucking you up. Man, I thought she was going to shit her pants."

Evan laughed and moved away from the three. Everything was working perfectly. Evan smiled inwardly. If everything continued on course, tonight would be Christmas.

30

On January 20th, Thursday morning, Avery Beck felt good for the first time in two weeks. Last evening he had called the newspaper and issued an official statement concerning prisoner Eric Moore's suicide. Now his comments had been printed and he was satisfied with the story.

Avery entered his office and took a pen and paper and outlined how he would handle Paulson. He expected Paulson to be argumentive and hostile. And Avery would deal with him as if he was a hostile witness on the stand. Avery would take quick shots, back out, bob and weave for a bit, and then attack again. Paulson would never know what hit him.

Beck heard the doors to the administration area open and knew Dennison was on his way to the coffee room. Ten minutes later Dennison entered Beck's office with two cups of coffee and placed one on the desk. He turned to leave but Beck stopped him in mid-stride.

"Did you see this morning's paper?"

Dennison turned slowly. "I saw it. It was a nice piece on the jail but I think it was a mistake."

"What do you mean you think it was a mistake?" asked Beck, completely caught off guard.

Dennison moved to the couch and sat down.

"You opened the flood gates. The newspapers got to you and they know it. They printed your story the way you wanted it, but what about the next story?"

"What do you mean, the next story? It's over."

"No, it's never over. There will be something else and, believe me, the newspapers will be looking. It might be Paulson's suit, or prisoner Mason Roberts' suit, or it may even be a disgruntled corrections officer who has an ax to grind. I guarantee there will be another story."

"So you're telling me you don't think it was a good idea for me to talk to the media."

Dennison hesitated a moment. "I didn't say that but you opened the flood gates. The reporters will be snooping around the jail, turning over every stone trying to find some dirt. And, believe me, they will find some dirt." Dennison took a deep breath and continued. "You may not see it as such but the bottom line is, you and the newspapers are at war. A war you cannot hope to win. Newspapers are after scandals, not facts. Tomorrow there's a good chance the news will read something like: "Jail Administrator Avery Beck contends his corrections officers handled the suicide of prisoner Eric Moore in a very professional manner. This writer wonders how prisoner Moore was able to commit suicide in the first place. If Mr. Beck's corrections officers acted so professionally, then why is a prisoner dead? Perhaps Mr. Beck himself is attempting to cover something up? This writer thinks the public has a right to know the facts."

"You really think they would print something like that?" asked Beck, stunned.

"I'd bet on it."

"What do you suggest?"

"Let it lie. You made your point. The staff is going to think you're wonderful. This is the first time in years anyone has publicly backed corrections officers. It will be one hell of a boost to morale."

Beck was gratified that he had done something right, something he felt good about. He knew Waterston would be upset but he had made a decision and he would make more decisions.

Beck pulled out his plans for the departmental reorganization and explained what he hoped to accomplish.

Dennison was impressed. Beck was sharp. He had reduced everything to the essentials, but Dennison wondered if Beck understood the implications.

"You realize, of course, if you do this, you are going to make some pretty big people awfully mad."

"I already have," snapped Beck.

Dennison tried again. "What I'm trying to say is, it's important to be aware of the "Brubaker Syndrome."

"The what?"

"The Brubaker Syndrome."

"And what exactly is the Brubaker Syndrome?"

"It's like the movie. You can make change in a bureaucracy as long as the change is done slowly and carefully. In the movie Brubaker took charge of a southern prison. Instead of waiting for the system to work, he took matters into his own hands. When he was warned to back off, he refused. He made changes, but the changes didn't last and neither did he. If you go off on your own and try to make changes too swiftly, someone is going to chop your nuts off. Politicians and bureaucrats don't appreciate people who make waves. If you submit this proposal for reorganization to the mayor's office, I figure he'll send it right back. There are too many people in the positions you intend to cut who have ties to City Hall."

"I'm not sending it to the mayor's office. He's already rejected the proposal. I'm sending it straight to the City Council. Not only am I sending the proposal, but I'm also going to send a request for an increased budget and increased staffing. Finally, I'm going to tell the city council just exactly what can happen if money is not forthcoming and changes in this jail are not enacted."

"You mean you're going to threaten them?"

"Not at all," Beck replied casually.

"They'll see it as a threat."

"Their choice," Beck replied, firm in his convictions.

"There is a high probability you will not be around to reap the benefits of any of those changes. If you make too much noise, the mayor will do everything in his power to get rid of you. If you appeal your case directly to the City Council, then that's occupational suicide. "

"But do you think my plans for a reorganization are operationally and functionally sound?" demanded Beck.

"Without a doubt," replied Dennison.

"I rest my case."

"You think it will do any good?" questioned Dennison.

Beck chuckled and replied, "If nothing else, it will stir things up for a while."

Dennison watched Beck silently. The man in front of him was a different man than the one who had walked in to the administrator's office a week and a half ago. Beck had changed, not just a little, but dramatically. Dennison stood up and wished Beck luck. As he left, he admitted to himself that in less than two weeks, Beck had developed one helluva set of brass balls.

Beck picked up the phone and asked Paulson to report to his office. "From now on you will follow my instructions and orders to the letter. You will not contact anyone in City Hall without first notifying me. If you have a problem, my door is always open and I will be happy to discuss the problem with you. I will not accept anything but total and complete loyalty. If you do not like the manner in which I run this organization, I will accept your resignation. Do I make myself clear, Mr. Paulson?"

Paulson's first reaction was shock, then anger, and finally agreement. "I would just like to say my loyalty to you has been, and always will be, total and complete. You're the boss and whatever you want or need me to do, just say the word. I'm really glad we had this talk. I was wondering if you were pissed off at me or something. There are a lot of personalities in this department and the administration of this jail has to work together. I'm on the team, boss, and you can count on me."

Paulson rose, shook Beck's hand, thanked him and strolled out of the office.

Avery Beck sat in surprised silence, wondering what the hell was going on. He had expected a major confrontation. Instead, he had received complete cooperation. The sincerity Paulson had expressed had touched Beck and he wondered if he had misjudged him.

Avery called his secretary and instructed her to make a dozen copies of his plans. He further instructed that a copy of a carefully worded memorandum fully detailing the jail's explosive potential, be attached to each plan and that a copy of the memorandum plan be hand delivered to the office of each city councilman.

Finished, Avery sat back in his chair and smiled. As soon as the city councilmen received his correspondence, they would call the mayor. The mayor would then call him. But unfortunately for the mayor, today was the day Avery Beck had elected to take a long lunch. He slipped into his coat, walked from his office and commented to his secretary, "I'll be out to lunch. If I get any calls, please take a message."

31

All night long, Georgie Byers sat in his apartment, thinking. At times, he would talk to Eric Moore. Moore made a lot of sense. Georgie learned that he and Eric Moore had a great deal in common.

Eric supported Georgie's belief. Eric told Georgie, "Nothing is real."

Georgie's eyes were red-rimmed from lack of sleep, his hair was matted and his clothes were wrinkled. Eric Moore and the jail occupied Georgie's thoughts. The jail, a place were all the failures came. A place where Georgie worked. He had to take care of all the failures. Some were mean, some were scared, some were angry. No, that's not right. They didn't exist. None of them existed. It was all illusion.

Someone was playing a cruel joke. Nothing existed. There was no beginning and no end. Everything was a circle. Everything repeated itself. There would always be a Georgie Byers. There would always be prisoners. There would always be a jail. Nothing could be done to change the cycle. Georgie was caught inside this never-ending circle.

"Have to break out of the circle," Georgie mumbled. "Jump over the boundaries of the circle and get free. Have to do it. No other choice."

The nickel-plated thirty-eight lay on the coffee table. Georgie's mind continued to whir. He picked up the pistol, opened the cylinder and removed the bullets. The gun was now capable of nothing. It held potential, but it was capable of nothing. It was just a worthless piece of metal.

Georgie peered at the gun intently. He could see his distorted face lurking in the nickel plating. He had become one with the gun. They had merged. The gun was of no use and Georgie was an empty shell.

The circle closed tighter, choking him.

Georgie carefully replaced the bullets, snapped the cylinder closed and peered at the nickel plated metal again. He was still one with the gun.

But now the gun was no longer powerless. The gun's potential could now be realized and Georgie 's potential could be realized.

Georgie smiled, then laughed.

Georgie held in his hand the power to escape the circle. Slowly and deliberately, he placed the muzzle of the shiny thirty-eight to his right temple and breathed deeply, relishing the ecstasy of escape.

Eric Moore stood beside Georgie. Eric was smiling. Georgie used his thumb to pull back the hammer. Eric was still there, still smiling. Georgie closed his eyes and relaxed.

His right index finger squeezed the trigger. A sharp crack echoed through Georgie's apartment.

A thirty-eight caliber slug plowed its way through skin, bone, hair and brain matter before exiting.

The thirty-eight dropped to the floor.

Georgie Byers slumped peacefully in his chair. Georgie Byers no longer had a heart beat.

Georgie's reflection was no longer in the thirty-eight. He had separated himself from the thirty-eight. He had escaped.

Georgie Byers had been right. There would be another Georgie Byers and there would be another Eric Moore. They might not look like the old ones, but they would be the same, nonetheless.

Georgie Byers was dead because he had refused to face the awful reality of the jail, dead because no one considered a corrections officer valuable enough to acknowledge the intense pressure and stress they experienced daily.

Georgie Byers did not want to play the game any longer. The game would continue without him.

32

Mason Roberts moved casually through the dayroom. For the past two days he had assessed the situation on the second floor and identified three groups of prisoners in the unit.

One was controlled by Jack Stilwell, a big, mean, muscular blond. The stocky, dangerous lifer named Leeks controlled another. The third group was made up of what was left.

For Mason Roberts, the situation was perfect. There was a chance the two controlled groups might never go to war. On the other hand, with a little help, Roberts could ensure an altercation. And would suit Roberts' ambitions.

Even if both Stilwell and Leeks survived, they would go to lockup and leave a power vacuum on the second floor that Mason Roberts would quickly occupy. Seizing power in jail was a complicated, dangerous process.

Roberts understood the paranoia, fear and distrust among prisoners. Roberts had met several during the past two days. Each prisoner wanted to know why he was in jail and what he was doing on the second floor.

Roberts made it clear that he was a jail house lawyer. He could prepare writs and civil suits as well as a professional.

In the eyes of the other prisoners, a "jail house lawyer" was not an ordinary prisoner but a valuable, well respected commodity. Once the word had been passed among the sixty-five prisoners housed on the second floor, prisoners had steadily come to him for legal advice.

Roberts told each of them that the first consultation was free. The second consultation would cost a candy bar. The preparation and filing of a writ would cost a carton of cigarettes. The preparation and filing of a civil suit would cost two cartons of cigarettes, depending on the complexities of the case. These prices were considered fair, reasonable and acceptable.

Meanwhile, Mason Roberts watched a young prisoner named Brad Wilson closely. Wilson had gone back and forth between Stilwell and Leeks, attempting to ingratiate himself into both factions, hoping to come out on top with whomever won the power struggle.

Wilson had the ear of both Leeks and Stilwell. He was someone Mason Roberts could use, but he would have to be patient. It was best to wait for Wilson to come to him, and he would. Sooner or later, everyone came to the jail house lawyer for advice.

On Thursday afternoon, January 20th, Brad Wilson's public defender entered the jail to offer a plea bargain to Wilson and Wilson responded that he would have to think about it.

After the meeting, Wilson approached Mason Roberts. "You're a jail house lawyer, aren't you.?"

Roberts responded casually, "Yeah, sure. You need something?"

"Well, I just talked to my public defender and he wants me to cop a plea for robbery and battery. My original charge is strong armed robbery. What do you think?"

Roberts thought for several seconds before responding.

"Look, I don't know anything about your case. Start from the beginning and tell me everything. I don't want to give you any bad advice."

Wilson explained the details of his arrest and several times Roberts asked for clarification. But mostly, he listened.

Wilson had been popped for stealing a purse which resulted in injury to an elderly woman. The deal was to plead guilty to robbery and assault, and the district attorney would drop the strong armed robbery charge.

When Wilson finished, Roberts explained, "If the robbery and assault charges are both misdemeanors, then plead guilty. Both crimes carry a maximum of six months in jail, which means you would do a year. The armed robbery charge carries a maximum sentence of two years in the joint. You want to stay away from all the felony convictions you can. Misdemeanor convictions don't mean shit, but felony convictions add up, and at some point in time, the fucking DA will throw the fucking bitch at you, contending you're a habitual criminal. Take the misdemeanors, but tell your public defender you want a few stipulations to go along with the plea bar gain. One, you want both charges to be misdemeanors, which they probably are. But make sure you get a guarantee. Number two, tell the public defender you want a recommendation for probation on one of the charges. That will cut your jail time in half. Number three, tell the public defender you want to be eligible for good time. If you get six months here, you'll really only do about four months with good time. If the public defender agrees, two good things happen. You avoid a felony conviction and you get out of jail after doing four months instead of two years."

"You think he'll agree?"

"Fuck yes, he'll agree. Look Brad, the jail is overcrowded. No one is going to kick about giving you good time. The jail people need your bed for someone else, so they want to get rid of you as soon as they can. The public defender will probably do some head-scratching and ass-picking, but he'll take it. You can bet on it."

"So you don't think I should go to trial?"

Roberts laughed. "Nobody goes to trial. Shit, if everybody went to trial we would be waiting ten years before we went to court. Maybe one percent of all cases, if that many, go to trial. The name of the game is plea bargain and it's a game everybody plays. Why do you think I file so many suits?"

"Beats me," answered Wilson.

"Because I never have to go to court and present my case. The judge looks at the case. Most judges are lazy fucks and don't want to preside over anything, especially when they could be playing golf or fucking some secretary. The judge calls a settlement conference and everybody talks about how much money it's going to cost to try the case. Then they take half that much and offer it to me as a settlement. I hem and haw for a while and I act indignant because my rights have been violated but eventually I take the money. Believe me, nobody, and I mean nobody wants a trial."

Wilson smiled and asked, "How much do I owe you?"

Roberts peered at Wilson intently and replied, "You don't owe me a thing. But I think you ought to know something."

Something in Roberts' voice put Wilson on edge and he peered suspiciously around the dayroom before turning back to Roberts and asking, "What?"

"I heard some dudes talking yesterday and they said something about Stilwell getting ready to fuck up Leeks. I know you and Leeks are friends, so I thought I'd let you know about it."

"No shit?"

"No shit," responded Roberts. "Oh, there's one more thing. I ain't saying who I heard it from, and I'll deny ever telling you. Understand?"

"Yeah, that's cool. No problem," replied Wilson.

"The only reason I'm telling you is because you got a chicken shit case and you'll be out in four months. I don't want to see you get caught in the middle of something. Know what I mean?"

"I appreciate that. I really appreciate that," said Wilson earnestly.

In a few short minutes Wilson had grown to like and trust Roberts. Roberts was smart. He could do things none of the other prisoners could. Roberts could manipulate the laws and the system.

Wilson thanked Roberts again and walked away to mingle with the other prisoners.

Fifteen minutes later, Wilson dodged into Leeks' room. Roberts smiled to himself. There had never been a question in his mind that Wilson would tell Leeks what he had heard. The only question was how soon.

Leeks wouldn't ask questions. He would listen and prepare for an attack. He would not wait for Stilwell to come to him. When the fight erupted, Roberts would make sure he was as far away as possible.

And Mason Roberts had nominated himself as the new leader.

33

A very ate lunch, read the newspaper and had several cups of coffee before returning to the jail.

Avery picked up his phone messages, noted that each call had een from Waterston or Waterston's secretary and dropped the essages in the trash. Turning to his secretary, he said, "I won't be aking any calls this afternoon. Just have them leave a message."

Avery knew he was playing a dangerous game. The rules re-uired department administrators to act in a certain manner. By oing around Waterston directly to the City Council, Avery had roken a very basic rule of bureaucratic etiquette. Not only had he voided Waterston, he had dropped all legal liability and responsi-ility for the jail's problems directly on the shoulders of the City ouncil.

If the council failed to act on his recommendations and a seri-us incident occurred at the jail, the City Council knew Avery would oint the finger at them.

It was a new twist for city councilors. Traditionally, they re-ained in the background waiting to criticize the department heads fter the fact. But Avery had enlisted them into the game and, like or not, they were now forced to play ball or suffer the conse-uences. Avery Beck was not going to be anyone's scapegoat.

The phone on Avery's desk rang and out of sheer habit he picked up. It was too late and he knew who was on the other end.

"What the fuck do you think you're doing, Beck?" screamed Vaterston.

Avery was not going to back down.

"I'm doing what needs to be done, Sam. I'm trying to put this il back on its feet. I believe I will save someone's life." Sarcasm dged its way into Avery's voice as he continued. "A life. You know hat that is, Sam, don't you? It's a warm-blooded, breathing voter."

Waterston was silent for several seconds and then spoke calmly. Look, Avery. I know you have some problems over there, but we

can work them out. Listen. Let me tell you what we're going to d
We'll get together and draft a letter to the city councilors. We'll te
them all the problems have been worked out, and to ignore you
earlier letter."

"You know, Sam, that sounds like a damn good idea. And I'll k
happy to do just that as soon as all the problems are worked out

"Now look, Avery, I've been patient with you. I've tried to wor
with you, but you're screwing with the wrong people. The city cour
cilors think you've lost your mind. They think you're threatenir
them and they don't like to be threatened. Some of these peopl
are very powerful and I mean all-the-way-to-the- governor's-office
powerful. You don't fuck with these people."

"Well, maybe it's time somebody did fuck with them, San
Maybe it's time they found out just what the hell is going on an
take some responsibility for a few things."

Before Waterston could respond, Avery plunged ahead.

"You know how it works, Sam. The politicians, including you
aren't interested until something happens. When somebody get
killed, the newspapers look for someone to persecute. All of a sud
den, everyone becomes interested. The politicians wring thei
hands, shake their heads and vow they'll get to the bottom of th
problem. Then they make their public statements. Their state
ments consist of self-righteous indignation. Why weren't they ir
formed there was a problem? An investigation into the matter wi
be initiated. And you know what happens, don't you, Sam? NAF
Not A Fucking Thing!"

Waterston tried to interrupt but Avery was on a roll.

"Not this time, Sam. This time, nobody can say they didn
know. Nobody can say they weren't informed. This time the cour
cilors and you, Sam, are holding the bag, not me."

Waterston burst through the verbiage with a roar.

"I don't know who you think you are, but you're crazy. Do yo
hear me, Avery? You're fucking crazy! You know that? You ar
fucking crazy!" The line went dead and Avery replaced the receive
and smiled. If nothing else, he had gotten their attention.

Waterston was livid. That son-of-a-bitch Beck was crazy. Thi
was not how things were supposed to be done. Beck knew how th
game was supposed to be played. So why wasn't he going along?

All eight councilors were demanding an explanation. They wanted to know what Waterston was going to do about Beck. None of the councilors liked being held responsible but that was what Beck had done. He had made them directly responsible for the jail.

Waterston's first reaction had been to fire Beck. A quick reconsideration, and he realized that was impossible. At least, right now.

Now Waterston was worried. If he fired him, Beck would take a copy of his memorandum to the news media. This was something Waterston and the City Council definitely did not want. No. He would have to wait. He would put together a task force to study the problems. While the task force was busy, he would make a public statement. Waterston would announce that Avery Beck had elected to step down as jail administrator.

Then if Beck decided to distribute the memorandum, Waterston would tell the press, "Yes, indeed, as Mayor, I am very much concerned about the jail. A task force was formed a week ago to study the problems identified by Mr. Beck."

He may have to wait a little while, but one way or another he was going to eliminate Beck.

Meanwhile, Avery stood at his office window watching dark clouds gather in the afternoon sky. Tomorrow was Friday. And then the weekend. Avery lit a cigarette, studied the clouds, and wished jails did not exist.

His mind turned back to his confrontation with Waterston. In a short week and a half, he had encountered more hostility, more anger and more aggressiveness than he had seen during his entire past forty-two years.

Suddenly, Avery's thoughts were interrupted by the phone. Maybe Waterston had decided to call back. Maybe Waterston had made a deal with the City Council.

He picked up the phone and listened. For several minutes Avery said nothing, he just listened. He then mumbled, "Thank you," to the caller and replaced the receiver.

Avery thought for a second, picked up the phone and called Dennison. Dennison appeared less than a minute later, spotted Beck staring out the window, sensed something was wrong and decided to wait in silence.

After several moments, Beck turned.

"Corrections Officer George Byers is dead. I just received call from the police and they claim Byers committed suicide."

Dennison pursed his lips and lit a cigarette. Both men wer lost in their own thoughts and in their own worlds. Dennison mind turned to Georgie Byers. Cool, calm, unemotional Georgi Byers, the Tin Man, the corrections officer everyone liked to hav around when things got rough. Georgie Byers, the loner. The on person few people, if any, knew anything about. Georgie came t work, did his job and went home. He never complained, he neve lost his cool and he never argued. Georgie Byers did his job an existed. That's all. He existed.

Dennison realized the effect Byers' death would have on th staff. The majority of the corrections officers had looked on Georgi Byers as a role model, someone who had all the answers and al ways maintained control. When word of Byers suicide was circu lated, the staff would be left feeling empty. The one person the had respected most had killed himself.

There was nothing Dennison could do about this, nor was ther anything he could do about the jail or, for that matter, Avery Beck Dennison was powerless.

Beck had become a strong, forceful leader. He had made som tough decisions and he had stood up to Waterston. Unfortunately Beck was killing himself in the process. His attempts to define th gray areas had ended in total frustration.

Beck was committing occupational suicide by his unwillingnes to bend and ignore the growing problems at the jail. Georgie Byer had committed physical suicide. These were two different kinds o suicide and they both led to death.

But Dennison admired Beck. If nothing else, Beck knew wha needed to be done and he was doing it. For the first time in years Dennison had found a ray of hope. Perhaps things would improve

Beck had turned back to the window, staring at the heavy blacl overcast. A few scattered snowflakes drifted lazily to the ground Dennison quietly put out his cigarette and left Beck with hi thoughts.

34

Lieutenant Frank Ivers reported for duty on the evening shift and was stunned when he heard the news.

There had to be a mistake. But there was no mistake. Georgie Myers had committed suicide.

Ivers sat in the lieutenant's office wondering if there might have been something he could have said or done. The other corrections officers were moping around in a trance.

The news had reached the prisoners and this was one of the few times they did not intentionally antagonize the corrections officers. They knew the staff was on edge. It would only take a little pushing to ignite a physical altercation. By nine o'clock the jail was abnormally quiet.

Ivers made the rounds on the detention levels but his heart wasn't in the job. Ivers investigated several prisoner complaints during the shift and automatically jotted them down on a piece of paper for future reference and documentation.

When eleven o'clock arrived, the evening shift passed their keys and radios to the night shift and left. Conversation was sparse as the evening shift filed out of the jail.

Each officer realized how fragile and precious life is. Each inwardly examined his own life and wondered what had caused Georgie to cross the thin line between life and death.

As Ivers watched the shift leave, he contemplated the plight of a corrections officer for the hundredth time of his career. They realize early in their career that working at the jail is laden with a high potential for death and serious injury. They do not carry weapons, nor do they normally receive any advanced courses in self defense, yet corrections officers are surrounded eight hours a day by killers, rapists, burglars and drug addicts. The only weapon they have is their wits. The thought of death is no stranger, but the reality of death, when death calls upon one of their own, is always a shock.

193

Soldiers fight side by side in a foxhole for each other. The loftier more noble causes of patriotism and freedom escape the soldier under the duress of combat. Under fire, the rationale becomes clear: Us against them.

In a jail, corrections officers are constantly under fire by the public, the prisoners, the administration, the politicians and the news media. In jail, there is never any confusion of values. It is always us against them. Now they had lost one of their own. It was not Georgie Byers' fault he had committed suicide. It was the fault of "them," anybody and everybody who did not belong to their select group.

As the last officer filed past, Frank Ivers anticipated an increase in the amount of force they would use in the coming weeks. For some inexplicable reason, the staff would make the prisoners pay for the death of Georgie Byers. It was Lieutenant Frank Ivers job to prevent this from happening.

Ivers walked into the darkened parking lot alone, unlocked the door to his Ford pickup and started the engine. Flipping on his headlights, he sat for several minutes watching huge snowflakes dance in the glare of his headlights. The white, clean coldness of snow always reminded Ivers of some sort of purification. By morning, the ground would be covered with a blanket of white.

Georgie was out of it now. The endless days of supervising prisoners were over for Georgie. No utility bills, no car payments, no rent payments, nothing. Georgie was free.

35

Carla Terwelp was nervous and scared. She had dressed for work earlier than usual and placed the envelope of pills for Evan Richards in her purse. She drove to work and nervously smiled at the officer posted in the lobby. Corrections officers, although required by department policy, rarely searched each other. The officer waved her through. She was one of "them."

Carla walked through the lobby and into the secure perimeter of the building. She was now inside the jail with contraband and could be charged with a felony offense. This was the first time Carla Terwelp had ever broken the law. She entered the briefing room and took a seat at the back, close to the corner.

She fidgeted uncomfortably waiting for briefing to start. She did not want to talk to anybody. She just wanted to give Evan the pills and then forget about it, put the entire episode behind her.

Carla hoped she would be assigned to the sixth floor again. Suddenly, the lieutenant called her name. It would be the booking unit. Friday nights in booking were the worst. Thursday nights were almost as bad. More than a hundred people were booked into the Coronado County jail during the night shift on Thursday nights.

Along with five other officers, she headed for booking. Sometime during the night she would have to find a way to slip up to the sixth floor without arousing anyone's suspicion.

Dawn Lammers had also been assigned to the booking area and she was telling Carla something about someone she had met the previous night. Carla nodded her head politely and gave Lammers a thin smile before moving away. Carla just wanted to be left alone.

Entering booking, the night shift officers groaned when they discovered C.O. Chris Keys at the window. Keys was working overtime tonight. C.O.s who volunteered to work overtime were generally afforded their post preference and Keys had elected to work the booking window. Keys was notorious for antagonizing prison ers. Everyone knew it would be a long night with a lot of fights.

Not more than five minutes had passed since the beginning o the shift when a police officer brought in an intoxicated prisoner Keys began asking questions. Each time the prisoner responded Keys followed up with a caustic remark or comment. The prisoner rather than getting angry, ignored Keys' inflammatory comment and belligerent manner. When the booking process was finished Keys leaned across the counter.

"Hey chump. Your parents ever have any kids that lived?"

The prisoner stared passively at Keys for several seconds and then responded, "No, but I got a brother who's an only child."

The other officers burst into laughter as Keys tried to fathom the meaning of the prisoner's response.

Keys shook his head, perplexed, knowing he had been had. He smiled and yelled, "Next!"

Forty prisoners and three hours later, Carla Terwelp slipped quietly to the elevator, pushed the button and rehearsed the story she would use if she was caught here on the sixth floor.

She would say she had lost a ring last night when she had been assigned to the sixth floor and had gone upstairs to see if she could find it. It was better to keep it simple. The more complex the story the harder it was to remember all the details.

Inside the elevator, Carla prayed Evan was not injured, and prayed she would not get caught. The door opened and Carla walked leisurely to the control room door and knocked.

The night shift control room officer opened the door and Carla quickly gave him the lost ring story and asked if he had come across it. The C.O. said he hadn't. Carla thought for a moment and then asked the officer to let her into the housing unit, stating she may have lost it when she was checking one of the showers the previous night.

He shrugged, closed the control room door and opened the heavy metal door to the housing unit.

Carla walked through the dark dayroom and headed straight to Evan Richards' room. She knew Evan would be waiting and hoped she was not too late. All day she had worried about his safety For the first time that day, Carla was not frightened.

Near Evan's door, she pretended to be searching for her lost ring. Carla dropped to one knee, took the envelope from her pocket and tried to slide the envelope through a small crack under Evan's door. The pills had bunched up in a corner of the envelope making it too thick.

Carla laid the envelope on the concrete floor and attempted to rearrange the pills evenly. She had already taken too much time. Frantically, she shook the envelope. But to her horror, the flap popped open and several pills spilled to the floor and rolled away.

"Damn it!" she exclaimed under her breath, as she tried to retrieve the pills.

Carla took a deep breath and tried to relax. There was no cause for alarm. If someone entered the unit she would know by the noise of the door and would have plenty of time to hide the pills.

She emptied the remaining pills onto the concrete floor. She would push them one at a time under Evan's door. It would take longer but it would work. So concentrated were her actions, she never heard the night shift lieutenant walk up behind her.

"What the fuck are you doing?" he demanded. Carla jumped, looked up, and saw Lieutenant Mack towering over her.

"I'm a..., looking for my ring...I lost a ring up here last night...and I'm looking for my ring...you know."

Mack leaned over and picked up the remaining pills.

"Come with me," Mack instructed.

She had been caught. If she told the truth, Mack would not understand. No one would understand.

Mack escorted Carla to his office, picked up the phone, reassigned several corrections officers and ordered an immediate shakedown of Evan Richards room. The shakedown found nothing. Richards had flushed the drugs down the toilet. Prisoner Evan Richards was clean.

Mack stared at C.O. Terwelp sadly. Mack had been on the sixth floor all the time. He had been checking a lock on one of the plumbing chase doors and had turned when the housing unit door opened and watched Carla head for the cell. Carla had failed to see Mack in the dark and the officer in the control room had believed her story about a lost ring. But he had failed to mention that Lieutenant Mack was on the unit.

Now Mack had no choice. He escorted Carla to booking. Standing in front of her, the police sergeant pulled out a Miranda card and advised Carla of her rights. Carla declined to make a statement and the sergeant booked her for bringing contraband into the jail.

It was an awkward situation for all the staff. This time Chris Keys did not make any sarcastic or caustic remarks while he booked Carla. He kept his eyes down. The others avoided Carla like she had a fatal, contagious disease.

Carla's uniform was replaced with a jail uniform and she was escorted to the women's unit and placed in protective custody. What had happened, she thought. An hour ago she had been a corrections officer. Now she was a prisoner. Her entire career was gone. Carla buried her face in her hands and sobbed. The shame and humiliation were overwhelming. She had been trusted and respected by her peers. Now she was nothing more than another prisoner. A prisoner who could not be trusted. Someone who did not deserve respect. She had betrayed the people with whom she worked and never again would she be a corrections officer. The love she felt for Evan Richards flickered like a candle in the wind. There was nothing else left except her love for Evan.

When Evan Richards saw the lieutenant approaching Carla, he quickly moved away from his door and swore under his breath. "The stupid fucking bitch is going to get busted." All his work for nothing.

It was a shame. All the work he had done. And for nothing. Richards knew Carla would be booked and assigned to the women's unit. She was no longer of any use to him. Richards flushed his toilet twice to make sure all the pills were gone and sat down to wait. There was no question in his mind that several corrections officers would arrive shortly to conduct a search of his room.

Richards lit a cigarette and sat in the dark, thinking. There would be another corrections officer some day, and next time he wouldn't push as hard. The problem this time was that he had hurried everything too much. Evan dropped his glowing cigarette into the toilet and waited.

Within minutes his door opened and two correction officers entered. After the officers left, Evan Richards climbed into bed and went to sleep. Carla Terwelp was not worth losing sleep over.

Mack made copies of all booking documents relating to Carla Terwelp's arrest and booking and attached them to his report. By morning the newspapers would have the story, and once again the jail and everyone working there would be suspect. Only when something bad happened in the jail did the public become interested.

The arrest and incarceration of a corrections officer was big news. The media would certainly sensationalize the story. This kind of thing had happened before and it would happen again.

Mack dropped the reports in the basket marked "Administration," called the women's unit, and instructed the officers to make fifteen minute checks on Carla Terwelp. Lieutenant Mack surmised that, by now, Carla would begin to realize what she had gotten herself into and would become desperate. The last thing he needed now was another suicide.

36

Friday Morning, January 21st, Dennison came to work, made coffee, checked the captains' logs and highlighted the log entry which recorded Carla Terwelp's arrest. Dennison knew Carla Terwelp vaguely but there was no question she had fallen in love and been conned.

It didn't matter how often corrections officers were trained and warned, the potential of being conned existed. Dennison had seen officers with more than fifteen years of service do things they would never dream of doing. Everyone was susceptible and everyone had to be on guard. Most people are inherently sympathetic and many are natural humanitarians. Prisoners see these traits as a weakness--a weakness to be exploited and used for their own personal gain.

Dennison dropped the log in Beck's basket and returned to his office. Today he would hand-carry a copy of the requisition for the boiler purchase to city hall. The original copy had been lost or misplaced. Fortunately, Dennison had made a copy of everything before it had been sent and this time he would make sure it landed on the right desk.

Dennison looked up and nodded as Beck passed by on his way to his office. Dennison spotted the newspaper under Beck's arm. The media had blasted the jail over Terwelp's arrest and Dennison anticipated that the mayor would be calling Beck soon.

Avery unlocked his door, picked up the log in his basket and scanned the highlighted areas rapidly. A corrections officer had been caught bringing drugs to a prisoner.

Avery had briefly glanced at the front page news article concerning corrections officer Terwelp's arrest and incarceration. His mind had examined every angle. The story cast doubt on the integrity of all the employees and corrections officers at the jail. Avery had mentally formulated a press release that would twist the slant of the story back to his favor.

"Due to a general increase of supervision at the Coronado county jail, and the high caliber of training in the supervisory ranks of corrections employees, a corrections officer was discovered bringing contraband into the detention center early this morning. This was the result of a long standing investigation by the department's Internal Affairs Department. Because of the vigilance of staff and their devotion to duty, the contraband was intercepted and appropriate action was taken against the employee. The staff at the Coronado jail have once again proved that the confidence placed in them by the taxpayers is well warranted. "

Avery placed his pen on the desk and smiled. He knew the part about a long investigation was nothing more than an outright lie. He could twist the truth as well as anybody. Avery understood well that the discovery of Carla Terwelp passing contraband to a prisoner had been nothing more than dumb luck. As far as Avery was concerned, that didn't matter.

Avery was learning to seize every possible advantage. To analyze every situation, to size up every person, to find a weakness and to use it to his advantage. It was war, and Avery Beck fought to win.

He sent his press release in his out basket and dialed the Internal Affairs Office. Roberto Romero answered and Beck asked Romero for an update on Mason Robert's case. Romero stated he would report immediately with the file.

Beck interjected, "Rather than meet here or in your office, I'll see you halfway at the coffee shop in City Hall. It will give us an opportunity to discuss the case away from the phones."

Secretly, Beck wanted to get away and avoid the call he anticipated from Waterston. He was in no mood to deal with Waterston this morning.

Avery grabbed his coat and in a few minutes joined Romero a block away and the two men walked together toward the coffee shop.

On the corner ahead, Beck sighted Deputy Chief Paulson standing by himself, obviously waiting for someone.

"What's up, Marshall?" asked Beck.

Paulson was visibly nervous. After several moments of stammering, he looked across the street and saw Dennison coming out

of City Hall after dropping off the purchasing paperwork for th
new boilers. Paulson mistook the presence of the three men a
some type of stakeout. Paulson's mind worked swiftly. Someho
they had learned he was meeting his confidential informant.

"I'm meeting my confidential informant," stammered Paulso

Beck looked at Romero, then back at Paulson and asked, "You'
what?"

"My confidential informant. An employee who tells me wha
the corrections officers are up to. I can't trust the captains and th
lieutenants to tell me what's really going on.

At that moment Chris Keys pulled up to the curb in a dark blu
Chevrolet sedan.

Paulson excused himself, quickly climbed into Keys' car an
they drove away.

Beck and Romero watched the vehicle drive away and wer
soon joined by Dennison.

"What's going on?" asked Dennison.

"Paulson just met his confidential informant, a C.O. who tel
him what's going on in the jail," Romero said between fits of laughte

"You mean Keys tells Paulson what's going on?" questione
Dennison, incredulously.

"That's about the size of it," replied Romero, wiping the mois
ture from his eyes.

Dennison burst into laughter.

Beck asked what was so funny and Romero explained. "First o
all, I'm sure Paulson thought we were out to bust him or some
thing. Here he is having this secret meeting with his "secret infor
mant" and who pops up from behind? You and me. Then, her
comes Dennison from the other direction. Did you see the look o
Paulson's face?"

Beck smiled and admitted, "He looked like a kid who had bee
caught with his fingers in the cookie jar."

"And of all the people to have as his informant," Romero inter
jected. "Hell, Keys is probably responsible for most of the prob
lems in the jail."

"Roberto's right," commented Dennison to Beck. "Keys i
trouble, but it looks like he's doing a pretty good job of conning
Paulson."

Beck pulled his coat a little tighter. Everything was a game, a
n. Nothing was simple.

Dennison left and headed back toward the jail, still chuckling.

Beck and Romero crossed the street and entered the coffee shop.
fter finding a table and ordering coffee, Beck said, "Now, tell me
out Mason Roberts."

Romero opened his briefcase and pulled out a thick file. The
le contained every scrap of information Romero had been able to
tain which related to Mason Roberts.

"Mason Roberts is a jail house lawyer. He will and does sue for
nything and everything. Ninety-nine percent of his past cases
ave been settled out of court. He knows the law and he knows the
stem."

"What about his allegation that some C.O.s entered his room
nd beat him?"

"I think he's being truthful about the beating. There's no
vidence to substantiate his allegation but my gut reaction is some-
ing went down."

Beck sat quietly for several seconds.

"If all the documentation says nothing happened, then the
epartment's position is that nothing happened. Go ahead and
urn everything you have over to the city's legal department. If
hat you say is true, the city will probably settle out of court. If
hat happens, I do not want the city to acknowledge any guilt on
ehalf of the jail or any of its employees."

Romero shuffled the papers back into his folder, lit a cigarette
nd changed topics. "That was a good bust last night by Lieuten-
nt Mack," commented Romero blandly.

Beck agreed and asked, "Is there generally this much going on
t the jail?"

"What do you mean?"

"Well, for instance, we've had a suicide, a couple of civil suits
led, a discrimination suit by Paulson, Byers' suicide and a correc-
ions officer arrested for bringing in contraband. Does this happen
ll the time?"

"Not all the time, but on the other hand I wouldn't say it's un-
sual. The general public has no idea what happens in a jail and
hat it takes to make a jail operate. In two weeks, you've learned

more about the inside working of a jail than most people will learn in a lifetime. The sad part is, it never stops, it just keeps going on and on, and no one, including the politicians, are interested in changing things. With some additional funding and a little interest on the part of the local politicians, we could avoid most of the problems. What we really need is another jail."

"I know. That's why I sent a memorandum directly to the city councilors."

"You what?"

Beck smiled and repeated himself. "I sent each city councilor his own personalized copy of a memorandum outlining very specifically what the problems are at the jail, and included the possible consequences."

Romero shook his head in amazement. Beck had done the unthinkable. He had made the politicians responsible.

Beck shrugged his shoulders, smiled a thin smile and continued. "It's time to either shit or get off the pot, and I decided to shit."

Beck drained the remainder of his coffee, rose, and left a stunned Roberto Romero sitting in silence.

37

Mayor Sam Waterston sat in his office and fumed. Avery Beck had been a good legal advisor during his campaign but now he was the enemy. The sooner he could get rid of Beck, the better.

All day Friday Waterston met with the eight City Councilors. Waterston had explained his plan to form a task force that would look into the problems at the jail and make the appropriate recommendations for change. One of those recommendations would be to replace Avery Beck as the jail administrator.

The eight councilors were alarmed over Beck's memo. They had never been placed in such an awkward and vulnerable position and they clearly indicated they did not like Beck's tactics. If something should happen at the jail and if Beck should provide a copy of his official memorandum to the news media, the councilors would look bad. This was something that could not be allowed to happen.

Waterston had waltzed and danced around the councilors, massaging wounded egos and muttering assurances that he would take care of Beck when the time was right. After all, Beck was a nobody. Waterston acknowledged that this incident with Beck was all his fault and he took full responsibility for Beck's appointment as jail administrator.

After hours of discussion, Waterston convinced the City Councilors to agree with his plan. After the meeting, Waterston returned to his office and carefully selected appointees for the task Force. The members needed only one qualification, complete loyalty to Sam Waterston. Once the members had been selected, Waterston carefully outlined the findings they would report to the City Council.

Finished, Waterston leaned back in his chair and sighed. Avery Beck had made a major mistake. He should have taken his advice. If Avery had only sat back, collected his check and let things slide, none of this would have been necessary.

Beck had been stubborn, had refused to cooperate and now he would have to face the consequences.

Waterston picked up the phone, made several calls and waited for the task force members to report to his office. Once he had briefed them on what their findings would be, it would only be a matter of time before Avery Beck was out of his hair.

Waterston decided the task force would begin meeting on Monday, January 24th.

* * *

Avery Beck woke early on Saturday morning. His head was throbbing from too much scotch the night before. He had not overindulged in years. He stumbled into the shower and allowed the tiny needles of hot water to massage his aching scalp. His thoughts turned to the jail.

Avery was uneasy. Waterston had not called his office so he must be up to something.

Avery turned off the shower, dried himself and dressed quickly. He walked into the kitchen and found Ann sitting at the kitchen table with two cups of steaming coffee.

Avery sat down, lit a cigarette, and picked up the coffee.

"Avery, I think we need to talk."

Avery looked up and inquired casually, "What about?"

"About you, Avery. About us."

Avery shrugged his shoulders and took another puff off his cigarette. "Go on."

"We've been married a long time and I have never interfered with your work. But, Avery, you've changed. In the past two weeks, since you started working at the jail, you've changed. We never talk. We never have any fun anymore. You don't like to go out in public. You started smoking and in all the years we've been married I have never seen you drink like you did last night."

Ann hesitated and then blurted, "Avery, last night you were drunk!"

Avery knew Ann was right. Last night he had lost control. Avery was angry and he almost told Ann he didn't need to put up with her shit. Instead, he kept silent.

"You kept mumbling something about hands in the cookie jar, nd you were going to get Waterston, and some other things that idn't make sense."

Avery tapped the ashes lightly from the tip of his cigarette into ne porcelain ashtray on the table and replied. "I've got a lot of nings on my mind right now, that's all. You're right, I did drink oo much last night, but like you said, it's the first time since we've een together. After forty-two years I think a man's entitled to cut oose, don't you?"

Ann sat quietly, staring at Avery with large sad eyes. He met er gaze defiantly but after several seconds he looked away and oyed with the ashtray on the table.

"Avery I don't want to fight with you. I'm only trying to point ut that you've changed. Working at that place is tearing you apart. ven when you're not working you're mind is still on the jail. If ot on the jail, then it's someplace else."

Avery admitted to himself that Ann was right. Since he had tarted working at the jail he had experienced an undefined sense f uneasiness as if some sort of pending disaster was about to oc- ur. It was an irrational fear that defied explanation.

Avery pursed his lips and spoke, "You're right, Ann. I have hanged. To see and hear and witness all the things I've experi- nced in the past two weeks would change anyone. I've seen the ery dregs of humanity coming in and going out of the jail on a aily basis. I'm responsible for everything. I'm not sure how to escribe it, but the jail is an evil, terrible, exciting place. It gets nto your blood and you can't shake it. I don't suppose I'm making nuch sense, am I?"

Ann reached across the table and placed her hand on Avery's rm. "I don't care what the jail is, or isn't. What I care about is ou. I don't like what you're becoming."

"And just exactly what am I becoming."

Ann shook her head sadly and said, "Avery you're like a wild nimal. You're tense and strained, and there is no spontaneity or umor in you. Everything is planned. You act like everything is a attle and you're planning for an attack."

As Ann spoke, the image of Jeff Powell, the former jail admin- strator entered his mind. Had he really become like that? Avery

207

recalled his original assessment of Powell: fierce, cunning, animal like. Always looking, searching, trying to find a weakness, a place to attack, an avenue to exploit. Had he changed so much in two short weeks? The thought was frightening.

Avery sat for several seconds before speaking. "There's something I suppose I should mention. I pissed off Waterston the other day. I think he'll be asking for my resignation as soon as it's politically feasible to do so. There are a great deal of problems in the jail. I suspect something very serious is going to happen, and happen soon."

"You mean a riot?"

"Could be a riot, an escape, it could be anything. The problem is someone is going to get hurt and no one wants to do anything about it. I've tried to enlist Sam's help and his advice is to ignore it, and maybe it will go away. Anyway, I pushed the issue and went around Waterston directly to the City Council. Waterston is pissed and the City Council is pissed. They would rather not know and right now I strongly suspect they are trying to figure out some way to get rid of me without causing any major flap in the newspapers."

"Do you really want this job, Avery?"

It was a good question. One he had asked himself more than a hundred times. Did he really want the job?

Avery smiled, ran his fingers through his uncombed hair and replied, "In some ways I do. In some ways being the jail administrator is like being the mayor of a warring city. The excitement, the danger, the hazards and the pitfalls all become unbelievably narcotic. On the other hand, I hate it. I hate the violence, the anger, the frustration and the politics. Mostly, I hate the insensitive public who don't give a shit about the jail. I suppose, in many ways, it's a love-hate relationship. You ask me if I want the job and frankly, I don't really know."

"You could always go back to private practice."

"I suppose so," replied Avery thoughtfully, "But it would be different. After working at the jail, I don't think I'll ever see things in the same light."

"So, what are you going to do?"

Avery smiled across the table and replied, "First, I'll try to keep from getting so wrapped up in my work. Secondly, I'll wait and see if Waterston can figure out a way to fire me. Lastly, I'll start giving you a little more attention and try to concentrate on being a little more spontaneous." Avery stood up and walked around the table.

Ann tilted her head upwards and met Avery's lips. He ran his hands down Ann's neck and gently slipped her bathrobe from her shoulders. It fell softly to the kitchen floor, without making a sound.

Gently Avery picked up his wife and sat her on the kitchen table. Ann protested mildly but he continued to trace the contour of her neck with his tongue.

Avery was determined. If Ann wanted spontaneity, he would damn well give her spontaneity. Avery laid Ann gently on her back and for the first time in their marriage, Avery and Ann Beck made love on the kitchen table. Avery whispered in her ear, "Ya can't get more spontaneous than this."

38

I t was January 22nd, Saturday afternoon. Greg Leeks remove the eight-inch by one-half inch metal arch support from h right shoe. He began scraping the edges of the support on th concrete floor in his room. Within hours he would have a raz sharp weapon.

Donald Macon sat on his bunk and watched. For the past se eral days, he had faced each day with dread. Sooner or late Stilwell's attorney would obtain a copy of Donald's statement an give it to him. In legal terms it was called "discovery." The defens was entitled to everything the prosecution had. When Stilwe learned about Donald's statement, there was no question in Donald mind what would happen. Stilwell would kill him. The entire se ond floor had learned about the bad blood between Leeks an Stilwell and were on edge with anticipation.

Donald's thoughts were interrupted when Leeks rose from th floor to test the edge and point of his homemade knife. Satisfie with the weapon's killing ability, he placed it on his bed and bega to tear his pillow case into half inch strips and then wound ther tightly around the butt of the knife. Fingerprints were hard to pic up from cloth. It absorbed the skin chemicals quickly and made good handle.

Leeks held the finished knife up for inspection and asked Donal over his shoulder, "What do you think, wino?"

"Don't call me wino."

Leeks turned to face Donald with the knife pointed. "What di you say?"

Donald met Leeks' cold stare. It was the first time in years h had stood up to anyone. After seconds of tense silence, Donal replied firmly, "Don't call me wino."

Leeks studied Donald grimly.

Donald sat frozen, wondering if Leeks would use his knife or if he would just beat the shit out of him. It didn't matter. Donald knew he was a dead man either way. If Leeks didn't kill him now, Stilwell would.

Leeks' faced widened into a grin. "OK kid. What do you think?"

Surprised, Donald studied the knife. "Looks good to me."

"Damn good," muttered Leeks.

Leeks had been involved in half a dozen stabbings in the past and one more didn't bother him. The battle lines had been drawn. In jail, there was no place to run. Leeks had never walked away from a confrontation. It was one of the main reasons he had been able to survive so long. He didn't seek confrontations, but he didn't run from them either.

"Uh, if you need any help or anything, you know, I could maybe help."

Leeks studied Donald suspiciously. "Why would you want to help?"

"I have my reasons."

"Such as?"

"Just reasons," mumbled Donald.

"I think maybe you and me need to have a little heart to heart," said Leeks as he placed a large muscular arm across his shoulders.

In a fraction of a second, Leeks could snap his arm in and break Donald's neck. Donald stood with his head down, wondering what to say. He could smell Leeks' acrid, stale cigarette breath. The smell and the fear made Donald's stomach heave.

Donald looked up and muttered, "I'm not a snitch, OK?"

"Sure, kid," replied Leeks as his eyes narrowed.

Donald licked his lips nervously and continued, "I was in the dumpster when Stilwell killed the guy at the convenience store. I saw him leave and I saw him with the gun in his hand. The cops, they busted me for criminal trespassing and I told them what I saw. That doesn't make me a snitch."

Leeks jerked his arm away and moved several paces from Donald.

"So what you're telling me is, you fingered Stilwell for a murder. If Stilwell finds out it was you, you're one dead motherfucker."

"That's about the size of it."

Leeks thought quietly for several moments. The wino had bee[n] in the wrong place at the wrong time. The kid wasn't a crimina[l] he was a wino. He could be useful.

"Here's what you're going to do, kid," ordered Leeks. "Eve[ry] night at nine-fifteen, the C.O.s bring out the brooms and mops an[d] get everyone to clean. Tomorrow night at nine-sixteen, you're g[o]ing to start a fight with one of Stilwell's buddies. Understand?"

"I don't know how to fight," protested Donald.

"You got a day to learn, kid."

"But the guy...he'll beat me up."

Leeks put his face close to Donald and whispered, "What's wors[e] catching a few punches, or getting killed?"

"Why do you want me to get into a fight? It doesn't make an[y] sense."

"You do what I say and everything will be fine. If you don't, I'[ll] put a fucking jacket on you and you won't last ten minutes."

Donald sat down heavily on his bunk. He was more than scare[d.] He was terrified.

Why did Leeks want him to start a fight? Who would he start [a] fight with? He didn't know anybody. None of it made any sense.

Donald Macon lay on his bed and covered his face with his blan[ket. None of this was happening. It was all a nightmare and soo[n] he would wake up and find himself back in his dumpster. Th[at] thought was no longer any comfort. Donald Macon wanted ou[t] out of jail and away from everyone here. But there was no escape[.] Like all the other prisoners, he was trapped.

Meanwhile, Tommy Brown sat in Jack Stilwell's room, munch[ing on a Zagnut candy bar, a gift from Stilwell.

Stilwell studied him quietly, anticipating the sexual pleasur[e] Tommy Brown would provide. Stilwell edged over and casuall[y] draped an arm across his shoulders. Tommy looked up and smile[d] at Stilwell with wide, innocent eyes. Stilwell smiled back an[d] slipped his hand to Tommy's crotch.

Shocked, Tommy jumped to his feet. "What are you doing, Jack?["]

"Aw, com'on Tommy. Don't act stupid."

"I'm not into that stuff, Jack. I'm straight. I think you got th[e] wrong idea or something."

Stilwell's face changed as he moved in. "I've given you a lot of candy bars during the past week haven't I, Tommy?"

"Yeah, Jack, and I appreciate it."

"Well, Tommy, it's time to pay up. Nothing's free in life. You understand what I'm saying?"

"Jack, I don't do that kind of stuff."

"Fuck you," snarled Stilwell. "You try to fucking brush me off, Tommy, and there's a dozen guys out there in that dayroom who are going to gang-bang you. I'm the only thing that's kept you safe since you came on this floor. I'm your protection, Tommy. Without me, every guy on this floor is going to take a shot at you whether you like it or not. You ain't got no choice, Tommy. You either be my little punk or you can be a fucking whore and everyone out there can take turns with you."

Tommy Brown could not believe what was happening. Stilwell, his friend, wanted sex. If he refused, then he would be held down by some of the other guys and sodomized. Tears ran down his cheeks as he placed the half-eaten Zagnut bar on the counter.

Stilwell smiled menacingly. "You got until tomorrow night to make up your mind, Tommy. If you ain't back in my room by then, be prepared for a very busy Monday morning. Picture it, Tommy. Everyone will be waiting in line for a shot at your sweet little ass."

Tommy Brown stumbled from Stilwell's room. Several of the prisoners whistled as he moved past them. It was no longer a game. It was serious. Tommy Brown had to make a decision. Submitting to Stilwell was sickening to Tommy Brown. Being attacked and raped by dozens of other prisoners was even more repugnant.

He stumbled into his room, sat on his bed and cried openly. How he had ever gotten himself into this mess. Life was no good. He had no one to count on. Tommy Brown searched his mind frantically. There was no way out. There was no place to run. He was trapped. His sobs woke Donald Macon. Rising slowly from his bed, Donald sat up and stared across the space which separated them.

Donald was afraid to ask. He knew what Stilwell had in mind for Tommy and he wondered if it had happened.

"What's wrong, Tommy?"

213

"Jack wants me to be his bitch. He says if I don't then he going to let all the prisoners on the unit loose on me. What am going to do, Donald?" Donald had no illusions. Stilwell was bi strong and mean. Tommy Brown and Donald Macon togethe wouldn't stand a chance.

Donald shook his head. "I don't know, Tommy."

Both men sat on their bunks lost in their own thoughts of in pending doom. Donald Macon would die. Stilwell would sure kill him. If Stilwell didn't kill him, then Leeks would. Tomm Brown would either become Stilwell's punk or he would be rape by the other prisoners.

Suddenly, Leeks appeared and checked out the two. "What th fuck's going on here?"

Tommy looked away and remained silent. Donald looked a Leeks, then Tommy, and back to Leeks.

There was a chance both he and Tommy might come out of th situation alive, but it all depended on Leeks. Donald Macon ros "We need your help."

"What's in it for me?" demanded Leeks.

Donald smiled for the first time in weeks and explained hi plan. Greg Leeks smiled contentedly. He liked Donald the Wino plan. Sunday night would reveal just how good a plan it was. Unt then, Greg Leeks would continue to prepare for Jack Stilwell.

Leeks ran the plan through his mind a dozen times. Stilwe was younger and probably stronger, but Leeks had the advantage He had a plan, and he would attack first. He would attack vi ciously and swiftly to eliminate any retaliation. As far as Gre Leeks was concerned, there was no place like jail.

A savage fury welled up inside him as he anticipated the com ing battle. It was a feeling Greg Leeks savored. The raw anima instinct of survival.

39

On January 22nd, Saturday, the evening shift settled in for their eight hours. Normally, the corrections officers assigned to the second floor would have detected the growing tension and hostility among the prisoners. But the death of Georgie Byers was still on their minds and they failed to notice any problem.

Prisoner Mason Roberts sat on the dayroom floor and watched the three prisoner groups. This had become his main past time.

He was amused by the body movements and the intensity of the three gatherings. Everything had gone as planned. A major disturbance was imminent. Leeks and Stilwell had no choice but to have a confrontation. Roberts had planted the seeds of doubt and fabricated rumors he was sure had reached the ears of both Stilwell and Leeks. If either of the two tried to back out now, their positions here in the jail and later in the joint would be destroyed. There was no way for either one to escape the destiny Roberts had carefully planned for them.

Roberts looked forward to taking control of the second floor. He would then file another suit based on living conditions and it would specifically cite the disturbance as a basis for cruel and unusual punishment. Mason would obtain affidavits from every prisoner on the second floor supporting his suit. Then he would have the power, the control and the money.

Mason Roberts watched as Tommy Brown sidled up to Jack Stilwell. Brown was a cute-looking little punk. Someone would have to take care of Brown after Stilwell was gone. Mason Roberts was not interested in punks but he had the good sense to realize that a punk as attractive as Tommy Brown was a valuable commodity. Tommy Brown was something Roberts could always use as a bargaining chip later.

Nine-fifteen arrived and the corrections officer assigned to the second floor distributed brooms and mops to the prisoners for

nightly cleanup. Roberts watched, almost holding his breath. Th
was the ideal time for an altercation. Twenty minutes later tl
cleaning was completed, the gear secured and all prisoners we
instructed to return to their rooms for headcount. Disappointe
Mason Roberts shuffled to his room. As Mason entered, he turne
and saw Jack Stilwell on the far side of the dayroom staring towa
Greg Leeks' room. For one brief moment Roberts detected a look
indecision on Stilwell's face. But the look was quickly replaced by
savage ruthlessness and Stilwell disappeared into his cell.

Roberts smiled to himself. What the hell, if it didn't happe
tonight, it would happen sooner or later and Mason Roberts ha
plenty of time.

The night crew reported to their assigned posts at ten minut
after eleven, were briefed, conducted their headcounts and settle
into their routine.

Outside, the wind was rising and snow was falling heavily. B
morning, the streets would be filled with white powder and trave
ing home would be difficult. Many of the night shift officers we
trying to snatch short naps, gearing up to stay and work overtim
on the morning shift. They knew many dayshift officers would ca
in and claim they were unable to report for duty because of th
heavy snow.

If there weren't enough, the shift captain could declare an eme
gency and order the least senior people to stay. If they refuse
they could be fired. For all practical purposes, the jail owned the
and they had no choice. Outside, the wind howled and snow pelte
the brown concrete structure. Like a giant brown ulcer, the ja
stood out against a sea of white, denouncing its purity. Insid
corrections officers dozed. Prisoners slept, moaned, wailed an
groaned. Others lay awake in anticipation, just waiting for tomo
row. There was nothing to look forward to, yet in the minds c
many, each day was waited as the day before had been.

Beneath the wind and snow, the jail pulsated and radiated it
evil. Finally, in the early hours sleep came reluctantly to the fe
who were still awake, but peace could not be found anywhere.

Breakfast arrived on Sunday morning, January 23rd, at five
thirty AM but none of the prisoners on the second floor made
move. All sixty-three stayed in their rooms, waiting.

The dayshift officers noted the strange fact in their logs, made several cracks about jail cooking and forgot the incident. It was not considered significant.

However, when lunch arrived, the officers clearly detected the tension. Each prisoner entered the serving line, took a tray and retreated to his group. The dayshift officer noted the three separate groups huddled together in the dayroom throughout the afternoon. This was logged and reported to the detention level lieutenant who made a note of the situation and passed it along to the shift captain. The captain annotated the fact in his log and indicated that a potential for violence on the second floor was being monitored closely.

Sunday afternoon, Tommy Brown stayed close to Jack Stilwell. Tommy's choice was clear. He finally realized he could be torn apart by dozens of prisoners or he could stick to Jack Stilwell. Tommy Brown wanted to stay alive.

Leeks and Stilwell eyed each other frequently across the dayroom. Both were aware of the stakes. Stilwell was confident. He was much bigger and stronger and he had no doubt he would prevail. Leeks was quiet and pensive. He had survived with brute strength as a youth but as he grew older, he relied more and more on cunning.

The lights winked off and on and the prisoners ambled slowly to their rooms. The dayshift was over. Tommy Brown smiled at Jack Stilwell as he moved away toward his room.

The evening shift reported for duty and for the third consecutive day discussed the suicide of Georgie Byers. Corrections officer Frank Willis was assigned to the second floor and corrections officer Sheila Watkins was assigned to the control center. After a ten minute briefing period, the officers reported to their assigned posts.

Willis was looking forward to working the second floor. During briefing, the shift captain had informed the evening shift about the situation. He had specifically instructed Willis and Watkins to maintain a close watch and to report any unusual events immediately. This was where Frank Willis liked to work. In the thick of things. If something was going to go down, Willis wanted to be there. He conducted his headcount, reported the number to Sheila Watkins in the control center and waited.

Tommy Brown, Greg Leeks, and Donald Macon sat huddled in their room. This was their last opportunity to go over their plans. If Tommy Brown spoke to Leeks while the other prisoners were out of their rooms, Stilwell would learn about it and would become suspicious.

For the last time Greg Leeks explained what Donald and Tommy Brown were required to do.

"If either one of you cunts fuck this deal up, and I'm still alive afterwards, I'll kill both of you myself."

Tommy closed his eyes and shuddered. Donald was no longer affected by threats and he merely rolled his eyes.

Donald was tired. He was tired of being in jail, tired of being frightened and tired of running. Now there was no place to run.

The electronic deadbolt on their room door clicked indicating the door was unlocked. Tommy Brown and Donald Macon left the room and looked at each other for one last time.

Tommy strolled through the dayroom and lingered nervously in the far corner waiting for Stilwell. Several other prisoners were also waiting for Stilwell. They spoke in low tones and one turned his eyes toward Willis as he spoke.

"If something goes down tonight, I'm going to take that cocksucker out."

The other prisoners followed his gaze to Corrections Officer Willis. Willis constantly harassed, intimidated and threatened the prisoners. There was absolutely no respect for Willis only fear. They knew Willis was responsible for several past beatings.

Stilwell joined the group, placed a large muscular arm casually over the shoulder of Tommy Brown and asked no one in particular, "What'ya hear?"

They shook their heads indicating they hadn't heard anything.

One asked, "When's it going to go down, Jack?"

Stilwell smiled his confident smile and replied, "Whenever Leeks wants. I think the old fucking con is scared and he's stalling."

Stilwell thought for a couple of seconds and continued. "As a matter of fact, I bet he gets himself thrown in lockup or something so he don't have to rock-n-roll. His time is over and he knows it."

The group smiled tightly. Stilwell would be the new barn boss on the second floor after he took care of Leeks. Those prisoners who had sided with Stilwell would be on the winning side and each would be in a good position.

Tension mounted throughout the night and tempers burned raw. Those prisoners who had chosen sides avoided each other. Those who did not want to get involved stayed in their rooms. Had Georgie Byers been alive he would have commented quietly that all the prisoners were wearing shoes. But Georgie Byers was not alive.

Frank Willis moved the gear to the dayroom and ordered the prisoners to begin cleaning. Donald Macon picked up a broom and began sweeping as did several other prisoners.

As Donald neared Stilwell's group, he looked up at one prisoner and ordered, "Get the fuck out of my way."

The prisoner eyed Donald evilly. "Fuck you, wino."

Donald let the broom fall and then he leaped. The attack caught the other prisoner off guard. They tumbled to the floor but Donald quickly scrambled to his feet and eyed his adversary. He had chosen one of the smallest members of Stilwell's group to fight in hopes of having some chance of survival.

Suddenly, the Leeks and Stilwell groups converged on the two fighters. The other prisoners shouted, stamped their feet and watched the brawling masses.

Donald was not a member of either faction and the fight was considered as nothing more than pure entertainment. A break in the monotony of jail life.

Donald was breathing hard. He eyed Stilwell's man as he circled expertly and exploded into him. Once again both fighters fell to the floor, gouging, kicking and clawing each other. Donald Prescott Macon--the Wino was struggling for his life.

Tommy Brown clutched Stilwell's right arm tightly. He did not have to pretend to be frightened. Stilwell glanced over at Brown and sneered. "What a fuckin' pussy."

Stilwell turned back to the fight as he watched the wino put up a surprisingly good defense. The wino was fighting a meaner, quicker and deadlier opponent. A mere ten seconds had elapsed since the fight had erupted when Willis walked quickly across the dayroom and called for assistance on his radio.

This was great. Adrenalin pumped through Willis' body as hi orders echoed through the dayroom and went unheeded. Fifty pris oners had now formed a circle around the two fighters and Willi hesitated before plunging in.

Watching others fight and seeing blood would often send pris oners into a frenzy. They would lose every last bit of rationalit and might well turn and attack a corrections officer. Willis quickl backed out of the group and waited for assistance to arrive. Hi mind moved quickly. The moment he heard the heavy metal doo moving, he would plunge back in. The other officers would arriv and be amazed at Willis' bravery.

All eyes were now riveted on Donald and the other fighter Donald's mouth and nose were bleeding and his breath was comin in gasps.

The prisoners watched intently, knowing that at any momen additional corrections officers would arrive and the fight would b stopped. Quietly, Greg Leeks wove his way through the crowd to ward Stilwell. His right hand was in his pocket, the shank hel tightly.

Instinctively, Stilwell sensed someone behind him and tried t turn but Tommy Brown clung tightly to his arm, restricting hi movements just enough to allow Leeks to close the distance quickl and sink the shank into Stilwell's back. The pain was intense an crippling. Tommy Brown made every effort to hold Stilwell's arm but was flung several feet while Stilwell tried to defend himself.

Stilwell doubled up in pain as Leeks continued to plunge the knife repeatedly into his body. Crimson flowed freely, staining the concrete floor of the dayroom. The other prisoners quickly grasped the deception. Both groups surged violently forward in a savage and bloody battle.

Wooden broom handles were broken and became spears. The entire dayroom was now a battlefield. Meanwhile, Donald Macon was forgotten as the battle coursed over him. He crawled on all fours through the mass of legs and kicking feet trying to find an escape.

The sound of the heavy metal door opening went unnoticed. The fight had gone too far. All sense of humanity had evaporated. The passion to kill and maim had gripped the prisoners.

220

Willis heard the solid metal door opening and took his cue to enter the fray. He pushed, punched and struck bodies before his stomach was ripped open by a broken broom handle. His knees turned to water and he sunk to the floor, semi-conscious. Several prisoners kicked him in the head, knocking him into unconsciousness.

Stilwell lay on the cold tile floor, thrashing in his own blood.

One minute and ten seconds had elapsed. Additional corrections officers rushed the dayroom and pulled prisoners away from the fight, handcuffing hands and legs, and dropping them, incapacitated, on the dayroom floor.

Lieutenant Frank Ivers, along with Corrections Officers Jason Robbins, Chris Keys, Danny Pitts and Mike Stone all responded. Ivers spotted Willis, Macon and Stilwell on the floor and called for medical assistance on his radio.

What Ivers had feared had finally happened. This was more than a small fight. This was a full-scale war. Ivers keyed his radio again and requested additional units but the officer responded that there were no additional units, a response Ivers failed to hear.

Suddenly, Ivers was struck with the handle of a mop and knocked to the floor. He rolled, recovered quickly and sprang to his feet. Ivers estimated thirty prisoners were still fighting. He had only twelve officers and was outnumbered.

With blood running down his face, Ivers moved to the control window and spoke rapidly. "Sheila, pull the fire hose from the hallway in here and do it now!"

Sheila knew it was a last ditch attempt to regain order. The only way she could comply was to leave the door to the control room open, enter the hallway, pull the fire hose from the case and take it into the dayroom. The housing unit door and control room door would both be open at the same time. If the prisoners gained access to the control room, it was over. The whole second floor would be at the mercy of rampaging prisoners. She leaped from her chair, sprinted to the door, flung it open and jerked the fire hose out of the cabinet. Reaching the open housing unit door, she handed the hose to Ivers, turned back to the fire hose cabinet and spun the wheel.

Instantly the hose became stiff with pressure and Ivers aimed at prisoners and corrections officers alike. The stream knocked everyone off their feet. Ivers stood like a stone statue as he hosed any prisoner who tried to stand. Thirty seconds later, all officers were able to stand alongside Ivers. He moved slowly forward, forcing the prisoners into their rooms. Two minutes later, the fight was over.

Officer Danny Pitts dashed to turn off the water and then returned to joined Lieutenant Frank Ivers and the other officers. The dayroom was now deathly silent. Six inches of water covered the smooth concrete floor. Cigarette butts and scraps of paper floated on top.

The corrections officers stood in an eerie, frozen silence for several seconds. Ivers then slowly roused himself and ordered, "Get the medical people in here now!" Officers Pitts and Robbins guided the medical staff to where C.O. Willis lay unconscious, the broom handle still protruding from his abdomen. The medical team packed the edges of the wound with sterile gauze, placed him on a gurney and wheeled him to booking where he would be taken to the hospital.

Donald Macon lay in a corner of the dayroom, where the high pressure hose had deposited him. Semi-conscious, Donald watched as medical people hovered over him trying to determine his injuries. Donald closed his eyes and let the warmth of unconsciousness wash over him. He had found a way out.

Jack Stilwell lay on his side, nearby, the shank still buried in his back. He had a dozen stab wounds and had lost a lot of blood. The water around him was pink. He was barely conscious. Leeks had surprised him. The motherfucker had slipped up behind him and the little bitch, Brown, had been in on the entire thing. Stilwell would kill them both.

Stilwell and Donald Macon were quickly moved out and transported to the hospital.

Lieutenant Ivers was given a sterile compress for the three inch gash on his head. Several other corrections officers had injuries but none were serious.

Ivers instructed Robbins to bring a team of prisoner trusties from the first floor to mop up the water. Turning to Pitts, Ivers asked him to contact the master control officer and have a police officer dispatched to initiate an investigation. There was a good chance Stilwell and Willis might not make it, which meant a homicide investigation.

Ivers then assigned four corrections officers to work as a team and check each prisoner and each room to make sure none had been injured. Two other officers were ordered to pick up the broken broom handles and anything else which could be used as a weapon.

There was nothing else for Ivers to do, except collect reports and write his own. He splashed through the water and walked shakily out of the dayroom. In the hallway, he paused and moved to the open control room door.

"We almost lost it tonight," he said to Sheila who was sitting at the control panel.

She looked up and stared. There were a thousand things she wanted to say, but nothing would come.

"You did one hell of a job tonight, Sheila."

Sheila tried to smile but failed. Ivers caught the elevator and headed for his office. It was time to notify Paulson and Beck. He sat down heavily, picked up the phone and dialed. It was only a job. At least that's what he kept telling himself.

On the second floor, Mason Roberts watched from his window as Stilwell, Donald Macon and Frank Willis were wheeled out on gurneys. It wouldn't take long for the corrections people to find out Leeks had been involved. After that, he would be placed in segregation and Roberts would have the second floor to himself.

Roberts smiled as he recalled Leeks sliding up behind Stilwell. "That fucking Leeks was one dangerous son-of-a-bitch."

40

Avery Beck was watching television when he got the call. Ivers quickly explained the incident and Beck said he would be down right away and hung up.

Turning away from the phone, Avery felt Ann standing behind him.

"What's wrong?"

"What I've been afraid of has finally happened. That was one of the lieutenants from the jail on the phone. There was a riot tonight. Two prisoners and one officer are in the hospital."

"How bad?"

"I don't know, but I'm going down."

Ann didn't say anything. The worry in her eyes said it all. While putting on his coat, Avery commented, "Don't worry. I'll be careful."

The blinding snow turned a twenty minute drive into an hour. Avery pulled into his parking spot and walked quickly inside. It took several minutes for the master control officer to locate Ivers.

Before Ivers could speak, Avery asked, "Any word from the people at the hospital?"

"No, nothing."

Noting the dried blood on his face, Beck asked, "Are you all right?"

"I think so," responded Ivers. "Maybe a little dizzy, but nothing serious."

Ivers took Beck to the second floor and explained step by step what had happened.

When he finished, Avery asked, "Is it standard procedure to use a fire hose to control a situation?"

Ivers smiled and replied, "No, it's not, but it was the only thing I could think of at the time."

Switching topics, Avery questioned, "You told me what happened, but you didn't tell my why." Ivers lit a cigarette and offered one to Avery.

"My best guess is this was a power play. Two heavies, probably Stilwell and Leeks, went at each other. From the looks of things, I'd say Stilwell lost."

"What about Leeks?"

Ivers blew out a steady stream of smoke and answered, "I moved him to segregation, but he ain't saying nothing."

Two weeks ago, Avery wouldn't have understood. Now he knew exactly what Ivers was talking about. Two big, seasoned, hardcore cons were vying for control. With control came power. And with power came the ability to dictate the actions of every other prisoner on the unit.

Avery thanked Ivers and left. Driving home, the picture Ivers had described stayed in his head. Why the corrections officers, the lieutenants and the captains stayed at the jail was beyond him. There had to be a better way to make a living.

There was no question in Avery's mind. Ivers' resourcefulness had averted a full-scale disaster. Had it not been for Ivers and Sheila, the whole damn jail might have been overrun.

Avery pulled into his driveway, cut the engine and sat for several minutes in the dark. Tomorrow, he would have to brief Waterston. Maybe, now, Waterston would listen to what he had been trying to say for the past two weeks.

The following morning, Avery rose, showered, shaved, drank his usual cup of coffee and drove to the jail. On the way, he stopped and bought a package of cigarettes and a newspaper. The front page carried the whole story.

Avery scanned the article. The reporter had called Waterston, and the Mayor had made a statement:

> *"I anticipated something of this nature occurring at the jail, which is why I developed a task force not more than two days ago to study the problems at the jail. Avery Beck is a good friend of mine, and he's done a good job during these past two weeks. A number of problems have been brought to my attention during the past week, and I think it's time we find someone who is qualified to take the jail administrator's*

slot. Avery Beck has done a good job and I was pleased he accepted the position until we could find a full-time permanent replacement."

Avery sat in stunned silence. There it was. He had been fired. Waterston had publicly fired him and covered all the bases in the process. Avery could say whatever he wanted but it wouldn't make any difference. If he went to the news media now, the general public would construe his comments as nothing more than sour grapes. Waterston had used last night's altercation as a way to rid himself of Avery Beck, knowing there was no way Avery could retaliate.

He drove to the jail slowly. Traffic was light because of the snow. Avery parked in the administrator's space and entered. Dennison was at the coffee pot.

Dennison handed him a cup of coffee and followed Avery into his office.

"You see the paper this morning?"

Dennison took a sip and replied, "Yep."

"And?"

"And you committed occupational suicide. You also got fucked."

"So what happens now?"

Dennison peered out the window at the new falling snow. Beck was a good man and a good administrator but he had made a mistake. Beck had believed he had the ability to change things.

Dennison turned to Beck and answered, "Nothing happens, nothing at all."

"Even with three people in the hospital, you don't think somebody will do something?"

Dennison shook his head. "Nobody's done anything in over two hundred years, there's no reason to think they'll do anything now. In over two hundred years, the penal system in this country hasn't changed a bit. People continue to commit crimes and we keep locking them up. It costs over twenty-thousand dollars a year to lock up one prisoner. The same people who complain about high taxes are the ones who want everyone locked up. It doesn't make sense."

Beck pursed his lips. "If you were king for a day, what would you do?"

Dennison smiled. "I'm not sure. I suppose I would focus on kids. Instead of trying to change things in the system, I would try to decrease the number of people coming into the system. Unfortunately, under my plan a decrease in prison and jail populations wouldn't be seen for maybe ten years. None of the political offices have ten-year terms, which means it wouldn't work. Politicians want something now. They want some miracle cure they can give to the public and use for reelection."

Beck lit a cigarette and spoke. "If nothing else, it's been an interesting experience."

Dennison smiled. "You know, in the beginning I figured you for just another political hack. I was wrong. It's too bad for everyone that you're going. For the first time in fifteen years I really felt like some good things were possible. Now everything will stay the same. The mayor will find someone who will do what he wants, which is nothing. Everything comes down to politics."

Beck drained the last of his coffee, rose and stared out his window for several seconds. Outside two sets up footprints were still visible in the snow. One set belonged to Beck and the other to Dennison. In a week the footprints would disappear without a trace. In a month the memory of Beck would disappear from the jail.

Avery Beck was no longer the jail administrator. He felt empty, yet elated. A gigantic burden had been lifted from his shoulders and he no longer felt trapped.

Beck put on his coat, tossed the empty styrofoam coffee cup into the trash and walked out.

Dennison watched him leave and then turned his attention back to the falling snow outside the office window. Beck was gone and he would be replaced by someone who would be willing to cooperate with the mayor's office. The mayor would make a lot of noise over the incident on the second floor, but ultimately the public would forget and the publicity would die down and nothing would change. Dennison turned off the lights in Beck's office and closed the door.

The logs he had placed in Beck's basket stood untouched. Dennison picked up the logs, tore them in half and dropped them in the trash. No one would be interested.

In a couple of days he would have a new boss. He hoped the new administrator had half the balls that Beck had. But he doubted it. This time Waterston would make sure he was not appointing a maverick. This time Waterston would appoint some panty-waist wonder.

Dennison sighed and walked to the coffeepot. He was trapped. There had been a spark of hope. A hope that things would change.

I'm a fool, he thought. Nothing really ever changes.

-EPILOGUE-

Sam Waterston's bid for re-election four years later failed dismally.

Avery Beck returned to private practice and is now employed by a prestigious law firm in the Coronado, Arizona, area. He quit smoking but is still plagued by memories of the jail.

Deputy Chief Sam Dennison still works at the Coronado County Jail. In five more years he will be eligible for retirement.

Deputy Chief Marshall Paulson dropped his lawsuit against Beck. Since then he has filed a total of five more suits citing discrimination, harassment and a hostile work environment. Paulson is still employed at the Coronado County Jail.

Roberto Romero, head of Internal Affairs, retired six months after Beck's departure. He presently lives in Las Vegas, Nevada.

Paul Rivera, the department's fiscal analyst, transferred from the jail to the City's purchasing department. He is still employed by the City of Coronado.

Lieutenant Frank Ivers, "The Preacher," is still working at the Coronado County Jail. Ivers continues to comfort prisoners in need. As of this writing he has successfully conducted an additional six exorcisms.

Classification Specialist Victor Moss resigned from the Coronado County Jail and currently sells computer equipment for a large firm in Denver, Colorado.

Although Corrections Officer Frank Willis recovered from his injuries, he never returned to work at the Coronado County Jail. He is presently employed in retail sales.

Officers Danny Pitts, Mike Tombstone Stone, Jason Robbins, Chris Keys and Sheila Watkins are still employed at the Coronado County Jail. No significant operational or policy changes have been made.

Corrections Officer Dawn Lammers remains at the Coronado County Jail and is presently the Administrative Assistant to the new Jail Administrator. How she was chosen for this position and promoted so swiftly, is a matter of speculation among staff.

Corrections Officer Carla Terwelp was convicted of taking contraband into a jail, a felony. She was sentenced to eighteen months in the state penitentiary. Her repeated attempts to contact prisoner Evan Richards were unsuccessful.

Prisoner Jack Stilwell died on the operating table three hours after his arrival at the County Hospital. Cause of death was listed as acute trauma, shock and loss of blood.

Prisoner Greg Leeks agreed to a plea bargain for the slaying of prisoner Jack Stilwell. Greg Leeks pled guilty to manslaughter. Prisoner Leeks received an additional two years for the killing of prisoner Jack Stilwell. Leeks is currently serving time in the state penitentiary and has become something of a legend among the other prisoners.

Donald Macon recovered from his injuries and was released from jail. Donald Macon rented an apartment, obtained a job as a janitor and is still employed. Donald Macon has not consumed any alcoholic beverages for the past four years. Donald Macon never speaks of his time in jail or of his seven years as an alcoholic.

Tommy Brown received a two-year suspended sentence for his burglary charge. He was released from jail and placed on probation. Tommy Brown enrolled in a vocational school and is presently an electrician's helper. Tommy Brown specializes in the installation of burglar alarms.

Brad Wilson plea-bargained his strong armed robbery charge and was placed on two years probation. Six months later, he was arrested again and sentenced to one year in the state penitentiary. Brad Wilson is assigned to the same cell block as prisoner Leeks in the state penitentiary.

Prisoner Mason Roberts became the barn-boss on the second floor. He maintained control of the second floor until he was sentenced to four years in the state penitentiary. The city of Coronado settled with prisoner Mason Roberts and paid seven thousand dollars as a settlement. Presently, prisoner Roberts has four civil suits pending in state and federal courts.

Prisoner Joe Hicks was deemed incompetent to stand trial and is presently in the state mental hospital.

Prisoner Evan Richards was sentenced to seven years in the state penitentiary. While serving his sentence, Richards initiated a fraudulent mail order scheme, was caught and received an additional six months.

The citizens of Coronado, Arizona, and the citizens across the country quickly forgot the incident which occurred on the second floor of the Coronado County Jail. As of this writing very few people are interested in the nation's penal system. The Coronado Jail is still under budgeted and overcrowded. Another serious incident possibly resulting in the death of a prisoner or corrections officer is anticipated to occur at any time.

Prisoner Eric Moore's survivors filed a wrongful death suit and agreed to a twenty-thousand dollar settlement.

Georgie Byers, may he rest in peace, was correct. Nothing ever changes.

GLOSSARY OF JAIL TERMS

Bay Orderly: Prisoner who has been assigned to perform cleaning and sanitation duties for a particular housing unit.

Barn Boss: The prisoner who is in charge of a particular unit. Although the formal jail and prison structure will not acknowledge this distinction, in reality each housing unit has one prisoner who controls the other prisoners.

Bitch: An attractive, experienced, homosexual male prisoner who is able to pick and choose his mate. Also, a criminal charge, denoting habitual criminal. This charge is routinely filed by the District Attorney's Office after a prisoner has been convicted of a number of successive felony offenses.

Blue Veil: An unwritten code of secrecy among correction officers.

Booking: The place in jail where all prisoners are initially processed.

Can: A term denoting jail, prison, or some other place of confinement.

Cherry: Anyone who has never been in jail. A first-time employee or a first time prisoner would be considered a cherry.

Classification: A system utilized to group certain types of prisoners within a jail or prison. Similar charges, criminal backgrounds, and ages are grouped together.

C.O.: Abbreviation denoting correction officer.

Con: Short for convict. Any prisoner who has been convicted of a felony offense and has served time in the state penitentiary. Can also be used as a verb: To con someone into doing something they would not normally do.

Contraband: Any item not specifically authorized for issue or retention by a prisoner.

Dirty: Commonly used when referring to drugs. If a prisoner is given a urine test and narcotics are discovered the prisoner is considered to be "dirty."

D.L.: Abbreviation for Detention Level.

Headcount: A physical counting of all prisoners in custody. A physical counting of all prisoners is conducted frequently on each shift.

Heavy: Denotes a well established prisoner. Someone who has done a great deal of prison time and is highly respected by other prisoners. Sometimes used to indicate a prisoner who is being held for an extremely serious or capital offense.

Housing Unit: A secure area where prisoners are assigned to live.

Jacket: A reputation for being an informant.

Joint: Prison or Jail.

Lifer: Career criminal. Someone who has done, or will do the majority of their life in prison or jail.

Lockdown: A period of time when all prisoners in a housing unit are locked in their assigned rooms. Lockdowns occur during every headcount.

Maggot: Derogatory name sometimes used by some corrections officers when referring to a prisoner.

Master Control: A secure area in a prison or jail from which door elevators and internal communications are controlled.

Punk: A weak or young looking prisoner who provides sexual favors to one or more prisoners.

Rat: A prisoner who is an informant.

Ratting Off: The process of one prisoner informing on another.

R&D: Letters stand for "Receiving and Discharge." The term is synonymous with booking.

Rig: A complete set of tools and materials required for tattooing.

Rock-N-Roll: Physical altercation.

ROR: Release on own Recognizance. Releasing a prisoner from custody without requiring the prisoner to post a bond.

Sallyport: Two doors, which do not open simultaneously.

Scrubboard: Term used in jail denoting oral sex.

Shakedown: A systematic search of one room, a specific area or the entire jail.

Shank: Home made knife, or crude weapon.

Snitch: Informant.

Streets: Anywhere outside jail or prison.

Them: Anyone who is not a corrections officer.

Trusty: A sentenced prisoner who is required to work. The name Trusty is a misnomer and does not automatically imply trust in the prisoner.

Unit: Housing area/housing unit.

Us: All corrections officers who can be trusted.

Virgin: Anyone who has never been in jail before. See Cherry.

SUNSTONE
PRESS

Send for our **free catalog**
and find out more about our books on:

- ❖ The Old West
- ❖ American Indian subjects
- ❖ Western Fiction
- ❖ Architecture
- ❖ Hispanic interest subjects
- ❖ And our line of full-color notecards

Just mail this card or call us on our toll-free number below

Name

Address

City   State   Zip

Send Book Catalog _____ Send Notecard Catalog _____

Sunstone Press / P.O.Box 2321 / Santa Fe, NM 87504
(505) 988-4418   FAX (505) 988-1025   (800)-243-5644